BLOOD RECRUIT

By
Murphy Morrison

To my parents, and the most supportive family
in the world.

Prologue: April 3, 1991

He regretted the ten shots of tequila. He definitely regretted mixing them with two whiskey and waters.

"Could you at least tell me your name?"

"Peter."

"Last name?"

"Donahue."

"I'm Theresa."

Peter's head was spinning fast, and the woman speaking to him became less and less audible.

"You have the most beautiful eyes, do you know that?" She tried a more direct approach. From a young age, Peter's pure, hazel eyes never failed to attract girls from across the room. The woman squinted her features in an attempt to appear cute. The effect was lost on Peter.

"Thank you," Peter answered, giving no compliment in response.

Peter never asked for her last name, did not know her favorite color, and her occupation certainly never came up. He didn't care to hear the details. In fact, this would be his first time sleeping with a woman despite lacking any emotional attachment. Peter felt that the act should be sacred, between two people both pursing an equal level of commitment. He had only experienced that feeling with two other women.

"Want to get out of here?" she asked in her most sultry voice, hiding her annoyance at Peter's wandering attention, but not yet ready to quit the pursuit.

Peter ordered two more drinks instead, although he fully intended to take her home in due time. Tonight he needed an escape from the stress of his job, and this woman had appeared at the bar as if on cue. Anyone within eyesight could have seen from Peter's demeanor that he was uninterested in the woman. She simply failed to care.

"Okay, you win. Let's get out of here."

The couple didn't bother shielding themselves from the rain before running to catch a cab. Drops fell in a straight path to the ground. This spring shower brought no joy. It was windless and the night seemed darker than usual, blacker than black.

Theresa's high-pitched screech sounded throughout the first half of the cab ride. Her flirtatious efforts attempted to put on a show.

Peter's nausea took hold and he let loose a low groan.

"Hey man, you going to get sick in my cab?"

"Pull over."

The cab's interior could use a good scrubbing, but Peter didn't want to foot the bill. The taxi driver didn't take much convincing, and the car screeched to a stop. Peter emptied his stomach on the side of the road before climbing back into the cab.

"Sir, I think we will be making two stops tonight, if you don't mind." He looked at the woman next to him and willed his vision to stay focused.

"I'm not feeling too well; I'm sorry, but I think it's best if I just go home and get to bed tonight. I'll give the driver enough money to get you back as well."

Theresa looked wounded and upset. So upset that Peter lost any desire to be in close quarters with her. An air of resentment filled the car and Peter thought the ride couldn't finish quickly enough.

The cab arrived at Peter's humble home and Peter tipped the driver nicely. Reaching his door, he struggled to find the right key into his house—his coordination suffered after so much alcohol.

"Damn keys." Peter fumbled over three keys before finding the winner.

Just as the metal fit through the lock, the woman from the bar placed a hand on Peter's shoulder. He turned, startled by her presence. The cab pulled away minutes ago and she should have gone with it. Theresa kissed him and reached around Peter's body to open the front door.

Three hours later, Theresa stirred in bed and Peter rotated his body toward the wall, noting its rough texture: stucco. He had always hated stucco, considering himself more of a paint kind of guy—anything to distract his conscience from the blonde, delicate-skinned female next to him.

In spite of his efforts, Peter's mind refused to stop dwelling on the woman who he really loved—the woman he would forever push away. Her tan skin, calloused hands, and chestnut eyes were permanently embedded in his memory. She was a woman completely opposite in nature to the one currently beside him.

Deep down, Peter reminded himself of the single reason that he was forced to keep his love a secret. It was quite simple, actually.

You would put her in danger.

Threats to Peter's security accompanied his daily work in the CPD Intelligence Unit. If one revenge-seeking gang member discovered Peter's love life, any girlfriend would become a target.

Eventually, he assumed, the gaping emptiness would disappear. That, or he would become numb to the isolation. One thing was certain: his attempt to dull the pain with a one-night stand had failed miserably.

At 5:30 a.m., tired of waiting for sleep to come, Peter finally got out of bed. He dressed quickly to avoid any awkward morning conversation, while taking in the watermark on the ceiling and the large blue stain on the white carpet. Peter moved into his home only last week and had yet to make repairs.

He glanced in the mirror and grimaced at his black bed hair. *I am not this guy.* As Peter walked toward the bedroom door and pulled it open, Theresa shifted, turning her wispy hair in his direction. Her blue eyes held no draw for him.

"Goodbye, Peter."

Peter stepped into the hallway and closed the door with one, quick backwards glance. "Goodbye," he muttered quietly, speaking to both the woman on the other side of the door and the woman in his heart.

That morning, he drove to work in a much more distracted state than the day before. Peter never expected to hear from Theresa again, but he felt sick at having slept with her. Especially, he remembered, after seeing a triumphant grin spread wickedly across Theresa's face just before he closed his bedroom door.

Chapter 1

The sun rose, boasting a unique strength and a beautiful glow. An alarm sounded at 5:45 a.m. Had Cohen been sleeping, he would have pushed the snooze button, set at three-minute intervals, at least three times. The truth was Cohen hadn't slept a wink. Although he pretended to err on the side of confidence in light of his first real day of work, his body was racked with nerves. Cohen welcomed the alarm, picking his body out of bed all too easily.

Pulling on a University of Minnesota T-shirt and a pair of black running pants, Cohen approached his large kitchen window. Given his apartment's fourth-floor location, Cohen had traded the city view for a decrease in rent. In light of the tradeoff, Cohen actually didn't mind the distance from the city. Rather, he found the quiet and the natural light a perfect escape from Chicago's chaos.

His gaze swept across the rising sun and the bird's nest resting in a tree just outside the window. Paulina Street looked beautiful this morning. Cohen had a feeling he would appreciate his living quarters more and more as the months wore on.

Choosing to avoid the elevator, Cohen climbed down the four flights of stairs and stepped out into the neighborhood. Beginning at a normal jog, he headed east down Irving Park Road, hoping to have enough time to reach the lake. This five-mile morning routine began shortly after his father passed away. To those curious about his habit, Cohen would explain that he loved exploring the sights with no pedestrian traffic to slow him down. This explanation could not be further from the truth.

Switching to a slightly faster pace, Cohen only just felt the beginnings of short breath and tired legs. He smiled. His stride fit his build perfectly. He was tall but not lanky, toned but not buff. He jogged until he felt tired enough to turn around; then he sprinted. Cohen sprinted with all of his being, pushing harder as his body told him to stop. Maybe he loved the sense of control; maybe he was addicted to the accomplishment he felt from defying his limits. Whatever the reason, Cohen craved the power he felt while running. He decided exactly where his mind traveled, making the hour between 6 and 7 a.m. the only time Cohen felt pure.

Cohen continued his pace up the four-story flight of stairs and jumped into the shower, never giving his body the opportunity to rest. After a quick rinse, he stepped out and placed a handsome, small watch on his wrist and a necklace around his neck. 6:50 a.m. *Shit.* With an hour commute to the Chicago Police Department's location on South Michigan Street ahead of him, Cohen threw on a pair of khakis and matched them with a blue polo. He took in his appearance before heading to the train. His dripping wet, light-brown hair did nothing to help his confidence.

Well, I'm about to make a great first impression, he thought. Cohen took the brown line to Belmont before transferring to the red line. Reminding himself to set his alarm earlier for the next morning, Cohen rode the train, completely oblivious as to where his career would take him.

***

Cohen felt a rush as he walked through the Chicago Police Department's heavy doors. Entering the lobby, he took stock of the few chairs that acted as a waiting room, the front desk, and the spotlessly waxed floors. Immediately in front of Cohen, a woman sat behind a large, geometric front desk. She did not glance in Cohen's direction, unaware of his presence among the early morning commotion. Cohen watched as other officers in uniform paced throughout the building. Each knew exactly which direction to walk and Cohen felt anxious to join their ranks. Some stopped and shook hands with fellow officers, most kept moving toward their destinations. *Try to blend in,* Cohen told himself, looking left, then right, in an attempt to pick a route.

"Excuse me, sir. Hey, you!" Cohen's head snapped to the left. *Please God, don't let her be speaking to me.* The woman at the front desk glared bullets in Cohen's direction. "Yeah, blue-eyed wonder, are you going to stand there all day or can I give you some direction so you're not loitering in the lobby?"

Officers chuckled as they overheard the encounter. *So much for blending in.* Apparently, coming off as seasoned would prove easier said than done. Cohen closed the distance between him and the woman in two quick strides, hoping her voice's volume would decrease with the proximity. She had light blonde hair pulled back into a ponytail. Her long, angular face appeared as sharp as her voice. Cohen couldn't help but notice the dark circles and wrinkles lining the woman's features.

8

She looked exhausted and certainly not happy to be dealing with Cohen at this early hour.

"Um, yes. Hi…" Cohen hesitated before looking at the nametag on display, "Officer Turner. I'm Cohen Donahue; it's my first day on the job," he extended his hand, "and I'm—"

"Donahue?" Officer Turner questioned. "As in, Peter Donahue's boy?"

Here we go again. "The one and only." Cohen faked a smile, willing any blush to stay beneath the surface. His hand remained extended, waiting for a handshake. It was not reciprocated. A moment passed, and he placed his hand back by his side. After Cohen admitted relation to Peter, he watched as Officer Turner's face changed from indifferent to something else—something he struggled to understand. The flash of what seemed like rage illuminated Turner's features and disappeared just as quickly as it came.

"Did you know my dad?" Cohen tried, confused as to how Officer Turner could display such dislike toward him this early on in their professional relationship.

"Doesn't your orientation into the department start in about five minutes, Donahue? You better put your rookie head back down and follow the signs, kid." Turner extended one bony finger, signaling Cohen to start walking. Her tone of voice left no room for argument.

"Right, thanks." Cohen had always hated pet names: sport, chap, kid, and the like—well, ever since Peter died, that is. As a child, the pet names signified love and affection that a father had for his son. Now they served no other purpose than to

9

remind Cohen of his loss. It didn't help that something about Officer Turner's tone made him feel as if she meant to demean him. Perhaps, Cohen thought, it was the fact that she called him a rookie. Officer Turner used the title with no hint of endearment, but rather to remind Cohen of his place. His legs moved in the direction of her pointer finger and he made a right turn around a corner. A sign hung from the wall.

Below the words "New Recruit Orientation," an arrow pointed straight down the long and narrowly built hallway. Cohen picked up his pace after checking his watch and realizing that he had exactly three minutes to spare before orientation began.

What was her deal, anyway? Cohen thought back to the change in Turner's facial expression at the mention of Peter. He had expected to be recognized in the department, but not with such hostility. Again, Cohen found himself wondering if he had imagined Turner's dislike.

You're losing it, man, he told himself, before walking through a door at the end of the hallway. Stepping in the room, Cohen was immediately brought back to his high school days. Three horizontal rows of desks faced a central chalkboard at the front of the room. A podium stood to the left of the board and two long windows showed a brick wall outside. Out of habit, Cohen moved to the far left side of the room and selected a seat in the second row. He settled into his chair just as a man sat down directly to his left.

Cohen turned and held out his hand. "Hey, man. Cohen Donahue."

10

His new fellow officer looked at Cohen without taking the proffered hand. His gaze started at Cohen's shoes and continued to the top of Cohen's head. "Ya, so I've heard. Spencer."

Okay "Spencer," Cohen thought to himself, fully aware that Spencer brought his rejected handshake count that morning to two. The way that Spencer looked Cohen up and down made him uncomfortable. His hands subconsciously moved toward his hair to see if it had dried. It had. Either Cohen wore a sign printed on his forehead saying, "Hate my guts," or everyone in this place had serious attitude problems.

Deciding to cut his losses and save other introductions for later, Cohen stared ahead, trying to put his encounters with Officer Turner and Spencer out of his mind. So far, his first day had been anything but enjoyable. At exactly 8:00 a.m., a burly, white-haired man walked into the room. His triangular shape, coupled with arms crossed over his chest, demanded attention.

"Welcome to the Chicago Police Department. My name is Lieutenant Dolan. I've worked for the CPD for thirty years now and have the amazing pleasure of teaching all of you new hires the ropes. I understand you all maintain the absolute minimum requirements to be here, basically a graduation certificate from our very own Chicago Policy Academy. Out of the 150 registered rookies that signed up for the twenty-two weeks of training, you are among the 130 that graduated. Congratulations." The sarcasm clung to Dolan's words.

"In case any of you struggle to interpret my tone, I am not, in fact, impressed with your achievements thus far. Quite the contrary. As far as I'm concerned, you haven't proven anything yet."

Between Officer Turner, Spencer, and now Lieutenant Dolan, Cohen wondered if anyone in this department had a friendly demeanor.

"Seeing how this is your first day back from the Police Academy, from my perspective, you're all interns." Lieutenant Dolan continued, "In the real world, if an officer makes a mistake, someone gets hurt or killed. I won't accept that from anyone in this class."

Cohen thought of his dad and needed a distraction to stop the sudden grief spreading from his stomach to his heart. He looked at Spencer through his peripheral vision; Cohen noted a slightly crooked and lopsided nose, big ears, and a goofy-looking haircut. Just like that, Cohen simultaneously felt the pain subside and his confidence grow.

As if able to sense the animosity on the left side of the room, Lieutenant Dolan glared in Cohen and Spencer's direction. "If I see anyone step out of line, I will make it my personal priority to see you thrown out of this police department before you know what hit you." Cohen glanced around the dimly lit, stingy room at the ten new coworkers sitting to his right: six men and four women.

Lieutenant Dolan's monotone voice still had more to say. "Now, based on your graduation, I know you all passed defensive driving, handgun retention, and all of the other training the academy supplies these days. With that in mind, today

12

through Wednesday will serve as informational days relating specifically to this municipal. Thursday, you will be paired with a Field Training Officer. Based on that officer's notes, I will pair you Friday with a more permanent FTO, one that you will be working with until we both deem you ready to be turned loose on your own. Are there any questions?"

Cohen mocked surprise at Spencer's upward shooting hand.

"In regards to our assigned FTO partners, will there be any opportunities for us to list our preferences?" Spencer couldn't help but to shift his gaze to the right, sweeping his eyes over Cohen before resting back on Dolan's face.

This has to be a joke. Cohen looked around the room and waited for someone else to acknowledge the ridiculousness of the question. No one spoke up and Lieutenant Dolan took his time responding. "If you're expecting me to consider your 'preferences' while I assign a *rookie officer's* FTO partner, Spencer, I suggest you start keeping your head down and your mouth shut. Any officer I deem worthy of serving as an FTO will be more than adequate, considering their *years* of training, to show you the ropes."

Ouch. Cohen hid the smile from his face, but his eyes failed to recover so quickly.

"Should be one hell of a week," one of the female officers sighed.

"You can say that again," Cohen responded.

"Lastly," Dolan finished, "I expect all of you to follow directions exactly as they are stated to

13

you. Follow directions and you should experience minimal problems here."

Cohen nodded once—at a pace that might as well have been slow motion.

Easier said than done, Lieutenant. Cohen's ability to follow directions had never been his strong suit.

Chapter 2

Cohen walked into O'Reilly's Pub and took a seat at his usual, isolated barstool. After his first real day on the job since graduating from the police academy, he needed a drink. Sitting to the far left of the pool table, Cohen mentally blocked out the people around him. Being back in Chicago felt good. It felt right. Working in the Chicago Police Department should have felt the same, but something nagged at Cohen that he couldn't quite understand.

When Cohen first received word of his acceptance into the CPD, his surprise overshadowed his joy. Sure, his four-year criminal justice degree from the University of Minnesota no doubt gave him preference over the applicants with merely a high school diploma. That, coupled with the pull his last name must have in the system, meant Cohen had very high chances of being accepted. Still, after opening the letter, Cohen felt numb. He packed his bags for training at the Academy.

"Donahue? As in, Peter Donahue's boy?" He had heard the question all his life. The association with his father produced sentiments of pride and love in Cohen. Pride and love, but also pangs of sadness with which Cohen had recently become all too familiar.

Cohen returned to Chicago after receiving his acceptance letter to make a life for himself—to embark on an unknown journey. So far, his attempt to leave his past behind had proved anything but successful. In fact, it seemed that his new position in the CPD would connect him directly to his childhood.

When Cohen was younger, Peter tried his hardest to keep his son in the dark about the details of his work, often declining to tell Cohen about any of the cases he worked. Cohen's curiosity only grew over the years. After choosing to work at the CPD, Cohen had expected to hear stories involving his dad. Now, Cohen wasn't sure he wanted to hear the details. Turner's change in features at Peter's name made Cohen feel as if his dad hid more than just the details of the cases he worked.

Realizing his transition might be more difficult than he originally thought, Cohen set out to find closure in another form. After his experience at work today, he needed closure. Closure from the pain, from the disappointment, closure from his childhood.

A bartender with jet-black hair, tight jeans, and a deep red polo worked his way down the bar. He gave Cohen a nod, introduced himself as Tommy, and asked what he could get for Cohen.

"Three shots. Whiskey."

Cohen pretended not to notice the wary look Tommy shot his way. He knew his appearance might seem curious, a twenty-three-year-old man sitting alone at a bar on a Monday night. Cohen mentally offered Tommy a truce, hoping to keep the judgment at a minimum. He glanced around the room, searching for a distraction.

It must be family night, Cohen mused, looking at the tables filled with multiple generations. Sitting only ten feet away from him, Cohen watched a young boy play patty-cake with his dad, the child's innocence apparent in his features. The boy obviously admired his father with all of his tiny being. Cohen had looked at his own father in that way once. The familiarity coupled with the threat of surfacing memories momentarily overwhelmed Cohen. He turned back to the bar, suddenly very ready to drink. *In that case,* Cohen thought, *I better make this quick.* For someone determined to use the night productively, Cohen sure couldn't wait to crawl into his bed and forget.

Tommy placed the three shots in a straight line in front of Cohen. Whiskey filled the glasses to the brim and Tommy completely avoided eye contact. *Looks like Tommy accepted my truce,* Cohen guessed. Usually, Cohen didn't let himself look at the shot glass for more than a few seconds before gulping the liquid down. Imagining the taste of the alcohol always proved worse than actually taking the shot. Tonight would be different. Cohen took in the three glasses lined up in front of him, paying no attention to the small brunette sending seductive signals from across the bar. Cohen's blue eyes, although not as noticeable as his father's hazel, had an equally strong effect on women.

Placing his fingers around the first shot glass, Cohen mentally prepared for the memories to surface. Cohen usually suppressed these moments, but tonight he wanted to remember. His stomach muscles clenched and his breathing slowed. *Closure,* he reminded himself.

Cohen forced himself to remember his mother. Theresa's dead stare had lacked any hint of love or affection toward her son. Rather, in place of tenderness, she would glare openly at Cohen, her

17

black pupils sending an unmistakable message of hatred. What she lacked in motherly love, Theresa made up for in malice. As a young boy, Cohen worried that his eyes, the same shade as his mother's, contained an equally ugly stare. He would lie awake at night and beg God to change his eyes from blue to hazel, like his father's. Every morning had been a bigger disappointment than the last. Eventually, Cohen stopped talking to God altogether.

Ready to continue his memory ritual, Cohen squinted, focusing on the wooden counter that supported his forearms. A snapshot surfaced in his memory:

Peter opens the front door, letting four people inside. Cohen sits on the couch, bouncing with excitement as he looks at the food lining the kitchen table: hamburgers, brats, and watermelon— everything necessary to have a successful barbeque. His dad invited over some of his CPD coworkers to celebrate the beautiful summer weather.

Blackness overwhelmed the mental image and Cohen's memory skipped like a scratched record.

Cohen hides under the kitchen table, crying. A man turns to the seven-year-old Cohen before leaving and says his goodbyes. "Have a great day, son."

Cohen's small head turns toward the clock and he hopes that his dad will come find him. Nothing sounds from inside of the house, aside from his parents screaming. Something shatters and Cohen pushes himself farther under the table. He cries because someone threw the food to the ground

18

in anger before anyone at the barbeque had a chance to eat. He cries because his parents scare him when they fight. Cohen wishes his dad's coworkers hadn't left at the first sign of an argument. Peter's brown loafers move into the kitchen.

"Coh? Cohen, buddy?"

Peter bends his waist, scanning under the table. The sight of his seven-year-old boy finding refuge in a corner of the house threatens to produce tears. Peter reaches out his hand and Cohen allows himself to be pulled to his feet.

"How about we go get some dinner and ice cream for dessert?" Peter winks at Cohen, placing his hand on the boy's bony, fragile shoulder.

"What about Mom?" Cohen asks Peter as his innocent eyes spot Theresa shuffling into the bathroom.

Cohen's mind returned to the present. *Breathe.* Aside from Peter's coworker Bre, Cohen never saw any of his dad's friends from the CPD again. He inhaled deeply before submerging himself into another memory, a memory that took place the day after the barbeque.

Cohen stands on the paved road just outside of his house. Usually, he waits for the school bus with his neighborhood friends. Today, he watches the yellow bus pull away. His girlfriend for the week, Anna, waves to him through the rear emergency exit window. This would be the fifth time that month that Cohen missed the bus. He turns and walks back toward his house.

Cohen wonders what excuse he's going to tell his dad this time. If Peter found out that it took

19

Cohen an extra ten minutes to wake up his mom and help her move from the bathroom floor to her bed...Cohen couldn't handle another night of yelling. Especially not after hearing yesterday's argument that drew an abrupt halt to all barbeque festivities.

His feet walk back toward his house, kicking at the rocks as he formulates his excuse for being late to class. When Cohen raises his head, he stops dead in his tracks. His mother lugs a suitcase across the front porch. A black Jeep with tinted windows stalls at the end of the driveway. Cohen strains to see the driver, but the windows are too dark. Theresa steps into the passenger seat and Cohen drops his backpack, somehow knowing what would come next.

Cohen runs for the car as fast as his legs can take him. He yells to his mom, needing her to get out.

"Mom? MOM?! Where are you going?!" Theresa looks at her distraught son running in her direction. She sees the tears begin to stream down his face. The lines of anger etched around her cheekbones disappear momentarily, suggesting that Theresa may just change her mind and step out from the car. Just as quickly as they disappeared, the lines press back into her features again, foreshadowing her next movement. Turning her head away from her son, Theresa shuts the passenger door. The white scrape on the lower left corner of the door catches the sun, for a split second sending a distracting reflection into Cohen's vision.

The tires turn slowly, as if laughing at Cohen for his slow pace. As his short legs grow tired, Cohen follows the car for a block until he physically can't run any further. The Jeep drives away; his mother drifts into the distance.

That afternoon, Cohen returned home to find Bre sitting on his front doorstep. For some reason, the memory of his delicate hand in Bre's strong, calloused fingers seemed to appear more vividly in Cohen's mind than most of the exchanges he had with his own mother. Cohen kicked himself for losing touch with Bre. In working with Peter and watching out for Cohen, Bre had served as more of a mother figure than Theresa ever had.

Quite often, in fact, Cohen slept in Bre's spare bedroom—whenever his dad randomly disappeared for two nights at a time. Cohen would come home from school to find Bre in the kitchen instead of Peter. He understood his dad's need to get away once in a while, but his curiosity about Peter's whereabouts never faded. Despite Cohen's persistence, Bre always claimed ignorance with regard to Peter's retreat.

Cohen hated that the memory of his mother caused his shoulders to slump forward. He hated that his body felt heavy, as if lead ran through his veins in place of blood. It had been sixteen years since his mother left, yet she still had the ability to hurt him.

Not anymore, Cohen confirmed. Cohen raised the first shot glass and whispered, "Goodbye, Mom." The dark liquid burned his throat. Cohen welcomed the feeling.

No stopping now. "Dad, this one's for you." Cohen heard Tommy start cleaning tables. It was almost last call, but Cohen knew he needed these next few memories to surface; he tried to hurry them along. *For closure.* He found comfort in the idea.

These memories came more easily than the last:

All of Peter's coworkers surround Cohen, six years old, and his father. Cohen wears khaki pants and a light blue shirt. The shirt's hue, combined with a child's pure bliss, makes Cohen glow.

"Pete, Theresa couldn't make it tonight? Not even to celebrate your Sergeant promotion?"

"Theresa isn't feeling too well," Peter explains. Both the question and Peter's response sound too rehearsed.

Cohen turns to make eye contact with a man chuckling under his breath at Peter's response. He wonders if the man knows that his mother drank two bottles of wine before getting into bed at 4 p.m. He wants to ask the man why he laughs, because Cohen feels sad for his mother. She didn't even eat dinner, after all. Cohen makes a mental note to leave some extra mac 'n cheese on the second shelf in the fridge tomorrow morning. Theresa would see it there. Sometimes Cohen wonders if his mother sees anything unless it's on her wine shelf. His small head turns back toward Peter and smiles. Cohen feels like one of the grownups tonight.

"Alright, come on now, all of you get together for one picture. Hold up your shots!" the Gage bartender instructs. Cohen holds his Sprite in

the air, his smile overwhelming his entire face. The camera snaps the photo. Peter turns to his coworkers and raises his glass a little higher.

"Thanks to everyone who came out to celebrate with me and my son tonight," he looks down at Cohen and winks, "and to dodging the bullet."

Everyone tips back a shot glass.

"Twenty minutes, man." Tommy interrupted the memory.

"Alright, alright. Thanks, Tommy." Cohen placed a twenty on the counter and raised his glass, signaling that he would be finished soon.

Cohen knew he couldn't avoid the last memory. He felt the familiar tears tug at his lids and he blinked fast. They stayed below the surface.

Now eighteen years old, Cohen places a large box into the trunk of his car. Peter and Cohen had plans to drive to the University of Minnesota that morning. Excitement for freshman orientation mixes inside Cohen with guilt at leaving his father alone in Chicago. His phone vibrates in his back pocket and he recognizes the number.

Bre. Probably calling to wish me luck, Cohen predicts. "Hey Bre, you already missing me, huh?"

"Hey Coh, buddy, listen...don't freak out; everything is fine. Your dad was shot on the job about an hour ago. He's in the hospital—fully aware and conscious. He's going to be totally fine. The doctor said he will have a full recovery; nothing to worry about."

Just as Cohen frantically places his keys in the ignition, ready to begin driving to the hospital, Bre continues, "I'll pick you up in ten minutes."

Don't freak out? Not likely. Cohen paces for what seems like three hours before Bre finally pulls into the driveway.

When they arrive at the hospital, he rushes into his father's room, following Bre's lead.

Peter wears a big smile and tousles Cohen's hair. A white wrap covers his left shoulder, marked with the slightest pinpoint of red discoloration. Cohen sighs in relief, offering Bre a tentative smile.

"I'll meet you there, kiddo," Peter tries. "Bre will drive me to Minnesota as soon as I'm discharged and I'll come help you set up your room. Seriously," Peter continues, despite Cohen's wary look, "the doctor said the only thing between me and my discharge is a boatload of paperwork. Then I'm free to leave."

"But Dad, I don't mind waiting..."

"Plus," Peter's animation grows as he cocks his eyebrow, "you can't let the other guys find the pretty girls before you even get there."

Cohen laughs and reluctantly agrees to finish packing and then get on the road. It would be a lonely ride, but Cohen knows that Peter would do his best to get there as soon as he could. Peter had been talking about this road trip for weeks. As Cohen turns to leave, Peter calls out, "Hold up a second, I almost forgot to give you your graduation present. I know it's a little late, but..."

"Oh, come on, Dad. You know you didn't have to get me anything."

24

Peter pulls a small silver box out of the gym bag sitting on the bedside table and hands it to his son. Inside the packaging, Cohen finds a long gold chain with a pendant hanging from the end.

"Saint Christopher?" Cohen asks.

"Just in case you need some guidance. Your old man isn't right around the corner anymore, you know." Peter gives Cohen his famous wink and Cohen thinks back to the night many years ago that he found Peter praying. Down on his knees, with his fingers interlaced in front of his chest, Peter had been so focused that he didn't even notice Cohen's presence in the room. Cohen had wanted to ask what Peter prayed about, but the sight had moved Cohen into silence, creating a similar sensation to the one he felt now.

With that, Cohen hugs his dad, receives a kiss on the cheek, and walks out of the hospital room.

Keep going, Cohen urged, blocking out the sound of glasses clinking together as Tommy placed them in the sink.

Cohen guesses the reason behind Bre's tears the second he answers the phone. He just finished unloading his last suitcase from his car; Cohen left the hospital nine hours ago.

"Um—Cohen, your dad...he passed away. A blood clot traveled undetected to his heart. I am so sorry..."

Cohen's body goes slack as his hands reach for the hood of his car in an attempt to steady his body. The effort fails, and his knees connect with the concrete that paves the parking lot. Tears flow and show no sign of stopping.

25

Cohen's mind walked through the haze of events that followed. Bre bought Cohen a plane ticket home. She planned the funeral and the wake and packed all of Peter's belongings into boxes to be placed in storage. The funeral flew by in a haze that Cohen could barely recall. He remembered the smell of flowers, the flowers and the closed casket. His dad would not want anyone to feel uncomfortable at the sight of his dead body, and he certainly wouldn't allow himself to appear vulnerable and weak, even in death. Before Cohen returned back to school, Bre packed a small brown box containing a few of his father's belongings.

"Just a few things I thought you might like to bring back to school," Bre explains. "Nothing special, I know you love this shirt of his. I put the obituary in there, some jewelry, and an old photograph I found in your dad's wallet. Like I said, not much, but…" Cohen pulls Bre in tight for a hug.

The box now sat in Cohen's new apartment under his queen-sized bed. He continually found himself looking at the picture taken the night of his dad's promotion celebration: him, holding a Sprite, his dad, a shot of whiskey, surrounded by smiling coworkers. The picture was all happiness—well, aside from one frowning man standing in the corner. Cohen couldn't remember another time in his life that so many genuine smiles existed in one room. The picture stayed in Cohen's wallet and the Saint Christopher necklace around his neck.

Between swallowing the second shot and placing the glass back on the bar, Cohen made a mental note to call Bre now that he had returned to

26

town. Tommy came out of the supply room and made his way to the bar.

Quickly, Cohen turned to the third shot. *This one is easy.* Titling his head toward the ceiling, Cohen raised the glass. "To dodging the bullet."

Cohen hoped the toast would resonate enough so that he could avoid a similar fate to his dad's. He also hoped to pay many years of homage to Peter's life's work. Giving Tommy a two-finger wave, Cohen stood and began mentally preparing for his second official day at the Chicago Police Department.

Chapter 3

On Tuesday, Cohen listened as Lieutenant Dolan divided the new recruits into two groups. Cohen's consisted of Leila, Charlie, Scottie, Jason, and, unfortunately, Spencer. The next two days would be spent entirely within these groups. While group one received a tour of the surrounding Chicago area, group two listened to presentations involving the specifics of the department, and vice versa. The agenda was planned to help the officers gain familiarity with their new surroundings, with presentation topics ranging from a detailed history of the CPD to a personal account of a senior officer who had been held hostage.

"Sometimes," the officer explained, "officers find themselves in dangerous situations—in situations that classify them as the victim instead of the protector. Take me for example: one minute, I'm driving home from work, the next, I'm grabbed the second I step out of my car and held in confinement for three days. It is imperative that you understand how to best respond to these types of experiences in case you find yourself in a similar situation.

"I'll leave you with three useful points to remember if you're ever held hostage. One, avoid the situation at all costs. Two, find an escape route. And three, when all else fails, use momentum." Cohen literally had to pinch his forearm in an effort to stay awake. Even if he found the presentations interesting, something about sitting in a stuffy room listening to a rather monotone voice all but put him to sleep.

28

Although Spencer's hostile demeanor toward Cohen had yet to dissolve, Cohen found the rest of his group to be rather enjoyable. Scottie and Charlie, friends since their high school days, had a sense of humor that Cohen appreciated. They found an excuse to use wit in almost any situation, often diffusing the all too obvious tension between Cohen and Spencer.

"Hey Scottie, are you retaining any of the information in there? Every time I look in your direction, it's as if you're dreaming about the girl from last night who got away. I mean Jesus man, get over it!" Charlie teased.

"Please. She could not have been more interested in me if I had been a Lieutenant. You're one to talk Mr. Suave, I didn't see you connecting with anyone other than that glass of beer you cradled all night." Scottie wasn't about to let Charlie win this argument, and the break between the presentations seemed the best time for them to duel it out.

"You weren't feeling it last night, Charlie?" Cohen joined in for the fun.

"If by feeling it, you mean having one drink and being a major buzzkill, then hell yeah he was feeling it!" Scottie added.

If Charlie wanted to come back with a response, Cohen doubted he would be able to put aside his laughter long enough to do so.

"Where did you guys hang out last night?" The quietest form of a question came from the opposite side of the room and all heads turned toward Jason. Since being back at the department, Jason hadn't been one to talk much. Well, at all. He

29

mostly minded his own business and kept any comments to himself. Hearing his deep monotone voice actually served as a bit of a shock for Cohen.

"Who the hell knows? Once you get down to your tenth beer, the details of the night tend to fade a little bit. Although I'm sure Charlie could tell you each and every bar we visited."

Cohen amusedly observed the exchange. He assumed that Jason played the quiet role out of habit, and predicted that he would balance the group out nicely.

Charlie looked pointedly in his high school buddy's direction before Lieutenant Dolan returned from his bathroom break.

"Alright everyone, what do we have next?" As Dolan looked down at the agenda in his hand, Scottie exaggeratedly imitated throwing back three beers big enough that he had to use two hands. Cohen couldn't help but laugh.

***

By the end of day two, Spencer and Cohen were getting on each other's last nerves. "Alright, Group A. I know we have been listening to a lot today, so I want to end the day with you each telling the members of your group something that would be helpful for them to know about you."

Cohen glanced at Spencer and threw him the most sarcastic smile he could muster. Spencer responded with a very casual middle finger. If these two had to speak to each other for any more than five minutes, all hell would break loose. Realizing the immature nature of his own actions, Cohen turned his attention back toward Lieutenant Dolan.

"Share any knowledge with your group that could benefit a future fellow officer in an emergency situation. Be honest, people; trust and transparency will prove absolutely essential in this profession."

A little vague, Cohen thought. Without missing a beat, Spencer opened his mouth and started babbling. Cohen immediately lost interest. He squelched his desire to inform Spencer that his pompous head had actually begun to look larger by the second.

"Alright, here we go." Spencer imitated a sports announcer, "I'm a Chicago native, attended the University of San Diego, and graduated summa cum laude." Cohen's silent laugh would have broken the surface had Leila's voice not interrupted.

"Thank God, Spencer!" Her sarcastic tone exuded irritation. "Tell you what, if a crook is holding a gun to my head and you're my only hope at survival, I'll be sure to remember that you graduated with an A in History 101."

Admiration trickled from Cohen. He had noticed Leila before, but not in the light he saw her now. Over the past ten years, remembering women's names had proved anything but easy for Cohen. Yet Leila's red hair, pale skin, and high cheekbones certainly grabbed his attention—not to mention her deep, blue eyes.

"Born in Minnesota, moved to Chicago during my fifth grade year," Leila continued; "my biggest fear is heights, so don't expect me to jump from building to building. Pet peeve is being

31

underestimated. Hobbies include kickboxing." She took a breath. "Oh, and fair warning to everyone in this room, do not talk to me before I've had time to drink my morning coffee; I can't promise you'll make it out alive."

With a final glance at Spencer, Leila nodded her head, signaling the end of her speech. Scottie chuckled at the shock evident on Spencer's face while attempting to hide his amusement with a fist over his mouth. Cohen trained his eyes on Leila and began his introduction.

"Born in Chicago, studied in Minnesota, scared of dark water, hobby is running—"

"Let me guess," Spencer interrupted, desperate to regain his lost ground, "your dad's name got you into the CPD and now you're expecting special treatment from the people who actually deserve to be here?"

"Pet peeve," Cohen continued with a slight cock of his head toward Spencer, "is douchebaggery." Although Cohen feigned indifference, his insides boiled and he legitimately considered knocking Spencer in the face.

Well, there you have it, folks, it's out in the open now. Cohen thought. *Now I'm sure no one will have a prejudice against me.* Based on Cohen's interactions thus far, he guessed his association with his dad would only result in more tensions. Thanks to Spencer, Cohen's relationship to Peter Donahue was now fully out of the bag.

In spite of not wanting to create friction with a coworker, Spencer's demeanor rubbed Cohen the wrong way. Spencer knew just how to push Cohen's buttons and get under his skin. Not to mention, how the hell did Spencer know about his dad? What had initially been an uncomfortable confrontation with Officer Turner had officially extended to Spencer. Cohen felt that he must have missed an important detail somewhere along the line. He attempted to focus on the rest of the introductions all while itching to be released for the day.

Just let it go, Cohen told himself as he changed out of his temporary uniform and into a pair of jeans and a long-sleeve, gray waffle shirt. For the life of him, Cohen could not figure out why Spencer hated him from the moment they met. Sure, Peter Donahue left quite a nice legacy at the CPD, but Cohen would have to prove himself just as much as every other new officer and he deserved a fair, unbiased shot. Due to the reputation that preceded him, Cohen probably deserved more of a clean slate than the other officers. He envied their ability to start in a completely new work environment where they could build themselves from scratch.

Losing himself in the silence of the locker room, Cohen almost didn't hear Scottie, Charlie, and Jason open the door. The chatter announced their presence as they approached Cohen's locker.

"There you are, Donahue! Put your shoes on, a bunch of us are walking over to Gage to grab a drink." *Gage.* Cohen thought of the picture in his wallet and smiled. He hadn't been back to that bar since his dad's promotional celebration. Despite Cohen's curiosity as to the state of the bar, the events of the day made him want nothing more than to go home and sleep. Realizing his lack of desire to socialize, Cohen attempted to back out of the invitation.

"I don't know, guys. I'm feeling a little bit restless. I think I'll just go home and relax for a while. Thanks for the invite though—have a shot for me."

Scottie acted as though he didn't hear one word of Cohen's refusal. "Charlie and I were just talking about how sick of these presentations we are. If we don't get some drinks in us soon, I'm honestly concerned about our welfare."

"Try and disagree with that," Charlie chimed in. Mocking Lieutenant Dolan, he continued, "Everybody hold hands now, look into each other's souls and say something really, really meaningful."

Cohen and Jason couldn't help but laugh as Cohen threw up his hands in surrender to their reasoning. He shut his locker door and forced his concerns about Spencer out of his mind. Having a beer did sound nice, and with a few more of Charlie's impersonations, Cohen's wandering mind could definitely be distracted.

"Hey! Are you guys coming or what?" Leila poked her head into the locker room and glanced at the four boys.

"For the love of God, Charlie, why don't you just put your locker key on your key ring?" Leila exclaimed just as Charlie placed his locker's key under the mat that lined the floor.

"What is life without a little adventure, Leila?"

"Well, let's hope Dolan never realizes that just about anyone can access your firearm if they just look under the mat."

Leila's eye roll ended when she noticed Cohen's shoes lying discarded to the right of his feet. "Let's go, Donahue." She twitched her left eyebrow playfully. Cohen didn't even tie his shoelaces.

Gage looked exactly as it had seventeen years ago. The green booths appeared a little more worn than before, with some of the cheap fabric ripping away from the frame. Aside from the updated stools and the younger staff, Cohen felt at home just walking through the doors. After witnessing so much animosity toward his father the past few days, this place successfully lifted his spirits. Scottie, Jason, and Leila grabbed a booth as Charlie and Cohen made their way to the bar. They offered to buy the first round.

The bartender did not hesitate before approaching Cohen, failing to supply Charlie with even a sideways glance. Charlie scoffed at Cohen, mocking him by acting jealous at the bartender's apparent lack of attention. Cohen ordered five beers for the table and felt his body relax, no doubt because of Spencer's absence.

As if the universe couldn't let Cohen breathe just yet, his relaxation was interrupted by the sound of the bar door opening. Spencer bounced through the frame and made his way straight toward the booth. He looked over at Charlie and Cohen standing at the bar and gave Charlie a wave. Cohen turned to Charlie, this time mocking jealously over Spencer's attention. Charlie laughed.

"Don't take Spencer too seriously, man. The guy has had a rough life."

Who hasn't? Cohen wanted to ask.

35

"I went to get drinks with him after our first day on the job. One drink led to another, and before we knew it, both of us were telling our entire life stories. His past is one for the books, man."

Despite his annoyance, Cohen couldn't quell his interest on the subject. He kept his eyes trained on the bartender and waited for Charlie to continue.

"Apparently, Spencer's lowlife dad drank away all of his family's money and abused Mrs. Hoffman pretty badly. I'm sure you can imagine the rest. Anyway, Spencer was determined to escape that life. He claims that his acceptance into the CPD is the best thing that ever happened to him."

Cohen watched Spencer as he listened to Charlie's narrative. When he reached the group, Spencer gave Scottie a high five and took a seat next to Leila, his arm casually resting on the section of booth behind Leila's back. Cohen's flare of jealously alarmed him; he had no right to feel possessive over a woman he hardly knew.

"So, on Monday, Spencer walked into the department feeling all blessed and shit," Charlie continued. "He walked by the front desk and overheard Officer Turner telling Dolan to 'watch out for Peter Donahue's kid. He's destined for greatness.'" Cohen nodded his head. "It's not that Spencer feels entitled to be here, but I'm sure you can understand his tendency to feel protective over the position."

Cohen sighed. "The name does seem to follow me…"

When Cohen spoke with Officer Turner, she seemed to genuinely hate his guts. Confusion settled as Cohen registered Charlie's story. Did Turner hate him or think he was destined for greatness? Cohen felt sure that Turner knew details about his dad, but what those details were he couldn't begin to imagine. Focusing on Spencer's role in the story, Cohen also began to think that he and Spencer may have more in common than he thought: a past to escape.

"Look, everyone else, we know you deserve to be here. I mean hell, based on name alone, there has to be some kind of cop gene in your blood. How I see it, with your reputation preceding you the way it does, you have a hell of a lot more to prove than the rest of us."

Cohen allowed himself a laugh and shook his head. "What did I get myself into?"

"Just give him some time, Donahue. He'll come around. I mean, he's a dick, yeah, but having animosity in the workplace won't help anybody…"

Cohen knew that Charlie's logic made sense. Constant bickering between new recruits would only draw unwanted attention from the officers higher up in the department. Cohen signaled the bartender. "Make that six beers, please."

Chapter 4

Wednesday finally drew to a close and Cohen's excitement about working with a Field Training Officer reached a whole new level. Learning about the law and a citizen's rights proved interesting enough in the academy, but Cohen itched to get out into the field. Physically putting a criminal away, Cohen imagined, had to be one of the most rewarding jobs available.

"All right everyone, your official uniform shipment finally arrived. Form a line and everyone take one of everything."

Cohen's anticipation as he waited behind Scottie and Leila only increased. With this uniform, he would be that much closer to starting his work in the city. Not even when Spencer budged in front of Cohen did he feel any negative sentiments. Cohen reached to grab his shirt and his fingers hesitated on the rough fabric.

"Psht, Donahue, please. Are you really reaching for a size large? With your small and delicate frame, don't you think a small would be a better pick?"

Leila's giggle sounded as the corners of Cohen's mouth inched upwards.

"Oh yeah, Charlie? Well while I'm grabbing the small, maybe you should just turn in your gun. Based on your lack of ability to throw a dart even remotely close to the bull's eye, not to mention the board alone, I wouldn't want to be within a mile of you using that weapon."

Dolan stood nearby appearing to invest the entirety of his attention on a document in his hands.

With one glance, Cohen noticed that Lieutenant Dolan's frown came dangerously close to bursting.

Dolan said a few parting words for the day and ended the session at 4 p.m., an hour earlier than usual. Cohen glanced at the clock on the wall and wondered how he would entertain himself tonight with his blood rushing so quickly through his veins. Distraction would be impossible. If the thought of working in the city gave Cohen this much adrenaline, he couldn't imagine how he would feel actually carrying out his duty.

"Go put these materials in your lockers. If your family members are coming to tonight's festivities, feel free to bring them by my office for a quick introduction. I find ample entertainment in meeting those responsible for putting up with your shit every day." Dolan couldn't help but let a smile slip through his tough façade. "More than anything, try and make the department feel like home to any family members coming today; you'd be surprised at how much that can ease a worried parent's fears."

Cohen turned to Charlie with a confused look on his face. "You forget, Donahue?" Charlie joked. "National Night Out: the night we invite the entire Chicago community to come see our department."

Cohen squinted his eyes in confusion.

"In other words, we have a chance to hand out candy and give tours as a way to convince our families that our job isn't a death wish." Charlie formed a pistol with his fingers and pretended to shoot himself in the head.

Right. Cohen now remembered that Dolan had mentioned something about National Night Out.

It must have been in between presentations—no wonder he had forgotten; Cohen had probably been mid snooze. That, or Cohen subconsciously chose to overlook the event, as if that would delay the inevitable.

"You got any family members stopping by?"

"Doesn't look like I'll have any today," Cohen replied, trying to insinuate that his parents would have eagerly waited for him in the lobby had the event been any other day.

Charlie reached over and gave Cohen a pat on the back. "Why don't you stick around for a little? Once my family leaves, we could grab a beer?"

Cohen nodded and carried his equipment to the locker room, passing through the lobby on his way. The tiny front entrance appeared overwhelmed with community members, especially children. Kids ran around, anxious for the grand tour of the department. Cohen kept walking, stifling the jealousy he felt at the sight of such expectant guests. Cohen imagined his dad in the department and smiled at the visualization of Peter's pride in Cohen's accomplishments.

As he passed the front desk, Cohen felt Officer Turner's glare burning into the back of his skull. He wished he could ask Turner some questions, although something told him the conversation should take place when fewer people stood within earshot. Chances were that Cohen would receive another verbal lashing when he approached Officer Turner. He couldn't help but chuckle at the same time; Turner didn't seem like the kind of person to enjoy screaming kids desperate for some candy and attention.

Cohen placed his equipment into his locker and changed into his standard look of jeans and a gray T-shirt. Right as he became used to the silence, Spencer entered the locker room accompanied by his mother. Mrs. Hoffman appeared pale and worn down to the bone. Cohen's heart went out to her fragile body and meek appearance.

"And this, Mom, is my locker." Spencer feigned excitement, putting on a show for his mom's benefit. Even in her rundown state and old age, Cohen still thought Mrs. Hoffman looked beautiful—Spencer definitely did not get his looks from this woman.

As they neared, Cohen reached out his hand. "Hello, Mrs. Hoffman. I'm Cohen Donahue. I'm a new recruit officer working with Spencer."

"Oh, how nice to meet you, Cohen!" Conflicting with her appearance, Mrs. Hoffman's handshake was as firm as steel. *She's a fighter*, Cohen thought, and smiled. "Now you watch out for my boy here, please, Cohen. I don't want to hear about Spencer getting into any trouble."

Spencer looked away uncomfortably. The blush on his cheeks betrayed his embarrassment. "I think Spencer will do just fine without anyone's help, Mrs. Hoffman, but I'll do my best to keep him out of any trouble."

Mrs. Hoffman nodded her head in approval and Spencer led his mother toward the exit. After Mrs. Hoffman walked through the door held open by her son, Spencer glanced back at Cohen and gave the slightest, almost non-existent nod before following his mother's lead. Cohen smiled despite himself and decided to head to Gage a little early. He took out his phone and sent Charlie a text message asking him to meet Cohen at the bar once his parents left the department.

The female bartender from the night before noticed Cohen the second he entered. Although hoping to avoid her, Cohen couldn't ignore the exaggerated hand motions she used when signaling an open chair for him at the bar. "Looking for some more whiskey tonight, kiddo?" she asked with the most animated expression Cohen thought he had ever seen. Cohen mentally added kiddo to the list of demeaning names he hated, especially when it appeared very obvious that the bartender must be around his age. Cohen actually found himself missing Tommy as he turned down the whiskey and ordered a Blue Moon instead. He would take an eye roll over aggressive small talk any day.

After the bartender introduced herself as Amelia, Cohen endured her babble for much longer than he wanted. Amelia took her sweet time in filling Cohen's glass, enjoying his company a little too much.

"You look kind of like a hockey player, do you play hockey?"

"Um, no I—"

"Soccer? Tennis? I bet you play tennis. Anyways, I've been trying to be more active lately and if you have any pointers...do you? Have any pointers?"

Noticing Cohen's stare directed elsewhere, Amelia only continued. "Hello? Are you even listening to me?"

Cohen zoned out of the conversation after attempting to answer Amelia's first question. In fact, his breath caught the second that he turned his head and spotted Leila sitting at a booth in the same corner as the dartboard. He didn't remember seeing her at the National Night Out and now wondered if her family failed to make an appearance.

"Okay..." Amelia continued without the slightest hint taken, "crazy weather we've been having recently, don't you think?"

"Sure, uh, yeah, crazy." Cohen stole multiple glances at Leila. She sat alone, just her and her beer glass. As he watched, Leila continued to stare into her cup as if she were studying something at its bottom. Just as he gained enough confidence to join her, Cohen scolded himself. *Of course she isn't here alone. Her date probably went to the bathroom.*

Cohen turned his head in the opposite direction, attempting to keep his attention from wandering Leila's way every few seconds. He had never considered the possibility of Leila having a boyfriend. He now realized his mistake. Leila had a beautiful personality with looks to match. For all Cohen knew, she might have a fiancé. His new friend Amelia broke him out of his trance. He couldn't have been more grateful.

"You looking at the girl over there, the one alone at the booth? The one with the red hair?" As if any other girls sat by themselves in the bar. "She got in about a half an hour ago. Came alone and has been sitting there ever sense. Are you two dating? You'd be an attractive couple if you were, maybe you should go talk to her. But if you don't want to you could totally stay here and—"

"Uh...thanks," Cohen said, giving Amelia a nod and acknowledging her advice. Besides, he realized, it wouldn't be the worst thing in the world if Amelia thought Cohen had a girlfriend.

So Leila did come alone, Cohen mulled as relief spread through his body. His heart rate decreased and he cautioned himself not to get too confident. He still knew nothing about Leila's love life. *So she came alone,* he told himself. *She could still have a significant other waiting at home.* He stood and prepared to interrupt her still-constant gaze into her mug. Attempting to look casual and confident, Cohen expected Leila to see him coming and offer him a seat. She didn't look up and he slowed his pace, wondering what she could possibly be thinking. Tilting his head toward her, Cohen softly announced his presence. "Leila?"

Leila looked up, her glazed stare slowly exiting a trance. Cohen's heart all but broke as he noticed her blue eyes lacked their usual strength and determination. Instead, they looked tired, scared, and lonely. Even in her pain, Leila remained the most beautiful woman Cohen had ever seen.

"Cohen! Hey, I'm just...what are you doing here?" At her attempt to appear light and nonchalant Cohen wanted to take her in his arms and hold her tightly. Where had all of these feelings come from?

"Hiding out from the National Night Out event. Not really my thing."

"You and me both." Her shoulders slumped the slightest amount. "If you're not with anyone and want to take a seat..."

44

Cohen sat across from Leila. It took everything in his being to restrain him from putting his hand over hers.

"Now, tell me this, Mr. Donahue, an attractive guy like yourself..." Cohen noticed a slight blush spread across Leila's face as she continued, "What are you doing at a bar alone?"

Cohen chuckled at her attempted banter. He felt Amelia's focus on him and hoped that she had moved on to the next man at the bar. Cohen wanted to be with Leila, and he had absolutely no control over his desire. "It's actually a long story," Cohen responded. "Let's just say I don't have a long list of family or friends here in Chicago—at least, not anymore."

"Anymore. You used to?"

Cohen's thoughts flashed back to his father's face and deep laugh. A smile spread across his face at the remembered image.

"Oh yeah, I had the best dad a kid could've asked for. Actually, one of my favorite memories with him happened here at Gage." Cohen found himself speaking of his father with ease. The memories he shared made Leila laugh and Cohen's lopsided grin stayed plastered to his face the entire time. Something about Leila made everything seem okay in the world. Very few people in Cohen's life had that effect on him.

"And your mom?"

Cohen stalled. He had yet to tell anyone the full story about his mother. During high school, Theresa's disappearance was common knowledge. The other kids would talk about it among themselves, sure, but never within earshot of Cohen.

At college, Cohen avoided speaking about family and found that lying often proved easier than telling the truth. Debating whether or not to sugarcoat the situation for Leila, Cohen decided on honesty at the last second.

"She left when I was seven. Haven't heard from her since." The other details would come in time, and Cohen certainly hoped that Leila would be onboard with spending more time together.

Leila reached her hand toward Cohen's upper arm but recoiled at the last second. Neither party knew the boundaries of their relationship yet, if they could even think of it as such. Cohen cleared the air quickly enough for Leila to avoid feeling embarrassed at her impulse.

"Alright, your turn now. What about your family?" He watched Leila bear the same struggle: truth, or lie? Cohen waited, hoping she would decide on truth.

"My parents moved to Florida basically the day after I graduated from high school. They said they would be back to visit, but it's been three and a half years since I saw them last. I mean, really though, can you blame them for wanting to stay in paradise?"

Yes, Cohen thought, *I can.*

"Anyway, they have a beautiful place and I'm welcome there anytime. It might take me a little while to save up with this 40K salary we're working with." Her left eyebrow arched and signaled sarcasm. Cohen couldn't seem to look away. He noticed her features take on a more serious tone.

"And then...there is Emmett, my older brother." Leila hesitated. Her mouth opened and then closed as she simultaneously placed her hands around her beer glass. Cohen waited patiently, encouraging Leila to continue with his genuine curiosity.

"Ever since I can remember, he's been running around with different crews in the city. It started in middle school with some petty crimes: shoplifting, selling alcohol to minors. Then in high school, he started selling drugs on the street. My parents stayed in denial about his substance abuse and Emmett shut me out. One day, I went to the corner that he ran and tried to talk him into coming home." She laughed at her apparent naivety. "Let's just say, I walked away having made no progress and sporting a new black eye. After that, I just—I guess I just stopped trying." Leila shrugged her shoulders and Cohen pictured Leila's determined self in a younger light. Cohen's insides crawled with anger at the thought of a child losing their right to innocence.

Despite Leila's efforts, she couldn't seem to stop the words from spilling out of her mouth. "I lied the other day in officer training. My worst fear isn't heights. It's that I'll be called to a crime scene and have to bring my brother into prison—or worse, that I'll find him dead. Then again, weirdly enough, I'm also terrified I'll never have the opportunity to put him behind bars."

Leila raised her gaze to meet Cohen's as if she had just admitted to murder. The guilt, plain as day, sounded thick in her voice. "I don't know, maybe he could finally turn his life around if he found himself in prison. God knows he won't do it unless forced.

"I want to laugh when I think about him, running around with his red hair—that's his street name, Red." She looked down again, attempting to lighten the mood before the tears showed. She didn't laugh. Instead, she spoke quietly, obviously embarrassed. "I really have no idea why I just told you all of that."

Cohen reached his arm across the table, fully aware of his movements and intending to keep his hand wherever it landed. As he squeezed Leila's hand and opened his mouth to offer support, a familiar voice interrupted.

"I'm with my family for all of a half an hour and you two couldn't wait long enough for me to lose them?" Charlie's sarcasm filled the bar as he walked over to Leila's booth. His eyes registered Cohen's hand leaving Leila's and he turned his head toward the bar, as if attempting to offer a second of privacy in exchange for his bad timing.

"It's about damn time, man." Cohen recovered quickly. "Get a beer and come take a seat." Cohen sent Leila an apologetic look and placed his hand back at his side.

Leila stood and said, "Here you go Charlie. I'm heading out—take my seat."

"You sure?" Cohen asked.

She nodded, "I've got to get going."

Charlie saw the bartender coming toward him with a beer and sent a confused look at Cohen. Last time Charlie and Cohen ordered beers, Amelia basically pretended that Charlie did not exist. Cohen chuckled in encouragement. Something told Cohen that Amelia had taken the hint and now found

Charlie a very viable option. Charlie walked toward Amelia to grab the beer halfway.

"Hey, your brother...he'll come around," Cohen offered as Leila placed her purse around her shoulder. "He'll find you when he's ready." Leila inhaled slowly as Charlie returned to the table and arranged himself comfortably in his seat.

"See you boys tomorrow."

Cohen didn't turn his attention to Charlie until he saw Leila step outside.

"I wish you'd look at me with those eyes." Charlie blinked his eyelids in mock flirtation toward Cohen.

Cohen punched him in the arm. "Oh, give me a break. How was the family?"

As Charlie rambled on about his parents, his sister, and his new brother-in-law, Cohen embraced the lightness that he felt after opening up to Leila.

Chapter 5

Cohen woke at 5:30 a.m. Thursday morning. He wanted to allow enough time for an extra mile to be added to his run. Today, Cohen would work with his Field Training Officer and he needed to pump himself up for the event. He ran and couldn't help but feel as if the weather reflected his mood. The sun shone through the occasional cloud passing overhead, and a brisk breeze washed against Cohen's skin. His run, shower, and quick breakfast flew by. Before Cohen knew it, he stood in front of the CPD doors. He made eye contact with Officer Turner as he walked through the lobby. She frowned and Cohen sent a smile her way; nothing could go wrong today.

In fact, he told himself, *maybe the conversation with Turner could wait until tomorrow.* Cohen knew that speaking with Turner would bring back some rough memories, memories that could potentially cause distraction. Today was not a day for distractions—better to just push the conversation back. Acknowledging that his delay in the exchange really served as a cop-out, Cohen promised himself that he would speak to Turner tomorrow.

Cohen sighed at the sound of Spencer's voice as he walked into the classroom. "Hey Scottie, check out your FTO. Hope you're ready to run some errands while the rest of us get some real action on the streets."

Could it be? Did Spencer finally find someone else to badger?

"You threatened by me, Spencer?" Scottie asked, throwing mock punches in Spencer's direction.

"You think I'm *threatened*?" Spencer let out a chuckle. "I'm about as threatened by you as I am by Sergeant's kid over there." Cohen looked up to see Spencer pointing at him. Although Spencer's comment still made him angry, Cohen could tell that Spencer's jokes were no longer personal attacks. The change in tone, Cohen realized, must be in response to the run-in Cohen had with Mrs. Hoffman the day before.

In an equally joking manner, Cohen responded, "I know you get pleasure out of hearing the sound of your own voice, Spencer, but do us all a favor and stop talking before we pass out at the high-pitched whine your vocal cords produce."

Laughter spread around the room, Spencer's included. Cohen took his seat and shook his head. His nerves threatened to show, and he wanted to appear calm and collected in front of his Field Training Officer.

Leila and Charlie walked into the room, the sight of them together causing Cohen to feel instantly jealous. Spencer let loose an obnoxious whistle as Leila walked past and Cohen held back from hitting him in the face. *Yup, still a dick.*

"Hey guys," Leila chimed in as she threw a smile Cohen's way and a grimace toward Spencer. At least he and Leila had one solid thing in common.

"Sup, Donahue." Charlie reached a hand out to Cohen. Cohen rewarded it with a strong shake. He had grown to really like Charlie over the past few days. In fact, Cohen enjoyed Charlie's presence

51

the most out of all of his coworkers. Cohen also knew that Charlie and Leila had nothing romantic between them, so why did he still feel competitive?

Shake it off, Cohen, he told himself and followed Charlie over to the bulletin board. Dolan would not be in the office today. In the place of his direction, he had left a sheet of paper on the bulletin board displaying FTO assignments for the day. Finding his name easily on the short list, Cohen's assignment leader didn't ring any bells.

Cohen Donahue: Kristy Duncan

Cohen walked down the hallway to the lobby, expecting to find Officer Duncan waiting for him among all of the other Field Training Officers for the day. Instead, he watched Officer Turner's neck snap in his direction the second he walked into her line of sight. He turned and willed Officer Duncan to emerge from the other officers, hoping it happened sooner than Turner's advancing comment.

"Donahue, what the hell are you looking at? Pick your head up and get over here."

In his few days at the CPD, Cohen had yet to hear Turner address anyone else in a similar manner. He guessed that she reserved her snide tone for Peter Donahue's son alone. With a nod, Cohen closed the space in two quick steps. Officer Turner flung a post-it note in Cohen's general direction. It hit him on the chin and an amused smile spread across Officer Turner's face. Cutting his losses, Cohen turned his attention to the note.

Donahue—meet me at Jackson and State. Get keys to car 56.

No signature or description. Cohen flashed Officer Turner the instructions. She let out a long, laborious sigh of annoyance. God forbid she had to tilt her head in order to read the twelve-word note *and* extend her arm ninety degrees to grab the keys to car 56. She placed the keys on the desk between them and turned her attention back to the computer screen sitting in front of her.

At least she didn't throw the keys.

"Thanks," Cohen mumbled, not expecting any sort of reply.

The air outside had turned warmer in the past hour and the sun shone with an encouraging intensity. Buckling his seatbelt and rolling the windows down, Cohen placed his not-so-encouraging interaction with Officer Turner in the back of his mind.

Tomorrow, he reminded himself, *I'll talk to Turner tomorrow.* Cohen put the car in drive and moved toward Jackson and State, mentally preparing for the day ahead of him. He hoped that he and Duncan would get along. It would be one hell of a long day if not. For someone who had never had trouble coexisting with people before, Cohen definitely lived in a different world now. He thought of Turner the entire drive.

Within seconds of reaching the corner of Jackson and State, a burly woman, debatably bigger boned than Cohen, reached her hand to the window and knocked once. Noticing that the woman wore no uniform, Cohen balked. He rolled down the window.

"Hey, excuse—"

"Kristy Duncan." She extended her arm into the car. Cohen reached out his hand, not surprised to feel a firm grip on the other end, but still thrown off by her running clothes attire.

"Cohen Donahue."

He unlocked the door and Duncan jumped into the car, quite gracefully considering her size.

"Alright Donahue, drive down this road until I tell you differently."

A true testament to how far Cohen had come within the past days, he had subconsciously begun to interpret an officer's lack of welcome as a sign of respect, assuming that no hostility entered the conversation. Cohen actually found exchanges with minimal amounts of talking preferable when on the job; people had fewer opportunities to dig into his past.

"Welcome to your first real day, Donahue. Sorry I wasn't there to hold your hand this morning in the lobby and walk you to our car." She tilted her head in his direction without fully looking at him. "I heard that I was assigned as your Field Training Officer and I thought I would take advantage of the situation to get in my run and grab some coffee."

In his peripheral vision, Cohen saw Duncan set a cup down in the cup holder closest to him. On a second glance, Cohen noticed that Duncan had brought two cups of coffee into the vehicle and still cradled her own as if waiting for some of the heat to leave the liquid.

"Thanks." Cohen gestured toward the coffee. "And yeah, no problem."

"Officer Turner give you a hard time about my note?" Finally, another officer acknowledged Turner's crummy attitude.

"She didn't seem exactly pleased with me."

"Don't sweat her, she can be a real pain in the ass." Duncan flashed Cohen a knowing glance. She reached over to the microphone, pressed the black square button, and stated, "Ten-eight. Car 56 on duty."

Returning to the conversation with Cohen, she said, "So anyway, let's dive right in here. I don't believe in any of that coddling bullshit they put new hires through. Which means you'll be driving today. I should probably explain my attire as well. Take a left on Wacker Drive then go straight. We'll stay in this area until instructed otherwise."

"Sounds good."

"With every class that comes in, I usually get assigned a new recruit. Every time, I also get permission from the Lieutenant to wear civilian clothing."

"Why is that?" Cohen asked, still not understanding the purpose.

"Simple. Civilians will think I am one of them. If they need help, they will approach you, and I can observe how you handle the situation."

"Makes sense."

Driving in the busy streets of Chicago made Cohen miss the roads in Minnesota. He certainly took the "Minnesota Nice" stereotype for granted while attending school. Getting used to blaring horns and aggressive driving would take some time. Before Cohen reached Wacker, the dispatcher jumped to life, bringing Cohen's heartbeat along with it.

"Car 56 to 1751 North Grove Ave. Reported robbery. Possible shooting. Backup requested." With one swift movement, Duncan hit the sirens and signaled Cohen to take a sharp left. "Ten-four. In pursuit."

"Damn it," Duncan complained, "all the way out in the Oak Park suburbs. At the rate you're driving, Donahue, it'll all be cleared by the time we get there."

Cohen stepped on the gas.

"Now, just because I don't look like an officer doesn't mean you're on your own out there. I am still in charge. You stay right beside me at all times, Donahue. I move, you move. I drop to the floor from a bullet wound, I expect you to drop dead right there with me. You understand that?"

"You got it." Cohen felt adrenaline prickle his outer extremities and burn its way throughout the rest of his body.

"Oh, and one more thing. I know you're a rookie and all, but try not to act like one."

Cohen took a sharp turn, making his way onto North Grove and flirting with an accident as he dodged a motorcyclist. "Fucking bikers," Duncan complained, "think they own the road." As Cohen put the car in park, it appeared obvious to both him and Duncan that the scene had been stabilized. Duncan stepped out of the car slowly and Cohen followed, wondering if Duncan's earlier warning still applied in this low-key environment.

"First thing any officer does at a scene, Donahue: take note of your surroundings." Cohen saw an ambulance parked right in front of a yellow, two-story duplex. Two EMT workers hunched over a man sitting on the front porch. The man appeared stable, but EMTs were placing a neck brace around his neck despite his protests. "Just to be safe," the EMTs explained, as they attempted to haul the man onto the stretcher.

One injured.

Another cop stood in the middle of the yard. His back faced Duncan and Cohen and he stood looking at the house while talking into the transmitter. A man stepped out of the house pointing an aggressive finger toward the third officer on scene. "You find him! You find whoever robbed my house! He tried to SHOOT me!"

"Him." The suspect is male.

"What's the story, Jacob?" Duncan asked the third officer.

"Armed robbery. The suspect was in the house, heard the front door open, and got spooked. While he fled from the scene, he managed to plow right through that guy on the stretcher, pushed him down the entire staircase." Jacob motioned toward the man still resisting the neck brace. "Our suspect apparently pulled out his gun and shot once." Jacob attempted to raise his voice over the victim who continued to shout. "Unfortunately, we have no hit on the guy yet, although we do know he wore a tan sweatshirt and had a black hat pulled over his face. The victim estimated him to be somewhere around six foot two, 215 pounds."

Cohen calculated the comparisons between their weights and guessed he would be able to outrun the suspect if it came down to it. Then again, the man apparently had a firearm; the matchup might be more even than he thought.

"Hmmm," Duncan responded. "Anyone on the scene for us to interview?"

"My rookie officer for the day is over at the neighbor's house. Duncan, why don't you stay with me, and uh…?" Jacob turned toward Cohen, searching for a name.

Reaching his hand out, Cohen introduced himself, "Cohen Donahue."

"Right, Peter's kid. Go join Scottie over there." Cohen followed the direction of Jacob's pointed finger. Right next to the yellow house stood its white neighbor, complete with a big porch and beautiful garden that put the yellow house to shame. As Cohen walked in that direction, he took mental snapshots of the scene.

The white and yellow houses were two of seven total houses on the right side of the street. A fairly high chain-link fence lined each backyard, making it difficult for anyone to escape too quickly. According to Jacob's story, the suspect ran into the injured man on the staircase, meaning he had been moving toward the front door. As Cohen's pace slowed, Scottie stepped off the house's front porch and nodded a hello toward Cohen.

"We've got nothing," Scottie stated, slightly louder than his normal tone of voice. Scottie neared and Cohen thought out loud, attempting to put the pieces together. "There aren't many escape routes the suspect could have used…even if he chose to follow the main road out of here, it's a pretty calm neighborhood. Chances are, someone would have seen the guy running and made another call to the department." Scottie nodded his head and looked around as if taking in the scenery.

"The house itself is even more closed up, only one way out and that's through the front door," Scottie added.

"Unless," Cohen continued, "the guy never ran." As if on cue, Cohen's instincts took control, shifting his body just in time to see a man duck out from under a set of bushes across the street. If the suspect had spooked earlier when the homeowners returned, Cohen expected similar results now. His actions were suspicious enough and the big man's tan sweatshirt sealed the deal.

"Hey, CPD, hold up for a second there." Cohen hoped this guy had enough common sense not to run after seeing four police officers. He hoped in vain.

The six-foot man took off running down North Grove. In spite of his weight, probably more around 200 pounds, Cohen guessed, the guy ran fast. Any delay in the chase could have meant losing the suspect. Cohen shot a quick glance back toward Duncan and saw her distracted with Jacob and at least 250 feet in the opposite direction. In that split second, he decided to take his chances and propelled himself after the suspect, surprised at the amount of adrenaline behind his speed.

"Duncan!" Cohen yelled before breathing into his dispatcher, "In pursuit of suspect. Caucasian male, six feet, tan sweatshirt, running east on North Grove. Haven't seen a weapon yet."

If Duncan was yelling after him, Cohen couldn't hear it. His heartbeat pounded too loudly in his eardrums.

"CPD, FREEZE!" Cohen shouted, knowing that at this point, his warning would have no effect.

The suspect, realizing his limited options, took a sharp left into an alley running behind the houses. *How predictable,* Cohen thought as he quickly followed suit, *the bad guy always runs down an alley.* The trashcans were not scattered haphazardly throughout the alley, but neatly lined along its side. Ahead, the end of the alley opened into another street.

Feeling Cohen's encroaching presence, the suspect shifted his weight to the right and reached for his back pocket, which was an excuse for Cohen to pull out his firearm. Cohen saw the shot coming and swerved behind a set of trashcans to his left. The bullet missed its mark. Hearing the shot was almost too surreal for Cohen to process. He pivoted around the cans and back into the alley.

His single bullet now discharged, the suspect dropped the gun and pushed on faster. The alley opened soon and Cohen knew this would be his only shot at securing the arrest. All of his morning runs finally paid off, giving Cohen a stride unmatchable by his opponent. Cohen closed the distance with a speed even surprising to himself. He lunged, connecting with the suspect's larger frame. The momentum sent both men sprawling to the ground.

"Stay on the ground or we'll shoot!" Scottie's voice sounded from behind. Cohen had been so involved in the chase he failed to realize that Scottie joined in the pursuit. Without having to be asked twice, the man held his defeated position on the concrete. Cohen moved in to place the handcuffs.

After securing the handcuffs and stating the suspect's Miranda rights, Cohen and Scottie turned back toward the house with the man they had pursued.

"You have one hell of a sprint, man. I thought you were a goner when I heard the gunfire." Scottie stated breathlessly. Cohen patted Scottie on the back, thankful that in the end he hadn't been on this one alone. As the adrenaline wore off, Cohen's hands began to shake and threatened to blow his seemingly cool composure. That chase had given Cohen a dangerously addictive rush.

As they emerged from the alley, Officer Duncan stood waiting, hands on her hips, scowl on her face. Cohen and Scottie froze at the sight of her authoritative stance. She stepped forward, grabbed the suspect in handcuffs, and dismissed Scottie with a glance so intense that it could have silenced an entire room. Cohen's rush faded just as quickly as it had come, a genuine fear taking its place. He had violated Duncan's order, and therefore Lieutenant Dolan's orders as well.

Scottie strode away, a little too quickly, and Cohen's mind replayed Duncan's initial demand: *"I go down, you go down."* Knowing very well that her direction had been lost on Cohen, he stood back while Duncan secured the suspect in the back seat and watched as she climbed into the driver's side door. One hour on the job and Cohen had already been demoted to the passenger seat. Meeting

Scottie's gaze just before he lowered his body into the car, Cohen interpreted Scottie's expression perfectly: *Good luck.*

Chapter 6

One sidelong glance from Duncan confirmed Cohen's fear; her face left no doubt that she was genuinely pissed off. With the suspect in the back seat, Duncan drove toward the Metropolitan Correctional Center. The twenty-minute car ride felt more like forty-five and Cohen stifled his urge to fill the awkward silence with a hum or whistle. Duncan made a quick ninety-degree turn into a parking spot, slammed on the brakes, and put the car in park. Cohen's body lurched forward at the abruptness of the movement while he cursed under his breath. Duncan smiled.

Within eight minutes, Duncan dropped off the man with the tan sweatshirt and walked back toward the squad car. Cohen braced himself for her wrath, praying that her scold didn't sting as much as her silence.

"Are you out of your goddamn mind, Donahue? What the hell kind of stunt was that? I've been with you all of one hour and you're already disobeying direct orders! Your sorry ass is not the only one on the line here, you know!"

Cohen assumed a defensive position readily enough. "With all due respect, Officer Duncan, you said you don't like the bullshit coddling they give us over at the CPD. Neither do I. I had a better angle, so I went for it. I really am sorry that I disobeyed your rules, but I would do the same thing again if I had the chance."

"Listen, kid. At the end of the day, I have to go write up a report on how well you did today. That report will determine who you spend your next few weeks with; so do us both a favor and pull your shit together."

"You're right, you're right."

Duncan's death glare remained so intense that Cohen worried his "sorry ass" would soon be fired from the department. Cohen's insides writhed in awkwardness at the ensuing staring match. *Stand your ground,* he told himself, although the temptation to break eye contact and admit defeat almost proved too strong. To Cohen's relief, Duncan's stare dissolved into something a little less aggressive. Not softer necessarily, just not as hateful.

"I swear to God, Donahue, if that happens again I will make sure you are held back as your colleagues advance throughout the program, if not kick you out all together. I do not tolerate disobedience, especially not on an officer's first day in the field."

"Won't happen again," Cohen confirmed, relieved to have reached some common ground. The word "disobedience" reminded Cohen of his dad's scoldings. "If you keep disobeying me, Cohen, you will be grounded for the next week." Peter had never actually grounded Cohen, but something told Cohen that Duncan wouldn't hesitate to follow through on her threat.

"And keep in mind, I'm only giving you a freebie because you remind me of myself at your age." Duncan rolled her eyes at the apparent strain in giving a compliment and put the car in drive. Cohen couldn't help but smile. He appreciated Duncan's spunk.

The remainder of the shift involved a few petty crimes—a shoplifter, an old drunk driver, a domestic disturbance—not to mention the arduous task of filing reports between incidents. Cohen made sure to follow Duncan's lead in each situation, not speaking unless spoken to and staying in very close range at all times. As a result, Duncan's body language began to suggest that Cohen's previous mishap had been forgiven, although definitely not forgotten. In spite of the low-key nature of the rest of their day, the rush Cohen felt from his first arrest never faded.

The shift neared an end and Cohen felt very lucky that Duncan had been assigned as his FTO. Through observation, Cohen leaned how to remain calm and cool-headed when arriving on each scene. Duncan taught him quite a lot about the job, and Cohen also realized some important things about himself in the process.

"Thanks for showing me the ropes today, Duncan. Trust me, I've learned a lot."

Cohen took Duncan's lack of a response as a "yeah, yeah." His mind wondered what he would make for dinner that night, pasta or pizza, when another call sounded in car 56. Merely two miles from the station, Cohen's stomach rumbled at the prospect of delayed food. It was 7 p.m. and it would only get later. The female dispatcher spoke calmly through the radio.

"Car 56. 4000 South Albany Avenue. Respond to drug bust. Further backup on its way to scene."

"The job never sleeps, Donahue. Ten-four."

65

Duncan slammed on the gas and Cohen immediately wished he had control over the wheel. "You drive like a crazy person, Duncan!" Cohen gripped the door handle as he watched the cars ahead pull over to the right side of the road in response to the sirens.

"Can't say that's the first time I've heard that." Duncan chuckled and Cohen wondered if she had taken his comment as a challenge. She stepped on the gas and drove like she was on a racetrack for the remainder of the ride. The dispatcher mentioned a drug bust. Assuming that Duncan and Cohen made the drive in good time, this crime scene would prove a little more dramatic than the others. Cohen reminded himself not to move without Duncan's command.

Lurching to a stop in front of the brick house, Duncan and Cohen drew their guns and hurled themselves out of the car. Cohen noticed three other squad cars surrounding the area, all with their lights flashing. By this point, the residents in the house had to be aware of the officers' presence. Cohen hoped they hadn't had enough time to plan a counterattack.

Cohen and Duncan met two other officers lining the front walkway. The four officers inched toward the front door. Cohen, holding his gun pointed up and increasing his step, felt the familiar rush of adrenaline through his veins. He couldn't help but notice a flash of red hair move toward the back door accompanied by another officer. *Leila.*

Focus, Cohen, he scolded himself; *you can't afford another slipup today.*

"Wait for my signal," Duncan whispered to the three surrounding officers.

"Shit!" Just as Duncan raised one finger, a rapid succession of bullets pierced the air, tearing through the front door. Without missing a beat, Cohen threw his body to the ground and rolled to the right toward a row of short bushes. He raised himself into a crouch only after he was positive that the brick wall lining the front step would provide sufficient coverage.

"Stay down!" Cohen hardly heard the warning as he looked around to see the other officers unharmed and holding similar stances. The bullets had yet to make contact with flesh. Cohen could only hope that the same proved true in the back of the house.

The sound of bullets leaving their barrels threatened to break Cohen's eardrums. He made eye contact with Duncan and waited for her instruction. From across the walkway, Cohen could almost guess Duncan's thought process as she looked at him with a torn expression. She could tell Cohen to retreat back to the car, but that would be equally dangerous considering the gunfire. Apparently deciding Cohen would benefit from the experience, Duncan nodded her head and Cohen nodded back in confirmation. Duncan shouted, "CPD, come out with your weapons and hands in the air!"

The shooting stopped suddenly, *too suddenly,* Cohen thought. Doubting the end of the bullets had anything to do with Duncan's warning, Cohen assumed the shooters ran out of ammo. No suspects emerged from the house and Duncan waited five seconds before she mouthed directions, "One, two...*three*!"

Without a second of hesitation, Cohen jumped onto the front doorstep. Arriving at the entryway first, he plowed his shoulder into the splintering black door now riddled with holes. The old frame fell after only one attempt and sent a shooting pain through Cohen's shoulder. Now with a visual of the house's interior, Cohen jumped to the right and walked quickly through the living room. As he fanned out right, Duncan moved straight ahead. The other two officers took a left.

"Clear!" Cohen yelled, finding nothing of interest in the living room and no major windows through which the suspects could have escaped. He kept moving, waiting to hear the others yell similar reports. Two other shouts of "clear!" sounded from the left side of the house. Cohen saw a door on the far end of the living room and moved toward it, assuming it must open to another room. Just as he reached the door, he heard Duncan yell, "Don't move!" from the other side.

He closed the distance between them in three quick strides, pushing through the door while holding his gun ahead of him, his finger on the trigger. As his mind took in the scene, Cohen stepped to the corner directly to his right. He now stood adjacent to the refrigerator, facing Duncan as she attempted to hold her ground across the room. Duncan stood under the opposite doorframe, not yet having fully maneuvered into the room.

Cohen now maintained the closest position to the Latino suspect. With the man's weapon aimed at Duncan, Cohen's breath halted and he waited for someone to make a move. Standing merely feet behind the man, Cohen watched fiercely for any twitch signaling that he would shoot his weapon. The stench of the room overtook Cohen's nostrils and he almost lowered his gun to gag. Dishes and food lay everywhere, the trash overflowed onto the carpet. As Cohen took a second look at the contents of the trash, he noticed tiny bags filled with white powder. Those bags, combined with the smell of weed, confirmed the dispatcher's initial description of a drug bust.

Duncan kept her focus and gun trained as her opponent mirrored her actions. Cohen guessed the suspect to be around twenty years old. Based on the amount of shaking in the suspect's hands and knees, Cohen assumed his experience with similar situations was limited.

"Put your gun on the floor."

Not once did the man look sideways in an attempt to see Cohen. As far as the suspect was concerned, there was no one else in the room aside from himself and Duncan. If he had heard Cohen enter the room, he gave no indication. The two other officers on scene squeezed past Duncan as they advanced through the doorway.

"Put it down. Now!"

The combination of four officers, all holding 9mms, convinced the scared man to lower his weapon to the floor and drop his head in defeat. Cohen pulled a set of handcuffs off of his utility belt and moved in. The second the suspect's gun hit the ground Cohen restrained the man's arms behind his back. The quick and almost nonexistent nod from

Duncan signaling a job well done caused Cohen's insides to surge with pride.

Cohen had followed Duncan's lead in a suspenseful case. That, in and of itself, proved an accomplishment. An even bigger feat, though, was that Cohen hadn't killed himself in the process.

"Put him in the car, Donahue. We'll drop him at Metropolitan Correctional Center on our way back."

Cohen walked the man to the squad car and stated his Miranda Rights. Through his peripheral vision, he saw Leila and her FTO for the day approaching the squad car adjacent to car 56.

"Watch your head, man." Cohen helped the arrested suspect maneuver into the car before shutting the door; the man did not even look at Cohen and had yet to say one word in response to his arrest.

"Nice work in there, Donahue," Leila said, a smile tugging at the edges of her mouth. Her left eyebrow arched and Cohen smiled as it did, recognizing her go-to, playful facial expression.

"You too, Herzog." Leila and Cohen rarely referred to each other by last name, and Cohen couldn't help but feel as if the extra formality was intended flirtatiously. He watched as Leila got into the passenger seat and waved goodbye. Despite his successful day, Cohen considered seeing her the best part. In the middle of his daydream, Duncan threw Cohen the keys. He mocked surprise in response and responded to Duncan's eye roll with a lopsided smile.

"All in a day's work, huh, Donahue?" Duncan rested her feet on the dashboard and turned the radio off.

"You said it. Off to the MCC it is." Cohen sighed.

Per Duncan's orders, Cohen parked the squad car and moved to escort the drug-bust suspect into the jailhouse. With the car door open, Cohen noticed the size of the man's biceps. The bulky young man glanced toward Cohen's face for the first time. Cohen guessed this guy was high out of his mind. Although the two made eye contact, the Latino man's pupils were as small as pinpoints, containing nothing more than a blank gaze.

"Hurry up, Donahue!" Duncan called through the open window of the squad car.

The suspect's gaze slowly but surely transitioned from blank to aware—very aware. It lingered on Cohen's facial features too long for comfort.

Cohen reached for the man's shoulder, wanting to ask him what kind of drugs he had been taking but deciding against it at the last second. Something told Cohen to keep his mouth shut, and he went about his duties of escorting the man out of the car.

"Alright, slowly now."

Equally as unsettling as the prolonged eye contact, a wicked smirk spread wide across the man's face. Cohen felt a chill through his entire core. He told the criminal to stand and walked behind him into the MCC. Although he couldn't see his face, Cohen knew that the smirk remained

71

plastered to the suspect's lips for the entirety of the walk.

Cohen handed the suspect off to the booking officer and waited until she finished searching through his pockets. The man's eyes did not leave Cohen's face once. Feeling challenged by his glare, Cohen returned an equally determined stare. As the correctional officer turned the suspect toward the cells, Cohen walked toward the front door.

"Don't I get to make a phone call?"

Cohen could almost hear the smirk through the question.

Chapter 7

Leila sat in an office chair, waiting for the clock to hit 8 p.m. Her rounds ended after the drug bust and she certainly didn't mind waiting around a few extra minutes. *Just in case they need me for something,* she told herself, *definitely not because I'm hoping to catch a glimpse of Cohen Donahue.*

Leila's romantic life until college could be summed up in one word: nonexistent. Not to say that Leila never had options; men waited in line for a chance to take her out on a date. The men always waited, but with her family drama constantly pilling up, Leila had found plenty of other things to worry about. Men and relationships definitely failed to make it onto her radar.

The University of Wisconsin changed all of that. Leila's indifference to men suddenly vanished. For the first time in Leila's life, she was able to completely focus on herself, placing her own needs before those of her family. Leila found a freedom and ease that finally made her life seem worthwhile.

During just her first week of school, Leila attracted much male attention. It soon became apparent that men looked at her differently when she wore certain clothes, when her mascara was thick, and when her hair bounced in curls as she walked. Almost immediately after freshman orientation ended, a man approached Leila during her third-period American Literature class.

Long story short, Oliver charmed his way into Leila's life and they dated for two years. Just after their second anniversary, when Leila considered herself madly in love, she found Oliver in bed with one of her best friends. The resulting pain crippled any chance of Leila letting another man into her life—she kept all chances of a relationship at a far distance. Leila put the makeup away and learned to feel confident with her natural self. For two years she hadn't felt ready to try again—until she met Cohen Donahue.

The first time Leila saw Cohen, he was standing in the CPD lobby looking around in awe. His demeanor appeared so sincere that Leila felt panic rip at her heart. She responded by quickly darting past Cohen toward the training room. Cohen hadn't even looked her way that morning, and Leila remembered feeling two feet tall. Despite the level of confidence that Leila developed after her four years of college, her foundation trembled upon merely seeing Cohen from a distance. Something about Cohen made her nervous to no end.

Thinking of their conversation at Gage made Leila's insides squirm so badly she had to reposition her body. She hadn't spoken of Emmett in such detail since high school. He never came up in conversations, and Leila liked it that way. In fact, Oliver hadn't even known about Emmett until six months into their relationship. Even then, Leila kept most of the details private.

Leila couldn't wrap her mind around why she told Cohen those stories. More importantly, why had she told him about her biggest fear? It was a nightmare that she constantly woke up to: arresting her brother. Not one person knew about that dream. Well, except for Cohen Donahue.

The way Cohen looked at her, as if he saw right down into her very being—Leila couldn't remember the last time anyone ever looked at her so intently, with such purpose. In that moment alone, Leila knew that something about Cohen would prove irresistible. Her determination to figure out just which qualities drew her toward him grew by the day, although she knew one already: his dreamy blue eyes.

Leila's attraction to Cohen differed from most girls, for she hadn't noticed his eyes until their conversation at the bar. Even after Leila spilled her soul to Cohen, the care and respect that Leila originally noticed in his gaze remained. Leila knew the scenario all too well: one second, her friends looked at her no differently from any other kid on the playground. Then, they heard about Emmett, and the next day their friendship transformed into judgment. Leila never wanted pity and she sure as hell didn't want anyone's sympathetic glance. She wanted understanding, and Cohen gave her that.

Looking at the clock, Leila decided it was time to leave work. She stood and put her cell phone and badge into her purse, glancing up just in time to see a streak of red move briskly down the hallway and toward the front door. *What in the world?* Leila thought. As far as she knew, there were no other redheads in the department, at least none that she had seen before. Her heart swelled with the unrealistic hope that she might see a familiar face. Running out of the office and into the lobby, she yelled to the back of the man's head.

"Emmett?" Leila's heart raced. The man stopped and turned slowly. His smile, unchanged from childhood, remained contagious.

"Hey, sis." Leila's heart immediately filled with love and concern, but her mind warned her to remain wary. Leila walked over to him hesitantly; Emmett pulled her in for a hug.

"What the heck are you doing here?" Leila asked. She realized that Emmett, a criminal on the streets, must have a very limited list of reasons to show up at the Chicago Police Department. With that realization, she forced down her optimism and acknowledged that he must have stopped by for reasons other than to catch up.

"Well, I just had to stop in and say hi to my little sister."

"Really, Emmett?" Leila asked in a slightly accusing tone. Emmett and Leila hadn't had a real conversation since high school, when Emmett's "brother" punched Leila in the face. This scenario seemed too good to be true. In Leila's experience, too good to be true meant just that: disaster must be waiting right around the corner.

"Alright, fine, you caught me." Emmett's grin appeared even goofier than Leila remembered. She couldn't help but mimic his smile. "Honestly, I remembered getting an invitation in the mail to your National Night Out. I planned on coming, but got a little caught up."

Silence filled the lobby as Emmett lowered his voice and edged to the far side of the room, putting enough distance between him and Officer Turner's front desk to prevent any conversation from being overheard. "I don't know, Leila. I guess...I guess I'm embarrassed. I don't really know how this works, I just know that I want it to."

Leila squinted, feeling confused and suspicious. "You don't know how what works?"

"You know, being a family again."

Leila gawked at her brother in disbelief as his genuine tone threatened to knock her over. In spite of her initial skepticism, Emmett might really have turned his life around. More than anything, Leila wanted to have a relationship with her brother again; she would give anything to rekindle her relationship with Emmett.

Emmett's phone rang and Leila watched his fun-loving attitude drain away into terror as he registered the name on the caller ID.

Or not, Leila worried, taking in Emmett's facial expression. Despite all of his past mistakes, Leila still found herself playing the part of a protective sister, although the roles should have been reversed considering Emmett's older age.

"You don't have to take that, do you? We could get a coffee and catch up for a little bit. I was just heading out when I—"

"Leila, look, I'm sorry. It was great to see you, but...I'm afraid I really do have to get going." He glanced at his phone one more time before answering on the fifth ring.

"Hello? Yes, I'm..." looking toward Leila he continued, "I'm with my sister. Okay, okay, I'm leaving. I'll see you in ten."

Emmett hung up the phone and looked apologetically at Leila. "Walk me to my car?" Leila knew her inquiries about the phone call would yield no results, and she felt desperate not to ruin the moment. A big part of her wanted to believe this would be the first of many conversations with

77

Emmett to come. She held back her desire to protest and reminded herself to take baby steps.

"Sure, why not?"

***

Just when Cohen thought his day could not possibly get any better, he pulled into the department parking lot and noticed Leila walking out of the front doors. With an equal stride, a man accompanied Leila toward a blue Saturn. Cohen parked the squad car and watched as the red-haired man pulled Leila in for what appeared to be an awkward embrace.

Duncan stepped out of the car without a goodbye and strode toward the building. Cohen didn't even notice her absence from the vehicle. He also stepped out of the car, watching Leila and the mystery man with a curious eye.

"Goodbye, Leila," Cohen heard the man say in a deep voice. Leila didn't respond as the man got in his car and drove away. She didn't move; she just watched the car until it made a left turn out of the parking lot, driving out of sight.

Cohen shut the car door and met Leila halfway on her walk back to the building. She read Cohen's curious stare and responded with a smile and small shrug.

"That was Emmett," Leila explained, looking more confused than happy.

"Just stopping by?"

"Apparently. Maybe you were right about him finding me when he was ready." Leila looked at Cohen in a puzzled manner, as if she were trying to put the pieces together, still not completely believing Emmett's appearance. "I don't know, something just felt different." She shook her head and looked back toward the direction of Emmett's car. Had Cohen not appeared just in time to confirm Emmett's presence, he probably wouldn't have believed that Emmett showed up at all.

Cohen pulled Leila in for a hug before letting his mind convince his heart otherwise. He held her tightly. Leila's arms fit around Cohen's body and her hands rested under his shoulder blades. He wanted so badly to pull her back and kiss her; by then, his mind had caught up. *Not now,* he told himself, somehow knowing that neither he nor Leila was ready for that yet.

"Hey," Cohen offered instead, pulling Leila back and losing himself in her presence, "whatever it was, it's a start."

Chapter 8

Cohen couldn't remember the last time he woke up in the morning feeling quite so accomplished. If working for the CPD meant mornings like this, he sure as hell chose the right profession. Cohen wondered whether his dad felt a similar love for his work. The alarm signaled that it was time for a morning run and he jumped out of bed with fresh energy.

Something about his pace seemed different that morning. Maybe it was simply Cohen's imagination, but he felt his stride elongate as his feet struck the ground with newfound determination. He embraced the change while willing himself to think about yesterday's accomplishments and, more importantly, his mistakes. Working under someone's command would be difficult for Cohen. More specifically, not having complete control over situations would require an adjustment period. The sooner he learned to trust his fellow police officers, the better.

Cohen's mind wondered for the thousandth time what exactly happened at the scene of the crime where a bullet hit his dad. He had never asked about the details, partly because he didn't want to picture the scene. Cohen didn't want his mind to conjure images of his dad in pain. Rather, ignorance served as Cohen's saving grace. Cohen was so wrapped up in his thoughts that he took a different route than the one he usually ran.

Cohen slowed his paced as he neared the edge of the water. Usually, stopping mid-run made starting up again much more difficult. Today,

Cohen felt a need to take his time in passing the water. He debated whether or not to take a seat on the large cement step facing the horizon when he heard someone calling from behind.

"Whoa! I've called your name five times, Donahue. You're that deaf and they still let you in the CPD?" Cohen smiled as Leila's voice registered; he simultaneously felt shocked at running into a familiar face this early in the morning—let alone Leila Herzog.

Leila sensed Cohen's discomfort and her laughter filled the entire morning. Cohen couldn't help but to join in. Their joy combined, draining away any morning silence. His nerves slowly began to fade.

"Sorry about that, I guess I'm not used to seeing anyone out this early," Cohen said, trying to regain his composure.

"No better time to take advantage of the city," Leila responded.

Agreeing by way of a nod, Cohen knew the interaction would come to an end soon. He didn't want to see that happen.

Apparently, neither did Leila. "Big day today, huh?"

Before Cohen had a chance to answer, his cell phone alarm sounded, signaling he had about half an hour to shower, eat, and get on the train. He hurriedly reached into his pocket to shut his phone off before the moment totally dissolved. Leila placed her hand on his arm and Cohen all but froze.

"No worries, I have to get going anyway. I'll see you at work, Cohen."

She removed her hand and Cohen felt a tingling in his arm.

"Yeah, see you soon." Cohen hoped Leila didn't sense the disappointment and longing in his voice. Based on the small grin Leila wore as she turned toward home, Cohen guessed she noticed. *Smooth*, Cohen thought to himself, *really smooth*. The pressure of Leila's hand over Cohen's forearm remained even as he watched her walk away. Approaching the park bench, Leila bent down in a way suggesting her shoelace had come untied. Cohen turned to face the opposite direction, knowing that his game would only suffer more if she were to turn and see him staring.

As if he had navigated down Irving Park with his eyes closed, Cohen failed to fully register the scenery until now. He stood inches away from the sidewalk's ledge, not stepping any closer due to the water washing the rocks directly below. The water looked especially ominous that morning and Cohen shuddered thinking about what could lie beneath. Goose bumps formed on his forearms.

Dark water had always been a fear of Cohen's, and not just any ordinary fear. For some reason, throughout his childhood, Cohen continually woke up to night terrors. Peter would come into Cohen's room and hold him tight, always offering the same advice. *"Remember buddy, next time you have a dream that you're drowning, just remember that you know how to swim. You can beat this fear, Coh. I know you can."*

The dreams eventually stopped, but Cohen's fear remained.

Guess you can't win them all.

A nearby shrieking of tires shocked Cohen out of his comfortable reserve. He swung his body around to look for the source of the accident. Fortunately, there didn't appear to be a collision, only a large black Jeep headed directly toward Cohen. Cars were not supposed to be on that sidewalk, yet the lack of anyone within eyesight meant no help would follow.

To Cohen's surprise, he had enough time to fully take in his surroundings: Leila's look of horror, barely visible now from such a distance, as she pivoted her stride in Cohen's direction; the accelerating Jeep; and the black water. With only two feet between Cohen and the vehicle, the driver floored the gas pedal.

Cohen propelled his body over the sidewalk ledge without a moment of consideration. The world continued to move in slow motion. Before his mind registered the nearing water, Cohen felt the freezing cold liquid shoot through his pores in a way that overwhelmed his senses. The initial shock at the impact kept him from swimming upward. Cohen sat suspended in water for ten seconds before kicking his way to the surface.

Gasping for breath while blinking his eyes for a clearer sight, Cohen caught a glimpse of the yellow emergency ladder and started to swim toward it. The shoes on his feet felt heavy enough to interfere with his speed.

"Keep going, almost there." Cohen didn't even realize he was speaking to himself.

Hearing no more sound from any tires, Cohen guessed that the Jeep swerved at the last second to avoid plowing over the edge and into the lake. Shivering, Cohen wondered if the driver would have done the same had Cohen's body remained standing on the sidewalk. Based on the precision of the driver's aim, Cohen doubted it.

"Cohen!" Leila's hands found Cohen's wrists, now halfway up the ladder, and latched on. She helped haul Cohen over the ledge while his entire body shook with shivers. He was close to having convulsions as he pictured the ominous water beneath his feet. Cohen's knees fell to the concrete and he placed his hands on his head, attempting to replay what just happened while simultaneously hoping to hide his irrational fear from Leila. Cohen's elbow bled although he didn't remember cutting himself. He felt Leila's hand on his back and his breath finally began to regain normal patterns.

"What—in the world—was that?" Leila breathed, breathless from her sprint to pull Cohen from the water.

Cohen looked to his left and then to his right. A few other runners had joined the path, but none slowed to check his status. The car appeared nowhere in sight. Upon further inspection, no standing water marred the sidewalk; no debris lay anywhere. Cohen found nothing to suggest that the driver had lost control on the road. He stood and pulled Leila up after him, looking around again in hope of finding some hint to explain the incident.

"Cohen…?" The concern etched into Leila's voice rang through Cohen's ears.

"I have no idea. But that car seemed pretty in control to me…"

Leila and Cohen shared a look of confusion. Cohen's phone alarm sounded again, this time from the sidewalk. He glanced down and noticed that it must have fallen out of his pocket and onto the sidewalk in the chaos, inches away from the water.

"Close call." He bent down to turn off the sound.

"Listen, Leila, I don't think we should tell anyone about that."

Leila's mouth fell partially open and Cohen knew he had an uphill battle ahead.

"What do we know about the situation, anyways? That a man driving a black car came close to hitting me on the sidewalk?"

"That car tried to kill you, Cohen," Leila reasoned.

"And I'm still alive. I'm still here, and there is no car in sight. No one besides us to even confirm that the incident happened. Before reporting anything, I want to make sure I have at least some proof to present with my case."

Leila couldn't argue with that point. She knew just as well as Cohen that Lieutenant Dolan would believe Cohen's story, but searching for the driver would be fruitless.

"You could at least mention it to Dolan."

"I'll tell you what, I'll stop by Dolan's office later and explain what happened, okay? At least someone else will know where to look for us in the off chance that the car comes back for round two and we go missing."

Leila punched Cohen's arm at his attempted lightheartedness.

"Or, better yet," Cohen smiled, "maybe I'll tell Spencer. I'm sure he would be really torn up if I didn't show for work one of these days."

Despite all efforts to suppress laughing at Cohen's lame effort to lighten the mood, Leila gave in. Her giggle immediately relieved the stress clinging to the air and Cohen straightened his shoulders.

After casting one last look around the area in search of the car, Cohen and Leila headed in opposite directions toward their apartments. Deep down, Cohen knew that Leila's argument made sense, and he definitely knew that he had reason to be worried. That alone scared him, much more than a large pool of dark water.

Chapter 9

A warm shower proved exactly what Cohen needed to put the morning's accident behind him. He walked into the CPD determined to turn his day around. Successfully ducking past Officer Turner, Cohen allowed himself to hope that the day might not be so bad after all.

Scratch that, Cohen sighed inwardly as he sat in the only open chair next to Spencer. Today, Lieutenant Dolan would announce the FTO assignments for the next few weeks. If this morning proved any kind of indication as to how the rest of the day would turn out, Cohen might as well be paired with Turner at the front desk.

Leila and Jason walked into the classroom together. Jason finished telling Leila a story, but Cohen could tell that she didn't hear a word of the narrative. Despite giving a little commentary here and there, Leila was focused on something else—and Cohen felt pretty confident in his ability to guess what that was. Her eyes wandered across the room and found Cohen. His sent her an inquiring glance. Leila nodded, *all good.*

Lieutenant Dolan made his way to the front of the room and the nervous energy grew thick.

"Without further ado, listen closely to your assigned Field Training Officer. I'm only going through this list once. If you hear your name, you may exit and go find your partner for the next few weeks." Dolan glanced at Spencer as if waiting for his hand to shoot in the air with another question. It didn't. Dolan placed glasses onto the slight bump protruding from his nose and unfolded the piece of paper in his hand.

"Connor and Officer Amanda Lucason, Scottie and Officer Thomas Rufous." Scottie shot Cohen a look of relief as he stood to leave the room. From what the new recruits had heard, Officer Rufous was a pretty stand-up guy; Scottie would learn a lot from him over the next few weeks.

Cohen almost stood from his chair in anticipation. Other officers filed out of the room as their names were called. Cohen sat in anticipation, watching six officers exit the room. After one minute passed, Dolan finished the list.

"And last but not least," Dolan announced, "Leila and Officer Chris Stanton."

Leila shot a quick glance of confusion Cohen's way. He returned an equal stare. The room would soon be empty, yet Cohen's name had yet to be called. As Leila grabbed her jacket and headed out of the room, Cohen remained the only officer still sitting. He began to panic, and his thoughts immediately traveled back in time to Duncan's scolding the day before.

Field Training opportunities existed so that rookie officers could learn the ropes. They also existed, Cohen realized, for the purpose of weeding out officers not cut out for the job. Perhaps Duncan had recorded Cohen's slipup in her report to Lieutenant Dolan.

"If I see anyone step out of line, I will make it my personal priority to see you thrown out of this police department before you know what hit you." Lieutenant Dolan's warning from day one rang clear through Cohen's mind.

Had Duncan told the Lieutenant? Cohen felt sure of it. Why else would he be the only recruit officer not paired with a partner? For someone yearning to blend in, Cohen sure did a great job of standing out. Lieutenant Dolan interrupted Cohen's thoughts and barked, "Donahue! Get that deer in the headlights look off of your face."

The door opened and a familiar face entered the room. A man, very built, probably around forty-five years old, offered Cohen his hand. The man's hair was black and peppered with patches of white. His blue eyes gave him an innocent look— their hue appeared quite similar to Cohen's own eyes.

"Well, I'll be damned," the man said, as Cohen shook his hand and waited for his mind to register the source of the familiarity.

"Cohen Donahue, my name is Griffin Mier." Still, the name did not ring any bells. "I am Sergeant of the Intelligence Unit. I worked closely with your father right up until he passed. We always talked about becoming partners one day. One hell of a man."

That's it, Cohen guessed. He must have seen Mier at one of his dad's work functions. Those days seemed so long ago now.

"After seeing your name on the roster of new recruits, I had to see you to believe it."

"Well, I appreciate you stopping by, Sergeant Mier. It is really nice to meet you," Cohen offered, temporarily distracted from his lack of an FTO assignment by his excitement at finally meeting one of his dad's friends in the department.

"I spoke to Duncan about your work yesterday...heard you demonstrated a little bit of an aggressive side," Mier continued.

So Duncan had reported the incident. *Shit.* Mier smiled mischievously; Cohen decided to proceed with caution.

"I learned a lot yesterday, Sergeant. Duncan was a great teacher." Cohen attempted to keep the conversation neutral. He definitely did not want to incriminate himself with the Sergeant of Intelligence, especially considering that Cohen planned to apply to the unit one day. Even with a good record, the chances of being accepted into Intelligence were extremely slim, especially considering the low turnover rate and high demand for the job.

"Well, up in Intelligence we look for officers to make aggressive, yet controlled decisions quickly and daily." Cohen tilted his head and nodded slightly, confused about the route that the conversation had taken.

"I just had a guy drop out of the unit this past week. He decided to move with his wife to Florida, the lucky son of a bitch. Anyway, I heard about your stunt yesterday and thought I'd see if you wanted to give Intelligence a shot."

Cohen stood completely stunned. How could this be happening? Yesterday, Duncan threatened to kick him out of the department, and now his misstep was serving as grounds for an early admittance into the Intelligence Unit? Cohen wanted to accept the job right off the bat, but something heavy weighed down on him and he felt the need to clear his conscience.

"Sergeant, I'm shocked, but I—"

"Hold up, Donahue. Before you make a decision you need to understand the dangerous and grueling nature of the Intelligence Unit. It is a risky job and officers die doing the work we do." Mier stopped, realizing he preached to the choir.

"Trust me, Sergeant, I've had enough secondhand experience to understand the risk involved."

Mier gave Cohen a knowing look and let him continue. "I'm humbled at the opportunity, I really am. I just want to make sure I'm getting this promotion based on my potential, and not because I share my dad's last name." As he spoke, Cohen thought back to Spencer's initial frustration at overhearing Officer Turner claim Cohen was "destined for greatness." Cohen needed to know that Mier's offer had nothing to do with his dad's reputation before he considered accepting the position.

Mier looked at Cohen and reached his hand out. He patted Cohen on the back, twice. "Welcome to Intelligence, son." The use of the word son failed to irritate Cohen this time.

Mier left Cohen with Lieutenant Dolan for the day, instructing him to report to the Intelligence Unit first thing Monday morning. Just like that, Cohen made the best and worst decision of his life.

Chapter 10

After informing Leila, Scottie, and Charlie of his promotion into Intelligence, Cohen was surprised to hear their genuine praise and congratulations. Cohen had been afraid to see their reactions, fearing they might see his promotion as a display of favoritism. Mier confirmed that the job offer reflected Cohen's efforts, letting Cohen feel confident that he really had earned the spot. Seeing that his new friends agreed only made the turn of events seem more surreal to Cohen.

"You're killing it, Donahue!" said Charlie as he pulled Cohen in for a hug. "Hey, what about we all go over to Gage to celebrate? Get a few drinks?"

Leila and Scottie agreed that they were available to celebrate. All three stared at Cohen, waiting for him to debate the outing. For the first time in his life, Cohen felt the potential beginnings of real friendships forming. Had he declined Mier's offer to advance into Intelligence, Cohen had no doubt that he, Leila, Charlie, and Scottie would have developed a camaraderie from working side by side. Cohen hoped that as long as their happy hour routine continued, ample opportunities to connect would still present themselves.

"Okay, fine." Cohen mocked annoyance. "On one condition—first round on me."

"No complaints there," Scottie said, as he shoved Cohen into the wall with his shoulder and Cohen lunged back in response. Although Leila gave Cohen a hug and said her congratulations, he could tell that something held her back from feeling as genuinely happy for him as Charlie and Scottie did.

"You okay?" Cohen asked in a tone reserved only for Leila.

"Cohen, did you talk to Dolan today?" Charlie and Scottie headed toward the door, ready to celebrate and trusting that Cohen and Leila would catch up.

"I got a little distracted…but I will on Monday. Besides, tonight will be a good night. Let's just forget about this morning, at least for the next few hours, agreed?"

Mier's offer really did catch Cohen off guard. By the time Cohen remembered his promise to speak to him, Lieutenant Dolan had already left for the day. It would have to wait until Monday, and Leila knew the same.

"Agreed." Her smile returned effortlessly.

As the four made their way past the front desk, Cohen remembered another promise he had made to himself the day before. This one he knew he must follow through on—if for nothing else, then for his own sanity. Charlie's words rippled through Cohen's body:

"He walked by the front desk and overheard Officer Turner telling Dolan to 'watch out for Peter Donahue's kid. He's destined for greatness.'"

Cohen stopped suddenly. He had to speak with Officer Turner; she knew something. Cohen guessed Turner worked with his dad, meaning she might have known Peter personally. Cohen hoped that tonight would shed some light on Peter's involvement in the workplace; he suddenly felt thirsty to hear stories about his lost father.

"Hey, um, I completely forgot, I have to finish up something before I leave. I'll meet you guys there."

Leila shot Cohen an interested glance. For someone eager to celebrate only seconds ago, Cohen's stalling must have seemed a bit odd. Leila's right eyebrow rose. *Left is for flirting, right is for curious.* Cohen made a mental note and avoided her glare, fearful of what Leila might see if she looked into his eyes.

"Ten minutes," Cohen promised. "I'll be right behind you."

Charlie's gaze wandered over Cohen's shoulder to Officer Turner's desk. Nodding his head in acknowledgement, he, Leila, and Scottie walked outside. Cohen turned around and saw Officer Turner already looking at him. Usually, Cohen felt spooked even thinking about Officer Turner, but today he felt only determination.

"So, you finally figured it out, huh?" Officer Turner began, as if she had been waiting for Cohen to approach her since his first day in the office. Cohen didn't see even one ounce of surprise in her features at his advancement toward her desk.

"Figured what out? That you and my dad worked together?"

Officer Turner shut her laptop and gave Cohen her full attention.

"Let me ask you something, Donahue. Do you think I chose to work up here at the front desk out of a longing to sit inside and stare at people and computers all day?"

Cohen balked. What could Officer Turner's position at the front desk have to do with anything?

He had never thought about it before now. Apparently, Cohen really did assume that Turner had selected her position, that she preferred the inside of the department to the streets of the city.

"Listen, Officer Turner, my dad kind of shielded me from his work, so I don't know much about what he did." He studied Officer Turner's face before continuing. "You seem to genuinely hate my guts, but I know nothing about you. I'm not sure how you could have found a reason to dislike me so quickly. Did you and my dad not get along?"

"Your dad, young man, saved my life. I owe him everything."

Cohen stepped a foot closer. He had not expected anything like those words to come from Turner's mouth. Cohen vaguely remembered hearing stories about his dad from Peter's coworkers when Cohen was a child, but Cohen didn't remember ever hearing a narrative like the one Turner hinted toward.

"Saved you? When?"

"The day that your dad died—the day Jeremiah Diaz shot him—the bullet wasn't meant for Peter. It was aimed at my head. Your dad saw it coming and he pushed me aside. I sat with him until the ambulance came, and when I heard the news later that night…I couldn't go back into the field. They placed me here instead."

Mean old Officer Turner now appeared as though she actually had a heart. Although she still showed minimal feeling, Cohen could almost see through Turner's tough façade. Despite her best efforts to choke any emotion off at the source, Turner's voice overflowed with feeling.

Jeremiah Diaz… Where have I heard that name? Cohen needed more information.

"Okay, so what, my dad saved your life and now you feel a need to pay him back somehow? Sorry, Officer Turner, but I don't see how going out of your way to get a jab in at me every time I pass by your desk erases that debt in any way."

"Let's just say, Donahue, if you end up quitting this position, I would consider my work a success."

First, Turner wanted to pay back Peter for saving her life. Now she wanted Cohen to quit his job? He did not see the correlation between her attitude and the shooting. Frustration spread through his body at her vague answer. "Right. Again, not following you."

"You shouldn't be here, Cohen. Your dad shouldn't have been here, and you shouldn't be here. Too many innocent people get killed on the job. It just isn't right, and in my opinion, you should pick another profession before you follow in your father's footsteps."

As soon as he heard the words, Cohen understood. Officer Turner saw Peter give his life so that she could live. As if that hadn't proven hard enough, she now had to watch as Peter's son put himself through the same danger. Her position at the desk hadn't been a demotion, but rather an adjustment of her priorities. Officer Turner learned the hard way that the job didn't play fair, and she hoped that Cohen would eventually come to the same realization. Although her reasoning remained sound, Cohen felt Officer Turner had forgotten one very important thing.

"My dad loved his work, Officer Turner." He felt bile rise in his throat and he struggled to keep his voice steady.

"Your dad loved you, Cohen."

A sharp pain hit Cohen's stomach and he feared losing control over his emotions. Officer Turner didn't have to tell him that much; Cohen knew his dad loved him more than anything in the world. The thought of Peter worrying about Cohen's career choice proved almost too much for Cohen to handle. If heaven did exist, Cohen did not want to cause his dad any stress. Deep down, though, Cohen knew that his father would smile at his choice. Peter would understand that Cohen couldn't work anywhere else.

Sergeant Mier came walking down the hallway.

"Goodnight," he called out to both Cohen and Officer Turner before exiting. Turner stared Mier down with such an intense look that Cohen knew his conversation with her would go no further. He turned his back and walked in the same direction as Mier.

"Donahue, I talked to your dad on the night he died." Turner still had more to get off of her chest. "I gave his hospital room a ring to see how he was doing."

*Okay…*Cohen thought, not bothering to turn around just yet, but stopping dead in his tracks.

"He seemed cheery as could be. Asking me about work and wanting to hear everything he missed. Then he asked me if I'd seen any black Jeeps while on duty."

Turner did not slow her pace as Cohen's body turned rigid.

"I laughed at first, telling him that I probably see around twenty black Jeeps every day. Anyway, after he asked, the conversation continued normally, but I just thought it was an odd question in the first place."

Cohen pushed his hands into his pockets so that Turner couldn't see how much they were shaking. The relevance of his father's question, when compared to the incident earlier that morning, dawned on Cohen.

"Have you heard anything about the case since then? I mean, you know, noticed a black Jeep or heard from Jeremiah or anyone?" Cohen attempted to muster any normalcy that his tone would offer. Thankfully, he didn't deliver the question with an ounce of trembling in his voice.

"Jeremiah died in prison a few months after he was put away. Another inmate apparently got out during break time and murdered him. No one ever contacted me further and I never saw a black Jeep. Are you okay, Donahue?"

Cohen had heard enough. He slowly yet firmly nodded his head before he walked out of the lobby and into the dark night. Turner must have sensed Cohen's worry, but Cohen knew she would mind her own business. Turner had delivered the message, finally giving her strategically sour mood toward Cohen some meaning.

Cohen welcomed the wind in the air as his strides grew smaller and smaller and his mind grew hazy. Eventually, he found himself sitting on a curb right outside of Gage. Cohen pictured the scene

Officer Turner described and clenched his stomach in an attempt to avoid vomiting. It reminded him of why he chose to avoid asking for details about that day. He wished Officer Turner had left them out.

"Then he asked me if I'd seen any black Jeeps while on duty." Cohen's mind spun in circles. How could a case from five years ago possibly relate to today? *Maybe it doesn't,* he reminded himself.

"Cohen?"

Cohen looked up to see Leila standing three feet in front of him. Her jeans hugged her thighs perfectly and she had unbraided her hair so that it fell onto her shoulders, cascading down her back. Cohen's appearance, on the contrary, must have been awful considering her next question.

"I saw you through the window. My gosh, Cohen, are you okay?"

Cohen could do nothing but lower his gaze. He rubbed his hands over the top of his head and nodded until he felt Leila sit down next to him. Cohen continued nodding, more to convince himself that he would be okay than to convince Leila.

Cohen felt Leila's body next to him and her arm exuding support as she wrapped it around his back. She rested her head lightly on his shoulder, understanding that he didn't need conversation; Cohen just needed her there. Her arm felt so strong and sure, it took everything Cohen had not to break down and tell her everything. Something about Leila's presence made him wish she knew—knew everything that Officer Turner just shared, everything about his dad, his childhood, and his pain. No one had ever inspired that feeling in him before and it made Cohen feel vulnerable.

He shifted his body and Leila slowly lifted her head. They made eye contact as she patiently waited for him to recuperate. Cohen closed his eyes before she saw too deep. He didn't even know what this new information meant. The last thing he wanted was to drag Leila into the mess. Lacing his fingers between Leila's, he stood and pulled her to her feet. Allowing himself ten more seconds of quiet, Cohen nodded and they walked back to the bar together.

"Does everything have to be this complicated?" Cohen asked. Leila rested her head back on his shoulder and didn't offer a response. He didn't expect one. Although no words were exchanged, Cohen felt as if Leila had just seen a small glimpse of his soul.

Scottie and Charlie had a booth reserved in the back of the bar. Four shots lined the table. Cohen and Leila made their way toward them and Cohen could tell by their expressions that Scottie and Charlie sensed the celebratory mood had changed. Cohen sat next to Scottie and waited for Leila to get settled across from him. Grabbing the shot glass—Cohen guessed it was whiskey—he made the only toast he knew how.

"To dodging the bullet." No one spoke. The four glasses clicked together and tipped backwards.

Chapter 11

Cohen felt tipsy by the end of the night, although by no means did he feel drunk. The four new officers sat at the bar for three hours before deciding to call it quits. By the fourth shot of whiskey, Cohen's worries about Turner's warning had all but disappeared. Charlie and Scottie's jokes grew more animated and Leila's cheeks blushed from the alcohol.

"Alright, alright. I'm calling it a night. Who wants a ride home?" Scottie offered.

"Are you okay to drive?

"Yes ma'am. Unlike Donahue over there, I know how to hold my liquor," Scottie mocked, imitating an extremely drunk man unable to walk. Charlie and Leila both accepted the ride home.

"I'm okay, but thanks." Cohen planned to be very productive the next day and wanted to allow the fresh air an opportunity to clear his system. He needed a chance to research the drug bust that Peter worked on four years ago, as well as a debatably relevant black Jeep. That kind of trip down memory lane would require rest, leaving no room for a hangover.

The morning's incident still present on his mind, Cohen felt a slight apprehension toward walking alone at night, especially considering that someone might be out looking for him. He seriously doubted that anything else would happen tonight, but Chicago streets were notorious for crime. Cohen made up his mind to take a cab to Southport and walk the remaining three blocks home. He would feel safe walking in the familiar setting of his neighborhood.

"See you guys tomorrow," Cohen called as he hailed a cab. As it drove over Lakeshore Drive, the scent of salami filled Cohen's nostrils. He opened the window to quell his urge to vomit. Just after passing Ashland, Cohen thought he might throw up. The corner of Southport and Irving Park could not have arrived soon enough. Cohen all but jumped out of the cab, anxious to get fresh air into his lungs in place of the rancid salami smell currently in his system.

The cab driver accepted Cohen's tip graciously and left Cohen to walk into the darkness, counting the blocks until he could see his apartment in the distance. No one else walked on the sidewalk at the late hour and very few cars were on the road. Cohen basked in the solitude while maintaining a quick pace. He was not naïve enough to assume he was completely safe. Glancing at his clock, Cohen realized it was 12 a.m.

As he turned the last corner, Cohen finally felt the alcohol beginning to wear off. Picking up his speed, he got closer and closer to the light that shone from his apartment's front porch. With only one block left, Cohen felt safe enough to lose awareness of his surroundings. He did not hear the man walk up behind him. He did not see the crowbar. Cohen wished he hadn't felt the object connecting to the back of his head, but the impact sent excruciating pain through his body.

Cohen's body collapsed on the grass and he hung onto consciousness by a thread. His attacker jumped on top of Cohen, working his hands roughly through Cohen's pockets. *He must be searching for a wallet*, Cohen thought. As if lifting his head even proved an option after being hit, Cohen attempted to fight back with no success. A hand closed over his small billfold and, to Cohen's surprise, moved on without extracting it from his pocket. Rather, the hands worked their way up to Cohen's front coat pocket and extracted what Cohen could only guess to be his phone.

A phone instead of a wallet? Cohen thought, baffled, waiting for the mugger to leave with his prize. Unfortunately, the man dressed in all black had different plans. He stood and Cohen raised his upper body now that the weight restraining him had been removed. A flash of light materialized in front of Cohen's sight at the movement and Cohen struggled to raise his body any further.

Pulling back his leg, the stranger's foot connected with Cohen's ribs and a howl pierced the still night. Cohen did not recognize the desperation in his scream.

The pain shot through Cohen's ribcage and his lungs gasped for air. He attempted to roll over onto his stomach, protecting the front side of his body. The man grabbed Cohen's shoulders and squared his back to the ground. Sticks and rocks poked into Cohen's skin from under his body. He didn't even notice. The man delivered a punch to Cohen's left temple, causing stars to form in Cohen's eyes. Still attempting to regain his breath and recover from the shock of the attack, Cohen couldn't move, scream, or breathe.

"Goodnight, Donahue."

The voice sounded odd but Cohen recognized it. The man, no longer a stranger in Cohen's mind, brought down the crowbar over Cohen's right ribcage and Cohen's eyes locked closed before his mind had time to comprehend the man's identity. The world went black.

***

Cohen woke to a wet tongue and rain splattering across his face. A brown, shaggy dog stood over his body with a tail wagging excessively. The night still remained dark; dark enough that no one would see Cohen's body unconsciously situated on the grass. Cohen struggled to regain his bearings. *There was a man*, Cohen remembered. His mind flashed back to the black mask and sweatshirt that the man wore.

Great, Cohen thought, unable to remember the details that he knew his mind had registered not too long ago. Before attempting to comprehend anything else, Cohen's body screamed with pain. He covered his mouth with his fist to block the yell from sounding from his vocal cords. His world went black again.

Three more times, Cohen endured this, gaining and losing consciousness. Each time, Cohen woke to the same dog licking his face and the same disabling pain. The fourth time Cohen woke, he knew he needed to get off of the grass and move toward his apartment. As if understanding, the dog began nudging Cohen's shoulders with his snout. Cohen eventually fought through the pain and lifted his upper body, the dog placing his head behind

Cohen's back and offering a slight push to help Cohen raise himself halfway.

"Thanks, boy," Cohen responded, feeling genuinely appreciative toward the animal and glad that he did not wake up alone. Placing his hands on the ground, Cohen pushed his way to his knees, then his feet, all while gritting his teeth. The dog remained right by Cohen's side, looking at Cohen the way a newborn baby duckling would look at its mother. Cohen realized that he needed help. He reached for his phone and found an empty pocket. *Right.* With no way to call for help, Cohen mentally prepared for the walk back to his room. He pushed one foot forward, this time unable to stifle the moan from escaping his mouth. *If you pass out, you have to do all of this over again,* Cohen threatened himself in an attempt to keep moving.

Half a block away, Cohen willed his feet to move as his hands grasped tree trunks for support. Cohen's new companion walked in perfect stride with him the entire way. *Please, keep it together long enough for me to get home,* Cohen begged his body, terrified of another blackout. The crippling blackness never returned, although a haze began to creep over Cohen's vision. The haze faded and Cohen found himself standing in his kitchen, not knowing how he got there or at what pace. The dog also seemed nowhere in sight. Oblivious to the pain and the blood dripping from his head onto his chest, Cohen took four ibuprofen tablets and passed out on the couch.

At 6 a.m., the alarm clock sounded, a completely different kind of hell than Cohen experienced any other morning. To say that Cohen's entire body ached would be the understatement of the year. Cohen's head throbbed as he reached to shut off the alarm clock. He forced himself from the couch.

"Whoa!" Cohen exclaimed after coming close to placing all of his body weight onto a furry mass parked on the floor next to the couch. The dog didn't budge and gave no inclination of being awake.

Stepping over the dog and walking to the bathroom, Cohen glanced into the mirror. Luckily, his face only had one bruise over his left temple. The man could have beat Cohen to a pulp, Cohen realized; yet his attacker passed on the opportunity to take the beating a step further. Instead, he only hit hard enough to force a blackout. Not to mention, it appeared that Cohen only had bruising in places not visible to third parties. The majority of the bruising appeared on Cohen's torso and would be completely covered by his clothing. Cohen guessed his attacker hadn't wanted to leave too much of a mark.

Taking off his shirt, Cohen saw that bruises lined his entire ribcage. Dry blood caked his hair from where the crowbar made initial contact. In the amount of time it usually took Cohen to run, shower, dress, and eat, he showered, took four more pills, and thanked God that it was the weekend. Sleep came too easily and Cohen woke again around midday. He let his hand fall over the edge of the couch, expecting to meet fur, but nothing rested on the floor aside from his shaggy black and white carpet.

Odd, Cohen thought to himself. He could have sworn he remembered a dog coming back with him last night. Almost as if reading his thoughts, the dog walked across the hardwood floor of the kitchen and stood at the edge of the couch. His tail wagged and he looked at Cohen expectantly. Cohen placed his hand on the dog and felt for a collar. No sign of ownership circled the dog's neck and Cohen removed his hand, alarmed at how thin and bony the dog felt.

"Alright, I'll tell you what, buddy. I'll put in a call to the humane society to see if anyone is looking for you. In the meantime, you can stay here with me." The dog whined and stared up at his new owner's face. Cohen assumed he wanted food. Knowing that the neighbors owned a large dog, at least based on its bark alone, Cohen knocked on their door and asked to borrow a few cups of dog food.

They gave it to him, glad to have another dog in the complex. As the dog ate and Cohen fell into a daydream, the man's words from last night echoed in Cohen's head:

Goodnight, Donahue.

The attacker had known Cohen's name. Cohen remembered the voice and felt a sinking sensation, knowing that his memory from last night lacked detail. Before passing out on the lawn, Cohen had recognized the man's voice. Now, following signs of fatigue and shock, he could only remember the man's black, indistinctive attire.

Two attacks in one day? Too much of a coincidence. Cohen's body forced sleep as a stall tactic, his subconscious knowing that the next few days would prove full of hellish experiences. He remained in a slumber, waking only to reposition his body, until 2 p.m. the following day.

Chapter 12

What the hell?

The doorbell jolted Cohen out of his deep and peaceful sleep. In the week he'd lived in this apartment, no one had ever rung the doorbell. The chime sounded odd and unfamiliar—almost cold— to Cohen's ears. Light shining through the window suggested the afternoon hour. For a split second, Cohen pictured his attacker on the other side of the wooden door, sending panic quickly through his limbs. Cohen shielded his eyes from the glare coming through the window and comforted himself with the thought that no one would come to hurt Cohen in broad daylight; it would be too risky, especially with all of his neighbors around.

Forcing confidence, Cohen stood carefully, acknowledging that his bruises had transitioned from intense pain to sore muscles. He walked slowly toward the door, a dull ache still preventing full movement. The dog's anxiety heightened as Cohen neared the door. Looking through the door's peephole, the round circle appeared to be covered by something, Cohen's sight was obstructed. *Great.*

"It's okay, boy," Cohen whispered to the dog now standing stock still at the door with him.

"We'll just be quiet and go sit on the couch; they'll leave eventually." Cohen and his new companion did not feel like inviting anyone into their home, especially if another beating accompanied the invitation. Unfortunately, the doorbell rang two more times, and Cohen knew his guest wouldn't be leaving anytime soon. The dog gave Cohen a look that he interpreted perfectly: *get some balls.* Cohen shook his head.

"Who is it?" Cohen called out, matched by a high-pitched whine from the dog. No one answered his inquiry yet the doorbell rang at a constant pace now.

"Alright, buddy, you with me on this one?" Cohen looked at the dog and made his way toward the door. He tucked his shirt into his jeans, fully aware of his disheveled appearance. As the bell rang for the twentieth time, now paired with obnoxious knocking to match, Cohen pulled open the door and braced himself.

"You really think the celebration of your promotion was going to end after a few shots at Gage, Donahue? Hope you're good at the grill."

Scottie, Charlie, Leila, and Jason noticed Cohen's flinch and broke out in laughter. Charlie stood in the front of the pack, holding up hamburger meat and buns. Cohen squinted in an attempt to adjust to the harsh hallway lighting. He forced a smile, but the usual genuine, lopsided nature of his grin failed to appear. At the sight of the food, Cohen's stomach growled loudly. He had actually never mastered the skill of cooking. In fact, Bre had always been the one to make Cohen and Peter meals on the grill. Cohen knew it would be rude to turn his friends away after they made the drive to his house; besides, he hadn't eaten since Friday.

"Are you going to invite us in, Donahue, or should we stand out here until you pull yourself together? You look like shit, you know that?"

"I was just ah…yeah, sure guys, come on in."

Not in the mood to celebrate, Cohen opened the door wide enough to let his friends file into his apartment. As Jason walked through the doorframe, he boasted a case of beer. Cohen suddenly felt slightly more game for socializing.

"We tried to call," Jason mentioned, "but after an hour went by with no reply, we just thought we would stop by."

"Was the phone on?" Cohen asked too hurriedly; his guests looked at him skeptically.

"I think I lost it last night, that's all."

"Oh, bummer. Yeah, it was on."

"Interesting. Well, make yourselves at home. I'll fire up the grill in one second." Cohen retreated to the bathroom where he took three more pills and looked at his reflection in the mirror. The only thing that would cure his bed head was a shower, and Cohen didn't have time for that. He decided to settle for a combing.

The dog's whines entered the bathroom. Cohen stepped into the kitchen, sure his companion must need rescuing from Charlie and Scottie. To Cohen's surprise, it appeared that his trusty sidekick had replaced Cohen the second Leila walked through the door. He couldn't blame the dog, but Cohen shook his head at the lack of loyalty. Leila bent down and rubbed the dog behind his ears. Her laughter filled the apartment and Cohen suddenly didn't mind the company.

"And who is this little guy?" she asked over the dog's constant whine at her attention. If Cohen didn't know any better, he would say his new occupant had a little crush on Leila. At the lack of an answer to her inquiry, Leila switched her glance toward Cohen. "Oh my God, Cohen, is that a bruise on the side of your face?"

Cohen had completely forgotten about the bruise coloring his temple. In fact, the marking was so light that he was surprised Leila even noticed. Wanting to change the subject before Scottie or Charlie had time to take a similar notice and ask more questions, Cohen casually responded.

"Just a little bump I got last night." Quickly shifting his attention back to the dog, Cohen added, "and I am actually not sure what the dog's name is. He kind of just followed me home."

Taking the hint, Leila didn't press for more details, though she did give Cohen a knowing look. She turned her attention back to the dog, "Mhm…well, I'm going to call you Pumpkin, if that's okay with you, mister." The waging of the dog's tail served as confirmation. Pumpkin liked his new name, and so did Cohen.

The afternoon quickly filled with card games, drinking, and eating. Scottie cooked the burgers and Jason handed out the beers. Cohen hadn't realized the extent of his hunger until food entered his body. After his first hamburger he had to eat another. Jason even let his guard down a little and told some jokes. Cohen found himself laughing so hard that he experienced an occasional wince in pain from the soreness of his bruises. In the relaxed atmosphere, Cohen felt genuinely happy, aside from the moments where reality would sneak back into his thought process.

Someone is out to get me, and I'm sitting here playing drinking games with my friends.

Although Cohen tried to push the thought completely out of his mind, it never fully disappeared. He hoped his guests couldn't sense his distracted state, but Cohen found Leila glancing in his direction on more than one occasion, wearing a worried expression. After three hours, everyone had eaten enough food to feed a small army and the beer ran out. Cohen walked Scottie, Charlie, and Jason to the door as Leila cleaned the dishes that Cohen had placed in the sink.

He shut the door and turned to watch as Leila's hands worked beneath the bubbles. She placed the dishes on a drying rack next to the sink. In her casual green dress, Leila looked absolutely beautiful. Her red hair had taken on a unique auburn glow, intensifying in a way Cohen had never seen. He swore Leila could wear rags and he would still find her stunning. His emotions stirred and he reminded himself that tonight was not the night to make a move. Cohen closed the distance and began drying the dishes.

Leila's intuition had kicked in the second that she entered Cohen's apartment, and he waited in silence for her questions that were sure to come. Cohen also prepared to share all of the details with her, not necessarily because he wanted to, but because he would be helpless not to.

"Mind telling me what really happened to your face?"

"Once you tell me your poker secret. No way did you win all those hands on luck alone."

Leila cast a look Cohen's way. Apparently, she did not find his response amusing. Cohen set down the towel he had been holding in his hand and replaced it with Leila's hand. Leading her to the table, Cohen took a seat in a chair on the opposite side and began telling Leila everything. He started with a description of his conversation with Officer Turner and finished with Friday night's attack. Wanting to spare Leila from the extent of his pain, Cohen left out some of the details from the beating. By the end of his narrative, the two sat in silence as the soap bubbles popped in whispers among the rest of the dirty dishes.

"Do you think this had anything to do with the other day? The car by the lake?"

"How could it not?" In reality, Cohen had no idea. He didn't like assuming that the two separate incidents correlated, but the two events happened too close to each other for them to be a coincidence. Leila sat in silence with Cohen—both trying their best to solve the seemingly impossible puzzle. Eventually, the combination of painkillers and beer caused Cohen's limbs to feel heavy with sleep. He didn't even notice that Leila's blank stare had shifted in his direction as she took in all of his features.

Cohen's breath caught as Leila stood from her sitting position. She walked over to his side of the table, pulling out the chair directly next to him and sitting so that her eyes fell parallel with his chin. Goose bumps formed over his body as she slowly extended a hand to his face, gently tracing the slight bruise on his left temple.

"Donahue, I'm worried about you."

It was as if all feeling, all pain, left his body. The discoloration traced by Leila's fingers remained, but Cohen could feel no discomfort. Instead, his blood rushed back and forth through his veins, the heat he felt internally increasing with each second. Leila's hand lowered and her gaze shifted to Cohen's. The intensity of the moment stifled the air. Cohen wanted nothing more than to wrap her in his arms. Moving as if afraid to disturb the air around them, Cohen placed his hand loosely around the back of Leila's neck. He gently pulled her to him as her hands reached toward his chest.

What resulted was the most delicate and deeply stirring kiss that Cohen had ever experienced. He lingered on the first, and on the second kiss, waiting for the kindling fire to burst into flame. Their chemistry undeniable and unstoppable, the couple moved in unison to the bedroom, their bodies fully accepting the need for intimacy—the hope for love. As the kisses deepened and their hands grew more and more confident, a tune sounded in the distance. Leila's body instantly tensed. She abruptly pulled back from Cohen, briskly leaving the bed and making her way to the kitchen just in time to answer the call.

"Emmett?"

Hearing Emmett's name, Cohen pulled himself together before joining Leila in the kitchen. He stood leaning against the wall, watching as her features, so blissful and relaxed only a moment before, took on a recognizable stress.

"Sure. No, no, it's okay. I can be there in ten minutes, okay?"

Despite the fact that he spent all day in Leila's company, the thought of her spending the remainder of her night with someone else made Cohen jealous, even in spite of the kin relation between Leila and Emmett. Almost as soon as the dread of Leila's impending departure appeared, Cohen's jealousy transformed to concern at her strained features. Leila hung up the phone and looked at Cohen apologetically.

"I'm sorry, Cohen. I recognized the ringtone. 'Man in the Mirror.' It was our favorite song as kids."

Cohen walked toward her and comfortingly grasped both of Leila's arms, enjoying the way that they fit into his hands.

"Is everything okay?"

"I'm not sure, he wants to meet up for drinks. Maybe I should have told him no, but—"

"Hey," Cohen reassured, "he's your brother. Family is the only sure thing we have in this world, trust me on that one. You should meet up with him."

Leila nodded her head with a mixture of agreement and regret. Had Emmett never called, the night would have progressed quite rapidly.

"I had fun tonight, Cohen." Leila walked toward the door while placing her black leather purse over her shoulder. Pumpkin moved in unison with her steps. "And please, tell someone about what has been going on with you recently. If not Lieutenant Dolan or Turner, then Mier. Whoever is out to get you sounds a little out of our league."

Cohen smiled at Leila's reference to "our league." If anything, he did not mind having her company throughout this whole mess, and she was one of the few people he trusted enough with the information.

"I've been thinking the same thing myself."

116

Clearly, someone wanted something from him, and Cohen seriously doubted that his cell phone would satisfy that want. He knew another incident would probably occur soon, and he hoped this time he would be ready. So far, Cohen had been alone during each attack. Sure, Leila had been present at the lake, but she stood too far away to be in any danger. What if the next assault took place in a more public environment? What if someone besides Cohen got hurt? He pushed the thought from his mind.

"First thing Monday morning, I'll drop by Mier's office and tell him what has been going on." Cohen opened the door and let Leila walk through first. As he shut the door, Pumpkin cried at Cohen's obvious attempt to leave him behind. Cohen laughed at Pumpkin's chivalry.

"Guess we better let Pumpkin walk you to your car as well." The door opened and Pumpkin wiggled his way through the opening. Cohen didn't bother to lock the apartment, knowing that the exchange to come would be quick. At her car, Leila stood on her tiptoes and gave Cohen a kiss on the cheek.

"Be safe tonight, okay?"

She turned, shut her door, and drove down the street after throwing a backwards glance and a slight wave in Cohen and Pumpkin's direction. Cohen stood watching her car disappear, the feeling of Leila's lips lingering on his cheek. Pumpkin's tail hit the back of Cohen's legs.

You better not mess this up, Cohen imagined Pumpkin saying.

"I won't, boy." Cohen started walking down the block and Pumpkin followed. With his new dog, Cohen saw a perfect opportunity for a nighttime stroll. Even with the still slightly dull aching of his injuries, Cohen felt completely alive. Despite walking in the same vicinity of last night's attack, Cohen felt no fear. In fact, when thinking of Leila, he felt nothing but peace. Besides Peter and Bre, Leila had been the first person to genuinely demonstrate care for Cohen. That, or Leila had been the first person Cohen allowed to demonstrate care for him since Peter died. Well, Leila and Pumpkin, for that matter. Cohen looked down at his new friend and smiled at the joy in Pumpkin's stride.

Cohen stepped to the beat of his thumping heart. He walked so fast that after ten minutes he looked up in surprise to find himself back at his apartment. Pumpkin bounded ahead of Cohen and, from memory, made his way up the steps. Still on the first flight of stairs, Cohen heard Pumpkin's bark.

"Come on, Pumpkin! You'll wake the neighbors!"

Pumpkin's bark took on a more urgent tone and Cohen sensed that something must be wrong. In the limited time Cohen had spent with Pumpkin, he had yet to hear him bark.

Cohen ran up the last few flights, his pain reaching higher levels at he neared the top. Reaching the last step, Cohen stopped as he noticed that his door stood wide open. He could have sworn that he closed the door before walking Leila to her car. In fact, Cohen remembered making a conscious decision not to lock the door as it shut. Pumpkin's barking continued from inside the apartment. Cohen entered and scanned the room for any disruption.

The kitchen and living room appeared exactly as Cohen had left them. The couches still sat in their original position. His TV and radio remained on the mantel. Had someone been in his apartment, they had clearly not been interested in stealing anything. Still with no sign of Pumpkin, Cohen followed the barking and walked into his bedroom.

"What the hell?"

He halted, not taking one step past the doorframe. Picture frames lay shattered on the floor, the contents of his dresser scattered across the carpet, and Cohen's bed rested on its side. Someone had been in his apartment all right, and they left angry. Cohen hadn't seen anyone during the ascent to his room, though he did acknowledge that the intruder could have used the elevator. Pumpkin frantically moved from one side of the room to the other, smelling the carpet as he moved.

"Come on boy, you'll cut yourself on something in there." Cohen coaxed his dog out of the room while observing the broken glass sticking up from the carpet. Cohen quickly searched the rest of his small apartment. Aside from his room, he found nothing else to be disturbed.

Cohen's mind raced. He and Pumpkin had only been gone for ten minutes, which wouldn't have left an invader with much time. Based on the destruction, the intruder must have gone straight for Cohen's bedroom. That made Cohen uneasy. Cohen looked again at the shattered fragments lining the floor and guessed that the person hadn't found what he or she had been looking for. A sick feeling filled Cohen as he considered a scary possibility. He hoped, despite knowing otherwise deep down, that whoever broke in hadn't been looking for the owner of the apartment.

Thankful that he now had something of a guard dog, Cohen triple checked the lock on his front and bedroom doors. After cleaning the mess and putting his bed back upright, Cohen and Pumpkin had one restless night of sleep.

Chapter 13

The first thing Cohen noticed about the Intelligence Unit was the air of freedom. Sergeant Mier hadn't been kidding around. Having observed the unit for only a few minutes, Cohen could already see that split-second decisions had to be made regularly. After being introduced to his new coworkers, Steph, Ajay, and Mike, Cohen took a seat in a desk on the left side of the small office. The room had no distinguishing features about it: two windows, three trashcans, five desks, and Mier's separate office. Cohen liked the quaintness of the room. Clearly, the officers in Intelligence spent more time outside of the office than in it.

Thankfully, his new team ignored the now barely visible bruise on Cohen's face. Cohen felt very appreciative that no one mentioned it. Sharing a story on his first day of work about how he had been unable to defend himself wouldn't leave the greatest first impression. Cohen meant to seek Mier's advice on the situation, but decided at the last second to hold out a little longer. Making a good first impression would be key. *Besides,* he reasoned, *how would Mier be able to help me, anyway?*

Then, the thrill of the job caused Cohen to forget his situation.

"Everyone, listen up," Mier began. "Now that you've all met Donahue, let's get started." He faced Cohen for a quick side note. "I know this is your first day, but I expect your learning curve to take all of about one minute. We don't have time for anything else, got it?"

Cohen gave one solid nod. Ajay leaned toward him. "Don't expect much more welcome than that," he joked. Cohen laughed, the speech sounding all too similar to Lieutenant Dolan's choice words on Cohen's first day as a new recruit. Mier lost no time in briefing Cohen on the current case.

"Donahue, you might see this case solved on your first day. We received intelligence on this yesterday and plan to wrap it up this evening."

Cohen's left leg started bouncing, a habit he constantly scolded himself for not kicking when it started. Not noticing the leg, or choosing to ignore it, Sergeant Mier continued, "Yesterday, two male bodies were found on the outskirts of the city. They looked pretty beat up: broken ribs, fractures galore, you can imagine the rest. Cocaine packets were also found in each of their pockets with traces of the drug in their systems. Reports suggest the victims were in their mid-twenties."

Cohen's leg stopped bouncing. Mier noticed. "We did some digging yesterday. All of our sources tell us that a guy named Jolt not only planned, but also executed the murders. In other words, we finally have enough reason to put Jolt behind bars."

"Sources?" Cohen questioned.

"Street people, gang members, ex-convicts, any acquaintances we kept in touch with who are willing to help us flush out the bad guys. They give us information, we cut deals with them, whether that means cash payments or decreasing their prison sentences." Cohen nodded.

"Jolt leads a gang known as the SC; we've been waiting for an opportunity to peg him for

122

something." Sergeant Mier pointed to a picture tacked onto a large rectangular bulletin board. The photograph showed a black man's face. Cohen instantly registered the tattoo of a cross over the man's left eye. *Jolt.*

SC: Street Corner. Cohen had heard of the gang before. As a kid, he would see them selling drugs, literally standing on street corners. Apparently, gang membership had grown over the past few years. Right before he left for college, rumors spread about an ambush led by the SC in which five people died. The SC had been the most notorious gang around during Cohen's childhood. Based on this case, not much had changed.

"As for Jolt's motive, we have no idea. Honestly, I couldn't care less. Two men were killed, regardless of their possible involvement in the cartel; motive plays no role in this case anymore. Now, a current inmate, Omar Ross, has old ties with the SC. He claims he can get us the information we need to put someone behind bars."

"Omar is in prison for robbery," Steph explained to Cohen. "He agreed to wear a wire. Omar gets Jolt to admit to the murder and his sentence will decrease." Mier looked at Cohen before offering further explanation. "I'll take a murderer over a thief any day."

And justice will be served, Cohen thought.

"I want everybody to take a break and meet me back here at 8 p.m." Sergeant Mier glanced at Cohen before grabbing his car keys and heading for the door. "We have a long night ahead of us."

The nature of the case left Cohen's nerves prickling. His first day on the job and he would

123

have a chance to help put a murderer behind bars. Intelligence had Cohen hooked.

***

"Ajay, Mike and Steph, take one car. Donahue, you're with me."

Cohen and Mier flew through the streets in no time. Mier drove a black SUV and followed the flow of traffic. Given the undercover nature of the case, the squad lights did not flash and the ride seemed to move in slow motion. The extra legroom didn't go unnoted by Cohen.

Despite working at night, Cohen welcomed the late hour. While waiting for 8 p.m. to arrive, he had buried himself so deep in old police reports that Cohen flinched when Ajay walked back into the office. If this routine remained consistent throughout his time in the Intelligence Unit, Cohen's mind might just get some distraction from his current situation—a very appreciated distraction.

Cohen listened as Mier barked orders into the transmitter. "Line the street outside of Jolt's place. Follow my lead, then fan out, one car in front, one on the adjacent corner. No one moves until I give the signal."

Cohen couldn't believe that this was his life; he felt like one of the main characters in a hit TV show. Hoping Mier didn't see his elation as immaturity, Cohen struggled to hide his joy. Mier maneuvered the car directly across from an old, rundown, two-story house. The blue paint was chipping away from the outside of the house and the curtains all appeared drawn. Cohen's head rotated in the direction of Mier's extended pointer finger. They watched as a man knocked on the front door of the house.

"8:30 on the dot, right on time."

Cohen heard four knocks through the transmitter, the sound mirroring the man's actions. *Omar Ross.* Omar's small frame worried Cohen momentarily; he had imagined Omar to be a larger man. Based on the size of Jolt's head in the mug shot Mier showed earlier, Omar's small frame wouldn't stand a chance against Jolt.

The night sounded so still that nothing else in the world possibly could have been happening at that moment. Someone opened the door and Omar stepped inside. Cohen listened attentively to the conversation that followed.

"Hey Oscar, long time no see." Omar's voice began.

"Well, well, well," Oscar's rusty voice welcomed Omar, "if it isn't Omar, back from the slammer. How you doin' my man? Welcome back. The SC family missed you over here."

"Hey man, finally got the hell outta there. I'm ready to start some new business. What's the word, what's been going on?" Cohen felt guilty for doubting Omar. Based on the apparent ease with which he approached the conversation, maybe Omar would be all right after all. If Omar felt nervous at all, his voice gave no hint.

"Relax, Omar, take it slow," Mier counseled. Cohen doubted that Mier even realized he had spoken out loud. Mier's intense stare at the transmitter mirrored Cohen's anxiety as he focused back on the activity inside of the house.

125

"Whoa, whoa now, easy, Omar. We just got you back here. We don't want Jolt to think you came back purely for the rush of the game. Like I said, we've been missin' you. Did you miss us?"

Jolt. Cohen's body clenched at the reference. Jolt must be inside of the house; Cohen could feel it.

"Take a seat, man, just got these forty-five cocaine rocks delivered today. They're fresh and I haven't even had a chance to break into them yet. Have a sniff; consider it a welcome home present."

The tension in Mier's shoulders grew as the conversation died for half of a minute.

"Damn it, Omar," Mier mumbled. Cohen knew well enough that Omar had no choice but to take the drugs offered to him. If he refused, Oscar would have sensed the sting operation.

"Where is Jolt anyway, dude?" Omar tried approaching the subject from a different angle. "People were talkin' in the cells about how the cops will be after him in a few nights. Sayin' they peg him as the one who killed two dudes or somethin'."

"Oh, that's what they're saying, huh?" Oscar's chuckle sounded raspier than his voice. "Jolt's around here somewhere; dragged his bitch downstairs an hour ago to shut her up. Apparently the whore just realized she is banging a fucking criminal or somethin'," the man explained, laughing at the woman's stupidity.

Cohen moved his hand toward the car's door handle until a harsh signal from Mier stopped him in his tracks. "But Sergeant…he could be killing that girl for all we know! They have drugs, it's enough for a bust." Cohen pleaded, shocked that Mier disagreed with his logic.

126

"It's not enough, Donahue. Remember why we are here: to find a murderer, not to put someone away for some coke use." Cohen pulled back. "Wait for my signal," Mier warned Cohen sternly, seeming annoyed that his authority had been questioned in the first place. *You're not in control here. Just accept it,* Cohen told himself, struggling with the concept. Disheartened, Cohen focused back on the wire. No conversation took place and Cohen wondered if Omar might be taking another line of coke. A door opened somewhere in the background.

"J, my guy, look who's back from his little vacation. Said he got wind that the cops would be after you come a few nights here."

J? Could that stand for Jolt?

The line was silent for the next twenty seconds and Cohen strained his neck toward the dispatcher. "That so, Omar? What brought you back this way?" J asked. His voice rang clear, laced with malice. Cohen's hair stood on edge at the apparent hatred in the man's voice. He guessed Jolt must have experienced some pretty terrible things to produce that much resentment.

"Just a little warning for ya, Jolt." Omar offered. "They said you killed two guys. They'll be looking to prove it. You got any idea how to get yourself outta this one? I want to come back to SC, man. I'm here to help."

More silence.

"So I've heard. Those cops ain't got nothing on me though, don't you go worrying yourself about it, Omar."

127

Cohen stirred, worried their window of opportunity had just closed. "Wait for it," Mier warned again.

"As for those two dead thugs," Jolt continued, "I couldn't think of a louder way to send a message. I think our supplier might finally take the hint. My guess is that our next shipment just might be free."

"MOVE!" Mier yelled into the radio.

Coming from all different directions, the Intelligence members surrounded the front walkway of the house within seconds. Everyone seemed to move in unison. No one waited for a "one, two, three" signal as Cohen had on his first day. Rather, they stepped on impulse with a connection that Cohen never before witnessed. His mind focused on his new team members, following their lead while moving in sync with Mier toward the front door. The mass broke off and took positions, securing the entryway.

Ajay stepped toward the door and the others fell in line behind his lead. With his gun ready, Ajay broke down the door after one swift kick. "CPD! Everybody freeze!"

The team fanned out, Ajay and Steph headed to the right, Mike to the left. One long hallway led straight into the house before splitting into an additional room on the right. Mier and Cohen strode forward, Mier staying straight and Cohen veering right. Cohen continued his pace through a doorframe and into the kitchen in a matter of seconds. The element of surprise had been their biggest advantage. Three cries of "clear" sounded just as Cohen found himself face to face with three men, each having stood from their seats around the kitchen table. Two chairs stood turned over. Cohen's adrenaline reached its height.

"Put your gun on the floor!" Cohen shouted. Of the three men standing before him, only one appeared to be holding a gun. Cohen aimed his weapon directly at the tattoo over Jolt's eye, right at the center of the cross.

Jolt mirrored Cohen's action and pointed his gun at Cohen's head with such intensity that Cohen barely heard Mier enter the room. Jolt then looked at Omar, realization of the sting crossing his features. He repositioned his gun and fired at Omar, the echo of Cohen's weapon simultaneously ringing throughout the house. Cohen's bullet struck Jolt in the left shoulder, causing him to fall against the wall as Omar's figure collapsed onto the floor.

Cohen stood stunned as the rest of the team jumped into action, maneuvering around his still figure as they moved throughout the kitchen. Ajay ran into the backyard after Oscar attempted to escape. Mike threw a struggling Jolt to the ground in one swift movement. Steph pulled his hands behind his back to secure the handcuffs despite Jolt's yells of protest at the apparent pain he felt from the bullet sitting in his shoulder. Mier walked across the kitchen and bent down to feel for a pulse in Omar's neck. He grabbed his dispatcher and pinched the bridge of his nose with his right hand.

"Sergeant Mier to Dispatcher, two ambulances needed at 4200 block of South Francisco. One shot, one dead."

Everything seemed to take place in a span of two seconds: two seconds, and not one more. Two men down, two shots fired, one dead. In two seconds.

"Fuck," Cohen whispered.

The rest of the team carried on as if this kind of thing happened multiple times a day. No one mentioned the elephant in the room, Omar's body. No one appeared affected at all by his death. Mier walked toward Cohen and gave him a stern look. "If you have the shot, Donahue, you take it."

Understanding completely, Cohen nodded and placed his gun in his holster. He saw the ambulances arrive outside of the house, their flashing lights disguising the darkness. Had Cohen shot Jolt immediately, Omar would still be alive. The truth struck Cohen's core and he attempted to hold himself together, suddenly all too ready to get home. Considering his shaking hands, Cohen seriously doubted his ability to shoot again, at least for tonight. After the crime scene reports were settled, Cohen climbed into Mier's car, thankful that the shift had ended—or so he thought.

Chapter 14

The second Mier fastened his seatbelt and started driving, Cohen lost sight of his surroundings. He willed the car to drive faster as images from the scene invaded his vision. Cohen didn't notice that Mier missed the left turn back to the department. He had no idea that the car took a right onto Rockwell Street. Instead of passing by the familiar Starbucks, a Dunkin Donuts advanced on the right. The street names would not have appeared familiar to Cohen and, had he been paying attention, he would have noticed the extra ten minutes added to the car ride. Instead of the scenery, Cohen saw Omar's body. He heard the paramedic declare the time of death and saw her cover the body with a fire blanket. He watched as the two medics placed Omar's body into the back of the ambulance, the motion illuminated by the bright flashing lights. Cohen looked down at his hands and imagined them covered in blood.

Mier pulled over and parked the car adjacent to a curb. Cohen glanced at the suburban setting outside of his window for the first time. He followed Mier's glance toward a yellow house across the street. All of the lights were still on, and the house looked hopeful and lovely, reminding Cohen of the safety he once felt as a child. That safety had been absent for some time now. He looked at Mier for clarification.

"Omar died serving the CPD, giving his life for the Chicago community. I think his family should know they have a reason to be proud of their son, don't you?"

Panic filled Cohen's insides. Mier had driven to Omar's parents' house. Cohen's mind stalled. Let Cohen file the paper work, place him on probation for a month, anything besides making him look into the face of Omar's parents and express condolences for their son's death. Cohen hadn't only witnessed Omar's murder; he firmly believed he caused the tragedy. "Sergeant, I don't know if I—" bile threatened to rise from Cohen's stomach and he clenched his fists and closed his eyes to steady himself.

"You're a police officer, Donahue. People die every day on the job. The sooner you get used to that, the better."

Cohen didn't think he would ever "get used" to seeing innocent people killed. Honestly, he didn't think he wanted to. Feeling pain at the loss of a life seemed so basic, so human. In discarding his ability to feel loss, Cohen knew a piece of his humanity would also be sacrificed. Then again, Cohen had no right to feel sad at Omar's death. A recurring message sounded again and again.

You could have stopped it.

Mier stepped out of the car and Cohen followed. His entire body shook. How could he stand in front of Omar's family? His hesitation only an hour ago resulted in their son's murder. Mier knocked on the door and squeezed Cohen's shoulder. Mr. Ross answered and Cohen subconsciously took a step backwards. Mr. Ross resembled Omar on so many levels: his mouth as round as a circle, his small red lips, and his long eyelashes. Cohen noticed Mr. Ross's attire and balked: he wore his pajamas. Mr. Ross had been ready for bed, his life completely undisturbed, and now Cohen would deliver the most terrible news he would probably ever receive. *He wore his pajamas;* Cohen's mind couldn't let the fact slide.

As far as Omar's parents knew, their son sat in prison, safe and secure. It made sense then, that when two police officers showed up on their doorstep, they would have some questions. Confusion was expected. Denial was understandable. It made the situation exponentially harder.

"Mr. Ross, I'm so sorry." Mier began describing the reason behind his visit and Mr. Ross stood unmoved. "Omar gave his life helping the city of Chicago. He died a hero, sir." Shock lasted all of one minute before Mr. Ross found his voice and launched into questions, convinced that his son must still be behind bars, safe.

"Omar was let out of prison?"

"He offered to aid us in a sting operation."

"Omar would have told us if he was getting out; I just talked to him yesterday. Someone should have told us!" The volume of Mr. Ross's voice rose with each sentence.

"Mr. Ross, we are extremely sorry for your loss and beyond appreciative of Omar's bravery—"

"Like hell you are!"

Mrs. Ross joined her husband at the door after hearing the commotion. The sight of police uniforms immediately connected in her mind. Without receiving an explanation, she dropped to the floor. Just dropped. Like a fly hitting a light bulb. The skirt of her nightgown spread around her body on the hardwood floor beneath Mr. Ross's feet.

Mr. Ross stayed standing; Cohen was sure the full effects of shock had yet to wear off. He wondered who trembled more, Mrs. Ross or himself.

Before Cohen knew what was happening, he found himself at Mrs. Ross's side. Now crouching at eye level, he placed his hand over her arm and squeezed it gently, partly to offer reassurance and partly in an attempt to steady his own body. Omar might have inherited his father's facial features, but his eyes definitely belonged to his mother. For a moment, in place of Mrs. Ross's face, Cohen pictured Omar's.

"Mrs. Ross," he choked. "Omar was a smart, intelligent, and loyal person. I...I am so, deeply sorry for what happened today." She looked at Cohen and for a moment—for just one second— Cohen saw a smile struggle to develop at the memory of her son. Her effort stirred a feeling deep in Cohen's heart; she forgave him. Omar forgave him. That moment between Cohen and Mrs. Ross, that small moment, allowed Cohen to begin forgiving himself, if only ever so slightly.

Cohen and Mier rode back to the department in silence. Cohen took in the neighborhoods, the street signs, and the green grass. He let the guilt completely envelop his entire body.

"From experience, kid, take the night to drown out your sorrows. A little alcohol might be just what you need." Mier offered as the car pulled up next to Cohen's car. Cohen shook his head. Getting drunk didn't sound like the worst idea in the world, and Cohen knew that he needed to be alone more than anything. He opened the car door and stepped into the parking lot without mumbling a goodbye. As Mier reversed back onto the street, Cohen walked to his Ford pickup, fell to his knees, and cried.

***

When Cohen arrived at his apartment, he threw up the lunch he had eaten earlier that day. Pumpkin, after waiting for Cohen the entire day, jumped onto Cohen's leg and whined for attention. Cohen patted him on the head before gently pushing Pumpkin's front feet to the floor. "Not tonight, boy." The bathroom swelled with steam as Cohen dragged his shower out for over an hour. Not even an hour was long enough to scrub the feeling from his already numb skin.

Cohen couldn't pinpoint which aspect of the night made him feel this nauseous. Whether the gruesome nature of the case or Omar's death at Cohen's hands propelled the feeling, Cohen didn't know. Maybe it was the fact that three people had died at the end of the day: two men and Omar. Cohen couldn't help but feel as though Jolt had won. He knew one thing for sure; he wouldn't get through the night without drinking a substantial amount of alcohol.

Stepping out of the shower, Cohen looked in his fridge for something to drink. He saw one old beer bottle pushed to the back of the second shelf. Pumpkin kept his distance and waited for Cohen to come into the TV room.

"Not enough," Cohen mumbled, knowing tonight would be more of a whiskey and Coke kind of night. He dressed in worn blue jeans and his go-to gray Blackhawks sweatshirt. Cohen grabbed a set of keys and walked the two blocks it took to get to O'Reilly's Pub.

He walked in a trance; three cars swerved to avoid hitting him as he crossed the street. One honked. A red Cadillac, a black car, and a blue something-or-other—Cohen saw the cars but didn't care if they hit him. He walked past the tall evergreen trees, crossed the street, and entered O'Reilly's within ten minutes of leaving his apartment. Cohen veered for the right side of the bar, not wanting to associate his usual spot with tonight's guilt. Glancing at the clock and noting the time—11:30 p.m.—Cohen guessed he had at least an hour and a half before his body began screaming for sleep. He started the night with two whiskey waters and willed the images of the day's case to disappear.

"This seat taken?" Cohen turned his head. A blonde-haired woman pointed to the stool next to him. She had curled her shoulder-length hair for the night and mascara lined luscious eyelashes surrounding two squinty eyes.

Cohen took another sip of his drink. He guessed at how the night would end and he felt disgusted at the thought. He nodded his head in welcome to both the woman and Tommy bringing another round.

"I'm Danielle, Danielle Smith."

Jesus, Cohen thought to himself, *first and last name within two seconds of meeting me?* Stories of women getting involved with the wrong kind of guy—rapists, killers, etc.—covered the news, and this girl just gave him her first and last name right off of the bat? Cohen could be a serial killer for all she knew. It was odd what the brain focused on when looking for distraction. Danielle took a seat and leaned her body ever so slightly toward Cohen.

"Let's have some shots, Tommy," Cohen ordered, tossing Tommy his credit card. "Keep the tab open, please." Tommy glanced at Cohen and the woman next to him, noting their equally desperate appearances. He laid the shots in front of Cohen and watched the rest of the night play out.

The remainder of the conversation between Cohen and Danielle contained no depth, nothing to suggest that any sort of IQ existed between the pair. Despite their intelligence, neither attempted to impress the other. Small periods of time passed in silence as they gulped down their drinks, both wanting to be as drunk as possible for what would inevitably follow. It was quite simple, actually: Cohen needed an escape tonight. Danielle did too.

"Where do you work?" The lack of interest in Danielle's voice could not have been more apparent.

"Does it really matter?"

"No, it doesn't. Are you going to bring me home or what?"

The kissing started in the elevator. Danielle closed the distance between them, placing her hands on his chest and parting Cohen's lips with hers. Cohen moaned, not because he felt turned on but because he needed this.

Cohen encouraged Danielle to keep leading as they hit the bed. Leila flashed into his mind for the tenth time and he pushed her away. Danielle

137

was aggressive. The kisses were rough and desperate, two people trying to forget their day's work. *You should be with Leila,* his insides screamed. Cohen stifled their cries. In seconds, Cohen's jeans were thrown beside the bed. Danielle barely removed the deep blue, clunky bracelet from her wrist before she pulled Cohen inside of her. The sex was quick and it was hard. Then it ended. No cuddling, no second round. Once was enough. Cohen lay naked on the bed, attempting to distract himself by focusing on the rain that fell straight down in the windless night.

He woke up to an empty bed, a cup of coffee on the kitchen counter, and a note:

"I'm sorry," Cohen read the words out loud.

Yeah, me too, Cohen thought. His mind flashed immediately to Leila and guilt crept through his entire body. He walked to the shower and turned the water to scalding, attempting for the second time within the past ten hours to wash his regret away. Danielle seemed like a sweet girl, the kind that would never hurt a fly, but Cohen felt nothing toward her. He avoided running that morning. After the night he'd had, the thought of being completely alone with his thoughts scared the hell out of Cohen.

Stepping out of the shower, Cohen felt a sudden urge to contact Bre. He needed to hear a motherly voice; maybe she would be able to knock some sense into him. Reaching for his phone, memories of the robbery came flooding back. Cohen still had yet to replace his cell.

"Great."

Cohen thought about the black car for the first time since the day before. It had been a while

138

since his last run-in with the vehicle; Cohen wondered what they could possibly be waiting for.

Chapter 15

"You have a good time last night? You look like hell, man," Ajay stated as Cohen took a seat at his desk. *If only you knew.* The energy that drew Cohen to the Intelligence Unit yesterday now threatened to suffocate him. At the sight of his new team members, Cohen felt overwhelmed with last night's case. He looked around and noticed that everyone else appeared normal, well rested. He couldn't imagine what he looked like. He avoided the mirror at all costs after waking up, assuming that seeing the guilt in his face might prove even worse than feeling it.

"Hey, Ajay, could I ask you something?" Cohen said. Ajay nodded, not moving his gaze away from his computer screen. A picture frame sat on his desk. It held a photograph of a beautiful woman and three little children, two girls and one boy. Cohen had no family and the job scared him— he couldn't understand how someone with loved ones at home could be successful in the profession. Then again, his dad didn't seem to have a problem knowing that Cohen waited at home for him each night.

Cohen lowered his voice, not wanting Mier to overhear the conversation. After his reaction last night, Cohen felt sure that Mier thought him weak. He didn't want to give him more proof. "How do you stomach it? The deaths, the innocent people dying, all of it. What's the secret?" Cohen asked, desperate for an answer he could apply to his work.

Ajay looked squarely at Cohen, apparently taking in his appearance for the first time. Cohen knew that Ajay heard Mier scold Cohen last night about taking the shot. In fact, Cohen was pretty sure that the entire team had heard it. Based on the way that Ajay looked at Cohen now, he guessed that Ajay couldn't have agreed more with Mier's words.

"The secret, Donahue, is that there is no secret. You can either handle it, or you can't. And if you can't, you better start packing up, man, because you won't make it in Intelligence."

At Cohen's dismayed look, Ajay's features softened. He offered more. "Listen man, the truth is, when I saw my first death in the unit, I wanted to quit. I went home that night and looked online for other job openings that might interest me."

"I know the feeling."

"Well, that feeling lasted all of one night. I just sucked it up the next morning and pushed the pain down, deep. Sure, it resurfaces every once in a while, but you have to push it away. "

"Right." Cohen breathed.

"Guys like us, we can't do other jobs. We need the satisfaction of knowing that our day-to-day work could save another life down the line."

Tilting his head back, Cohen wondered what the hell he had gotten himself into.

"All right team, here it is." Mier stepped out of his office holding a coffee. Cohen got the sense that Mier purposely avoided making eye contact with him, probably in an effort to help Cohen feel more comfortable. Cohen appreciated the gesture; had Mier looked his way an enormous blush would have spread across Cohen's face.

"Today should be an interesting one. We are dealing with the drug cartel again. Got word off the street that another big shipment, a thousand rocks, will be coming in today. The crack will be transported in a freight train scheduled to arrive at the shipping yard on 61st and Lafayette in the Englewood neighborhood at 7:45 tonight."

Pinning yet another man's picture on the bulletin board, Mier continued, "We have some information from the street, but not enough. Our main informant, Leo, arrested last month for his involvement in the cartel, said Tibo will be taking the lead on this one." The mood in the room immediately became more serious. Cohen assumed that Tibo must be a big player in the cartel. Mier pointed to the picture on the wall and Cohen tried to memorize the facial features, although no distinguishing tattoo existed this time.

Mier explained further, "I need all hands on deck for this one. You should all reach out to any street sources willing to talk—prostitutes, pimps, whoever. Find me more information."

"Who is Tibo?" Cohen's curiosity got the best of him.

"Tibo, Donahue, will be your worst nightmare if this opportunity to put him away slips by."

With that, everyone on the team jumped into action, grabbing their coats and leaving their desks. Having basically no experience, Cohen could only watch as everyone left the office, no doubt going to speak with the sources they had built up over the years. It would take many cases before Cohen could find anyone trustworthy enough to consider a source.

Mier watched as Cohen moved for the file cabinet.

"What's your plan, Cohen?"

"I thought I would start to familiarize myself with past cartel cases. At least until I build up sources, the best way to support the team might be to show up to stings as prepared as possible."

"I have other ideas. This Leo that I was talking about, I have a feeling he's not telling us something. He gave us just enough information to catch the shipment and nothing more. I trust my gut on this one: he's holding back on us."

"What do you think he's hiding?"

"No idea. I was going to go question him myself today, but I could use some time here to catch up on paperwork. Considering your lack of connections on the street, I'll send you instead."

Cohen looked up from the file cabinet.

"Unless, of course, you prefer to look through the file cabinet."

Cohen slammed the file drawer shut and stood straight. This would be the perfect opportunity to bury the feelings still lingering from last night. He wondered if Peter and Bre enjoyed their jobs in the CPD for similar reasons, for distraction. Considering his mother, Cohen guessed that his dad definitely needed some serious distraction from the hell waiting for him at home all of those years.

"I need you to go down to the MCC. Request to speak with Leo. He should be willing to cooperate considering the major decrease in prison time we'll be offering. You're flying solo on this one, Donahue. Don't let me down."

143

Cohen nodded his head, grabbed his keys, and walked briskly out the door. Halfway to his car, he remembered that he had left his wallet in his locker. Cohen reluctantly made his way back into the building to grab it. The worst-case scenario right now would be running into Leila. She would no doubt pick up on Cohen's guilt and ask for details. Trying to avoid conversation with anyone so as to keep his focus, Cohen ran right into Mier as he walked through the locker room door.

"Whoa! Mier, you scared the shit out of me. What are you doing down here?" Cohen's alarm at seeing Mier made the Sergeant jump as well.

"Damn it, Donahue! I just wanted to tell you something else about Leo. Jesus, I never knew you were so jumpy." Cohen immediately thought back to Omar's death the night before and realized the event, in combination with his recent problems with the black Jeep, couldn't be good for his stress levels.

"Anyway, I just wanted to give you a warning that Leo might be difficult to extract information from; feel free to use force if necessary. We really need the specifics, so don't let us down today."

Cohen nodded slowly, knowing well that using "force" on an inmate must be against the law. Apparently, the same rules held no standing in the Intelligence Unit. "Now that I'm down here, I might as well use the bathroom." Mier added as he walked through the locker room doors. "They still as terrible as they were twenty years ago?"

"My guess is they are much worse. Good luck in there." Cohen left the sergeant to his own business and jogged back to his car. Since he and

Officer Turner talked, she had yet to even look at Cohen as he passed her desk. If only she knew about the case last night. Cohen felt for a second that maybe Turner had been right. Maybe he shouldn't be here. Maybe he wasn't cut out for the Intelligence Unit.

Well, only one way to find out. Mier's mention of force stuck with Cohen, making him nervous. He couldn't let the sergeant down again, so if force proved necessary, Cohen would have to figure out quickly how much he was willing to use. But if he had to guess now, it would be none.

Besides, Cohen realized as he placed the keys in the ignition, at this point, he needed reassurance in his ability just as much as Mier did.

***

Cohen arrived at the MCC and approached the booking officer sitting at the front desk. Although not as slight and small as the usual officer behind the desk, the woman looked pleasant enough. Cohen flashed her his badge.

"Officer Donahue, CPD, here on Sergeant Mier's orders."

"Follow up questions on Michia, Officer Donahue?"

"Actually, no. I'm here to speak with Leo. He's helping us on one of our current investigations," Cohen countered.

"One moment, please." Cohen watched as the tall, very thin woman walked toward the jail cells. Leo needed to give consent before Cohen could talk to him. Cohen took in the sight of the office, noting its tidiness. Post-it notes lined the front desk, filled with messages written to various officers. No one else sat in the lobby. In fact, each time Cohen had been to the MCC, the lobby had been empty. The atmosphere seemed almost peaceful. Cohen laughed, considering that the inmates were no more than ten feet away. The booking officer returned and Cohen read her name badge: "Maria Swanson."

"Leo will see you now, Officer Donahue. If you would just follow me." Cohen stepped toward Officer Swanson just as her office phone began to ring. She signaled Cohen an apology and said, "It should only take a minute." Cohen took a seat in one of the chairs and waited for the call to end. Instead of hanging up the phone, Officer Swanson extended it to Cohen. "Sergeant Mier would like to speak with you, Officer Donahue." Cohen stood in confusion and took the phone. Maybe something had changed in the case.

"Hey Sergeant, I'm about to speak with Leo. What's up?"

Cohen could hear Mier struggle with the words about to come out of his mouth. "Donahue, were you with a woman last night by the name of Danielle?"

"Um...Danielle Smith?" It was a miracle Cohen remembered her last name, considering the amount of alcohol that had been in his system last night. He thought the question odd, but assumed Mier already knew the answer. "Yes...I was."

In an instant, his mind flashed back to the note Danielle left on his counter.

I'm sorry.

146

"Listen," Mier continued, the seriousness of his tone having increased dramatically. "I need you to get in the squad car and start driving back to the department. Drop the car off in the parking lot and leave the keys in the middle compartment. You're probably going to want to hide out for a little, so try not to run into anyone."

"Sergeant, what the hell is going on?" Cohen asked. A second ago, he had been asking Officer Swanson for access to question Leo, now he would "probably want to hide out?" Cohen waited for what seemed like three minutes before Mier offered an explanation.

"Danielle just showed up at the office. She said she wanted to press rape charges. I will explain—"

"Rape charges?" Cohen interrupted, paying no mind to Officer Swanson's look of alarm. "That's insane! Let me come in and give a statement. I'm completely innocent here."

"Cohen, you had sex with her last night. Your DNA would show up as a match if you provide it. DNA is the first thing any investigating police officer would ask you for."

"Okay, but couldn't we—"

"Listen up Donahue, because I don't have all day to explain. Danielle was also banged up pretty bad. Her right eye was black and she had a cracked rib, among other minor injuries."

What the fuck? Cohen thought. Danielle had been perfectly fine when they went to bed. Cohen's mind failed to comprehend what was happening; his head swam with denial.

147

"For now, stay somewhere safe and low key. Investigators called five minutes ago to provide me with a warning, but they haven't been to the office yet. My bet, they show up here in around an hour. So until I can find a way to fix this, I want you to talk to no one, especially not Danielle. I'll take care of the police."

"Jesus, Mier, take care of the police? Let's not forget that we *are* the police. I should just come in and give my statement. I really think I should. People will hear my side of the story out."

"Are you really that naïve, Donahue? Because let me tell you something, this world is anything but fair. Innocent people are locked up every day, okay? A woman came into the office saying you raped her, that you beat her. She took the rape kit test, Cohen. Danielle has proof whether the story holds or not. When the media gets wind of this, whose side do you think they are going to take? A cop, or an innocent girl lured by the dirty police officer who also appears to be a woman-beater?

"I can see the headlines now, kid: 'New police officer fails to cope with daily reminders of his father's death,' right smack above a picture of Danielle's black and blue face."

"You know that's not true, Mier."

"Sure as hell I know it's not true, but tell me that story doesn't have a nice ring to it. The media will eat you alive, Cohen."

Cohen lacked words to respond to Mier's claim, especially because he was starting to believe that Mier had a point. Once the media got hold of a story, they could convince a mass of people of an innocent man's guilt, especially when so many clues clearly supported the claim. If it came down to protecting a reputation, would the CPD consider believing Danielle's story over his?

Mier had much more experience in the field. If he said a situation wasn't safe, Cohen wasn't about to disagree. Besides, if Cohen could have anyone in his corner, Mier would be the best man for the job. Deep down, Cohen knew that Mier would put the cartel case aside and place all of his efforts into helping Cohen. He just knew.

"We should also take every precaution here because I'm honestly not sure how serious this could become. I would stop using your cell phone. Let me do some research. See what I can find. Call me from a pay phone in two hours."

Cohen almost told Mier about the mugging the other night. How, even if he wanted to, Cohen wouldn't be able to use a missing phone. Instead, he remained quiet and listened as the line cut. Cohen handed the phone back to Officer Swanson and walked out of the lobby into the dark and cloudy day.

Chapter 16

Mier hung up his phone and rubbed his hands over the top of his head in a repeated motion. He had stepped into the parking lot to get some privacy before calling Cohen on the phone. After retiring from the CPD, he doubted that the stress of the job would leave him with any hair on his head. In his entire career as a sergeant, Mier had never been involved in charges filed against his officers. The media would eat this story up and he had a feeling the attention would prove fairly biased in Danielle's favor. Mier made a mental note to warn Cohen's coworkers not to speak with reporters. A snitch within the office was the last thing Cohen needed.

Mier stayed sitting in his car, not yet ready to enter the building. As sergeant, he must fulfill his duty to stay focused on the job. His job description included maintaining the safety of everyone in his unit. Now, Cohen had made it very hard for him to do so. Mier's mind spun so fast he doubted his ability to focus on anything, let alone any new cases that would come in. Mier felt genuinely confused. Should Cohen be his priority or should he focus on the rest of his cases?

Cohen, he told himself, thinking of Peter. Until the whole issue resolved itself, Mier would focus on making sure that Cohen received only what he deserved; Mier knew for a fact that Cohen had no real role in these charges. Rape seemed out of the question. Even as a rookie officer, Cohen demonstrated incredible awareness toward humanity, especially human suffering, as was proved in his reaction toward the Ross family. Something about the way Cohen comforted Mrs. Ross over Omar's death, well, Mier questioned whether or not Cohen could handle the strain of the job. Then he remembered Peter, how he had operated with the same level of care, and Mier knew that Cohen would succeed.

Mier reached for the phone now sitting in his back pocket to make another call. This call would be more relaxed in nature. Mier knew that the integrity of his entire department would inevitably be questioned once the rape charges came to light. Before the whole world learned of Cohen's employment at the CPD, and Mier's job became a lot more stressful, he needed a strong dose of normality in his life. Without it, Mier knew that someone would notice his worried appearance the second he walked back into the department. The whole building would start talking. He could hear the conversation now.

"Did you see Mier this afternoon?"

"He stepped out to make a call and came back completely panicked. Something must be really wrong."

"I'll see if Lieutenant Dolan heard anything."

The gossip mill would do its work and, before they knew it, Cohen would be a murdering rapist with a drug problem.

Mier's anxiety also stemmed from the fact that he had yet to inform Lieutenant Dolan about Danielle's allegations. Honestly, he wasn't sure he would pass on the news. Mier dialed the number, hoping for a decrease in his heart rate to result. Doug and Mier had been best friends since high school, and Mier knew that speaking with Doug would solve some of his problems—put some of his worry to rest. The voicemail sounded.

"Hey Doug, it's Mier. Looks like I missed you. I'll give you another try later tonight. Hope all is well, man." Sensing the ominous tornado looming around the corner, Mier hung up the phone and opened his car door. He took a deep breath, straightened his tie, and walked back into the department. Mier almost felt ready to tackle Cohen's battle.

***

Rape charges? How the hell could this be possible? Danielle initiated everything last night. Even if she hadn't, Cohen knew for certain that the sex had been consensual. The rage flowing through Cohen's veins threatened to pop through his skin. The pulsing continued as he replayed the entire night in his head. From the beginning, Danielle played him. Cohen pictured himself responding affirmatively to Danielle's request to take her home. He had a sudden urge to punch something.

"You idiot! This could have all been avoided!"

In all of Cohen's life, he had never been in serious trouble. Cohen actually couldn't remember ever receiving punishment for any major wrongdoings. The main reason was that Cohen didn't act in a way that required scolding. Sure, he and Peter had a few typical father-son fights throughout his childhood, but Cohen had always made sure to keep a clean record.

This had to be the universe's way of catching up to all of those years Cohen slid past. That, or the Intelligence Unit was playing a prank on the new guy. Cohen mulled over the possibility and realized that Mier had known Danielle's name. No prank would've gone so far as to send a woman to seduce Cohen at a bar. It had to be the universe. In that case, Cohen needed a very solid plan to avoid being sent to prison.

Replaying the conversation with Mier over and over in his head, Cohen finally pulled himself out of denial and acknowledged his circumstances. Danielle pressed rape charges, he could be arrested, and now Cohen had to hide from the police. *The police.* Cohen felt his firearm in his utility belt and couldn't help but wonder at the strangeness of the situation: a police officer hiding from fellow police officers. Danielle must be a woman trying to make a few extra dollars by getting some face time on the news. The only thing Cohen felt confident about was his innocence.

Stay somewhere safe, Mier had said. *Call me from a payphone in two hours.* Cohen glanced down at his watch and noticed the early time of day. Not only did Cohen have two hours to kill, but he also had to find a secure place to do so. One of the hardest parts of the situation was Cohen's inability to determine how seriously the police would take the allegations against him. The police could be waiting to make an arrest until they had a chance to speak with Mier. Or they could be searching for Cohen at that very moment. Cohen sincerely hoped that Mier held them off long enough for Cohen to come up with a plan.

153

He turned on the car and began driving back to the department. *First things first*, he thought. Cohen needed to drop the car off at the department. Then, he would worry about finding a place to hide. Cohen stalled before fully acknowledging his lack of family and friends living in Chicago willing to offer aid. He certainly couldn't just go back to his apartment, no doubt the first place that any investigating officers would look. For someone surrounded by people all day, Cohen felt undoubtedly alone.

On the drive back to the department, emotions struggled for the limelight in Cohen's mind. Cohen jumped from denial, to panic, to numbness, before settling on confusion. Knowing he didn't have time to sit and sort out his feelings, Cohen parked the squad car, left the keys in the middle compartment as instructed, and quickly strode toward his car. He didn't want to see anyone in the parking lot and he definitely didn't have a good excuse as to why he was leaving work at midday.

Halfway to his car, Cohen saw Leila taking a phone call in the parking lot and he corrected his previous thought process. He didn't want to see anyone in the parking lot *besides* Leila. She would know a way out of this mess; even her presence would help Cohen to think more clearly. Before fully acting on his desire to speak to Leila, reality hit Cohen like a sack of rocks.

You slept with Danielle last night. Cohen now had no right to even look Leila's way, not to mention ask for her help. Although nothing constituting an exclusive relationship existed

154

between Leila and Cohen, he knew deep down that it eventually would have. *Would have.* Something told him that Leila wouldn't settle for any man treating her poorly. Cohen's actions had definitely placed him in that category. He did not deserve Leila.

Cohen guessed that he must have abandonment or commitment issues. *"It makes sense,"* his high school buddies would tell him, *"your mom left you and your dad, and now you don't want to find a girlfriend in case it happens again."* The simplicity of the complex situation described from a teenager's point of view made sense to Cohen. Naturally, when a functional relationship seemed to be forming, Cohen went and slept with another woman. Unfortunately, no matter how true the young diagnosis rang, Cohen knew it didn't serve as an excuse. Just when he thought he had hit rock bottom, his stomach continued to drop, as if without end. Knowing he deserved the pain, Cohen headed in Leila's direction.

Leila spotted Cohen jogging her way. "Hey, Dad, listen, I've got to go. Love you too." She had yet to see Cohen that day and as he drew close, Leila's eyes narrowed at the lines of worry framing his forehead. She waved in his direction and received a tentative response.

"Uh, hey Leila."

"Whoa, Cohen, what's with the rush? You look like you just saw a ghost from your past or something…"

Cohen wanted to tell Leila everything right then and there. To pull her close and wrap his arms around her as he explained how he messed up, how

155

his inability to have a relationship served as no excuse to treat Leila the way he had. Cohen planned to say all of these things. Instead, he decided on this:

"I can't explain right now..." *Stupid,* he thought, "but I am in a lot of trouble for something that I didn't do. Mier told me to hide somewhere until things blow over, but I don't have anywhere to go—"

Before Cohen finished his sentence, Leila handed him the keys to both her car and apartment.

"Say no more. My apartment is all yours."

Right, Cohen realized as he glanced at her car keys now in his hand. *If I can't use my phone, I probably shouldn't drive my car either.* He closed his fist around the keys and consciously avoided looking too far into Leila's stare out of fear that she would see right through him. Leila read him like a book. Cohen feared that the second he let his guard down, Leila would know about Danielle. She would know what happened last night and wouldn't want anything to do with him. Cohen couldn't handle that. Cohen knew he had acted selfishly, and that was the worst part. Leila deserved to know the truth, and he felt too cowardly to tell her.

Thrown off by Cohen's odd behavior, Leila offered, "My address is 3509 North Pine Grove Avenue. It's a duplex. Mine is on the left." She opened her car door as an invitation for Cohen to climb in. As if waiting for Cohen to say something with at least a small amount of substance, Leila held open the door.

"Is everything going to be okay, Cohen?"

Cohen could not exit the war taking place in his mind long enough to provide Leila with an answer.

When Leila finds out…What the hell have I done?

"Th—thanks, for the car. Well, the keys, you know." Cohen attempted to thank Leila. After mumbling the words, Cohen allowed himself one glance up toward her face. Leila's hair blew in the wind and Cohen's head began to spin. He pulled the door shut and left without any further interactions.

Looking in the rearview mirror, Cohen saw that Leila made no movement to head back into the department. The wind blew her hair and she wrapped her arms around her body. Not yet ready to watch her disappear, Cohen stalled the vehicle at the end of the parking lot. Leila straightened her shoulders and lifted her head before making her way toward the big wooden doors. Her stride lengthened with each step. Cohen stepped on the gas, easing his way into a gap in the traffic. He began the drive to Leila's house, his guilt sitting shotgun.

Chapter 17

Leila's duplex looked exactly as Cohen had pictured it. Quaint enough for one person, the brick façade belonged in a magazine. On the inside, two sofas faced a modest TV-stand beneath a small flatscreen. Cohen imagined Leila sitting on the sofa and saw her pale skin glowing against the blue velvet fabric. Even in his mind, she looked beautiful. The kitchen appeared small, but nice nonetheless. Green tinted granite covered the counters and the cabinets boasted a deep brown lacquer. Cohen almost opened the cabinets to see what lay inside, but something held him back. Cohen wanted Leila to show him, he realized, although he seriously doubted he would ever find himself standing in Leila's kitchen again. Not after she heard about Danielle.

Leila's shoes created a neat line by the door and Cohen felt comfortable with the clean nature of the house. It smelled as if a vanilla candle burned and nothing lay so far out of place that one would feel a need to pick it up. Cohen noticed three dishes sitting in the sink and took to finishing them. He set the dishes on the drying rack and continued to picture Leila in every scenario he could think of: Leila watching TV, Leila making coffee, Leila drawing the blinds at night and opening them in the morning.

Cohen didn't feel the lopsided smile coming but it spread across his face; he loved being at Leila's apartment. He loved seeing her life away from work.

After moseying around the duplex, Cohen found himself looking at the old photographs Leila had on display. In one picture, Leila's young, still slightly awkward form stood next to two adults. Based on the similarities between Leila and the woman, Cohen could only assume that the adults were her parents. The happiness radiating from Leila's smile appeared obvious in every picture. Cohen realized, to his dismay, that he had yet to see Leila that happy. Sure, she always wore a smile and seemed upbeat, but after seeing these pictures, Cohen knew she had been happier in the past. A knot of sadness built up in his heart.

Making his way toward the last frame in the row of six, Cohen saw Leila standing with her brother, Emmett. The redness of their young hair made the picture that much brighter. Cohen wished he could have seen the fiery color illustrated in the photo, as it now took on a more faded hue. Leila and Emmett couldn't be more than ten years old in the picture, and their smiles were beautifully naïve and youthful.

For the next forty-five minutes, Cohen's mind remained in denial of his situation while his heart felt blissfully at ease. At the sound of the neighbor's dog barking, Cohen thought of Pumpkin for the first time that day. Had he known that he wouldn't be able to go home, Cohen would have made other arrangements for Pumpkin. His mind flashed to the welcome note that his neighbors left for Cohen on his first day in the apartment. They wrote their cell phone numbers on the bottom of the page—if only Cohen had thought to add those numbers to his contacts.

Not that you would have a phone to call them with...Cohen's mind graciously reminded him.

Over the past few days, Pumpkin quickly had become one of Cohen's favorite companions. Despite his inability to speak actual words, Cohen felt like Pumpkin understood him better than anyone. Cohen made up his mind that he would return home that night to feed Pumpkin; hopefully, the whole mess would be over by then. The thought of Pumpkin waiting all night for Cohen to come home warmed a part of Cohen's heart just recently reserved for that dog. With only fifteen minutes to spare, Cohen grabbed Leila's keys and took off to find a payphone.

Sergeant Mier answered on the second ring.

"Griffin Mier here." Cohen felt a pang of guilt at the stress behind Mier's greeting. He had been on the job for all of one day; considering Omar's death and now the rape charges, Cohen hadn't contributed anything to the Intelligence Unit but trouble. Once news of the accusation reached the media, Cohen knew CPD management would have a negative connotation within the public.

"Mier, it's me. Please tell me you have some information."

Five seconds of silence.

"Come to the office as soon as you can. Use the back door and try to avoid bumping into anyone here. I'm not sure who has heard of your...predicament, but assume everyone knows." Mier hung up the phone.

Frustration filled Cohen's entire body. *I think this is a little more serious than a "predicament."* He jumped back into Leila's car

160

and shut the door, adding a little more force than necessary. The stress of recent events had Cohen feeling sorry for Mier one moment, and enraged toward him the next. Cohen wished Mier would put himself into Cohen's shoes. Informing a man about rape charges filed against him and not supplying any more detail seemed cruel to Cohen. Then again, maybe the information would be too sensitive to discuss over the phone. The thought chilled Cohen.

As he drove, he let his body calm down. Realizing that the next few days would most likely produce a few spiked-blood-pressure moments, he made a mental note to control his reactions. Cohen had never been one to take out his anger on others. He reminded himself that Mier offered to help Cohen out of the goodness of his own heart and, of course, because of Cohen's kinship with Peter. Cohen could be completely alone in this fight, and he appreciated Mier's support more than he could say.

He parked a block away from the police station to avoid any chance of someone seeing him step out of Leila's car. Cohen worked his way to the department's back door, avoiding the street and walking through the alley between the CPD and its surrounding buildings. As he walked, Cohen feared most that Leila would cross his path, especially since by now she would have heard the details of Danielle's story.

"Sergeant," Cohen gasped as he pushed through Mier's office doors and stood in front of his desk. It was now around 4 p.m., and Cohen realized that everyone must still be out in the city finishing up rounds before the end of the day.

"With all due respect, what in the hell is going on here?"

Mier walked to the door and turned the lock on the handle to a horizontal position. He looked through his office window at the empty Intelligence Unit desks and pulled the blinds closed. Cohen couldn't help but hope that Mier's actions proved to be more dramatic than necessary. Then again, he doubted that Mier would act in such a way unless required.

"Listen up, Donahue, we don't have time to play catch up here. Danielle is sticking to her claim that you forced yourself on her and then abused her." Although Mier seemed ready to explode with stress, he spoke in a controlled and relaxed manner. Cohen began pacing, Mier's calm voice the only thing providing him with the slightest amount of peace.

"That's absurd! She is lying!" Unlike Mier, Cohen's voice portrayed his feelings perfectly: panicked.

"It gets worse. Since this morning, two other women, named Grace and Laura, also approached the police. They told a very similar story." Cohen's mouth dropped to the floor. This had to be a joke, now there were three women? One look at Mier's face convinced Cohen otherwise.

"Danielle *and* Grace and Laura? And what story was that?" Cohen asked incredulously, afraid to hear the answer.

"That you found their apartment postings on Craigslist. You contacted them yesterday via their contact information provided online claiming interest in their apartments and asking them to meet you for further negotiations."

"Well, that should be pretty easy to solve, Mier." Cohen's words began slowly, picking up the pace as his mind started forming a way out of this mess. "My cell phone was stolen a few nights ago! Someone beat the shit out of me and they took my phone. Even if they do have text messages from my number, I couldn't have been the one to send them."

Mier stared at Cohen with the most outraged look Cohen had ever seen. So outraged, that Cohen literally saw a vein growing by the second in Mier's forehead. He took a step backwards as Mier moved aggressively toward him, pulling back at the last second.

"And you didn't think that was relevant information until now? You didn't think that having your phone stolen should have been grounds to create a police report?" Mier's once calm voice now shook with anger.

"Do you realize that, had you reported the incident, you probably wouldn't be considered a suspect for rape right now?!"

Despite the blinds and locked door, had anyone been at their desks, Mier's loud scolding would unquestionably be heard.

"I wasn't thinking! How was I supposed to know this would all connect? I am telling you now. Doesn't that count for anything?"

"Cohen, the investigators received a warrant to check your locker at work. Your phone was on the top shelf. Had you told someone about the attack…this all could have been over."

Cohen's mind acknowledged his fault in the situation. Had he reported the crime as Leila suggested, to either Mier or another police officer, his claim could have been backed by proof. Instead, Cohen stubbornly decided to keep the incident to himself. In other words, he now had no proof of the other night, only his word claiming that it took place. Sure, some of the bruising still lingered on his ribcage, but he could have easily picked up those injuries from somewhere else. Cohen waited for Mier to continue, feeling completely exhausted and deflated already.

Mier looked just as confused as Cohen at this point. "Conversations between you and Laura, Grace, and Danielle did happen yesterday, according to your text messages. In fact," Mier continued, "your last conversation with Danielle took place yesterday at 11:35 p.m."

Mier handed Cohen a piece a paper. As Cohen looked at a printout of the texting conversation supposedly taking place between him and Danielle, Mier took up Cohen's pacing.

Cohen Donahue: Hi. I'm interested in your property on 175 South Fillmore Street. Want to meet up tonight to discuss? I am heading to O'Reilly's to grab a quick drink now.

(312) 554-6776: Meet you there in ten.

Cohen slowly looked away from the piece of paper and let it drop to the floor. He mentally retraced his steps from that night, trying to remember if he had seen anyone familiar or anything out of the ordinary. Whoever sent these texts had to have seen Cohen at the bar that night. They had to have seen him walking into O'Reilly's. "I'm being set up here,

Mier. Someone must have been following me that night. I did not send that message."

"The other two women have similar conversations with you printed out, although they claim to be 'lucky enough' to have denied your request for a meeting."

"Of course they do," Cohen muttered. For the first time since this morning, Cohen considered how amazing it was that Mier believed his story in spite of all of the evidence suggesting his guilty status. All of the information presented by Mier added up to one thing: Cohen raped Danielle and also intended to harm two other women. Had Cohen been placed in Mier's situation, he wasn't so sure he would be buying Cohen's excuses.

"What kind of woman would meet up with a stranger, late at night, after receiving a mysterious text message without knowing anything about the person?" Cohen did not think the story sounded legit enough.

"I agree; this scam could have been set up better. What's worse, the O'Reilly's bartender confirmed that you and Danielle left together that night. Your credit card statement suggests you had enough drinks to be really intoxicated."

Flashing back to that night, Cohen remembered asking Tommy to keep his tab open. Ever since Cohen's first visit to O'Reilly's, Tommy regarded him with a certain air of judgment. Cohen knew that Tommy wouldn't hesitate to provide the police with any information related to the case, no matter how incriminating the content.

"Damn it, Tommy."

"That's as far as the investigation has gone, but everyone is pretty convinced you're guilty here. I'm with you, man; I smell a rat. All of these points, they add up to be far too convenient. Only an idiot would leave so many clues behind after committing a crime."

"Only an idiot would leave behind *clues*? Jesus, Mier, only a monster would *rape* someone. A woman is claiming I raped her, a woman who was severely beaten up."

For a brief moment, Cohen's mind thought back to Danielle. He realized for the first time, adding to his guilt, that another victim existed in this web of confusion. Danielle had been bruised when she showed up to report the rape. Someone used Danielle to mess with Cohen, and he didn't like the outcome.

"Okay Donahue; touché, touché. I'm just trying to wrap my head around all of this."

"Join the club."

"Well, I don't know much, but I do know for a fact that Peter couldn't have raised a son capable of the things that these women accused you of doing. I just need some more time to prove it," Mier offered. At the name of his father, Cohen grabbed his Saint Christopher necklace out of habit. He wished his dad were here to provide some insight.

"There has to be something I can do."

"Stop, Cohen, I know where you're going with this. If you do anything—try and prove your innocence in any way—these guys will catch you. Do you understand? You are not to make contact with anyone unless you're speaking to me. Even then, only use a pay phone or this disposable phone." Mier handed Cohen a phone still in its packaging. "Hang tight, Donahue, and keep that phone on in case I need to talk to you. I programmed my number into it."

Cohen stood dismayed and placed the box under his right arm. *More waiting.* He shook Mier's hand and thanked him for his help, restating his innocence one last time. Mier demonstrated more confidence than Cohen felt.

Bringing up Danielle had reminded Cohen that one person could put an end to this madness. One person knew the truth behind the rape charges and the stolen phone. Danielle could shed light on the black Jeep; Cohen needed to talk to her. As he headed back to Leila's car, Cohen acknowledged the determination building in his core.

"Don't do anything my ass. Sorry Mier, following orders isn't really my thing."

Chapter 18

Knowing that Leila had at least another hour at work, Cohen drove back to her apartment and let himself in. *Time to take matters into my own hands.* He walked past the blue velvet sofas and crossed the open floor plan into a small office. A computer rested on a petite, white table also supporting a wide vase filled with yellow and pink tulips. A wooden floor replaced the beige carpet, sending a creak into the silence as Cohen stepped onto a soft spot in the foundation. He reached the computer desk and jiggled the mouse, praying the computer was not password protected. After a minute of warming up, a background image showed a large town square boasting a fountain and what appeared to be architecture from the eighteenth century. Just in front of the fountain stood a beaming red-haired beauty. Based on the façade of the buildings, Cohen guessed the photo had been snapped somewhere abroad.

"Now what?" Cohen thought through a strategy. He had a name and a computer. These days, almost anyone could be found online.

"Once a picture finds its way online, kids, it stays there permanently." Cohen could hear his PR professor's warning now and he cringed at the memory of the monotone class. The words used to seem repetitive to Cohen. Now, he only hoped that the warning held true in this moment. Cohen opened up his Facebook page and was greeted by his profile picture. He laughed at the outdated picture of him and his father fishing; it had been a while since Cohen accessed his page.

Cohen typed "Danielle Smith" into the Facebook search bar. Apparently, over a thousand Danielle Smiths lived in the Chicago area.

"Shit." Already feeling the stifling limits of time closing in on him, Cohen reminded himself to stay calm.

Think, Cohen, think. Acknowledging that an arrest could happen at any time, Cohen knew he didn't have the time to sift through a thousand profiles. Assuming that Twitter would yield the same watered-down results, Cohen opened up Internet Explorer and took a deep breath as the loading symbol appeared. Finally, CNN popped up as the homepage and Cohen visualized Leila reading the news in the morning before heading to work. Since opening Leila's computer, Cohen had learned that she both traveled and kept up-to-date on the happenings in the world. He felt intimidated and impressed, all while wishing that he had learned those characteristics in a more intimate way.

The Google search bar swallowed the letters as Cohen's typed. He hoped that "Danielle Smith, Chicago, IL" would magically produce the right result. Still, too many options populated in the results, ranging from "Extraordinary Mommy" to another Danielle Smith's Wikipedia page.

"Damn it," Cohen muttered. He took his time reading each option, waiting for something to catch his eye. The first ten links held no relevance to his predicament. The eleventh listing, however, made Cohen's arm hair stand on edge. He looked closer at the link and his heart skipped a beat at the relevance: a Craigslist advisement.

According to Danielle's story, Cohen contacted her about a Craigslist posting. In order for her story to hold any type of standing, Danielle must have actually created a Craigslist advertisement. It seemed likely that, while the investigation continued, she also had to maintain her account for evidence. Cohen hoped against all odds to have found a clue, although he didn't let himself get too excited.

Come on, help me out here, Cohen thought as he clicked on the link, not entirely sure to whom the plea was addressed. After the Craigslist page loaded, Cohen read the general description of the apartment:

Apartment for sale: 2 Bedroom, 1 bath, garden view, tenant occupied: 175 South Fillmore Street, Chicago, IL. Contact owner:
Danielle_Smith@yahoo.com
(312) 554-6776 (cell).

Cohen now had an address, cell phone number, and an email; yet, based on the results of his earlier searches, chances were slim that this was his Danielle. He tried desperately to remember the cell phone listed in the texting conversation from the sheet of paper Mier showed him earlier, with no success.

Although his gut screamed relevance, Cohen acknowledged his lack of solid evidence. The tenant-occupied status of the listing gave Cohen a little hope. At the very least, he could check out the address and maybe, against all odds, Danielle would answer the door. The apartment's two bedrooms threatened to heighten Cohen's hopes even further. Danielle must have a roommate; even if she didn't answer the door at Cohen's knock, perhaps her roommate would be willing to fill in some gaps.

Don't get ahead of yourself, he cautioned.

Cohen stared at the description a little longer. The entirety of the listing appeared quite barren. The screen didn't display many details. In fact, Cohen mulled, there might be just enough detail for the listing to appear legitimate. Toward the bottom of the page the potential buyer had the option to scroll through photographs of the apartment. Cohen opened the pictures, his heart pumping blood quicker and quicker through his body. Although he had yet to view any information confirming Danielle's role in the listing, Cohen's gut already knew.

The apartment looked nice in the pictures. Its quaint two bedrooms definitely did not appear large and spacious, but they were homey—lived in. Someone had created a life in that apartment, from the odd patch of blue on the yellow kitchen wall to the floral painting that hung from the staircase. Through pictures alone, Cohen could tell that the apartment had, at some point, developed into a home.

As he looked through the photos again and again, Cohen subconsciously hoped for a glimpse into Danielle's life. Maybe something in the images could supply him with a clue as to what provoked Danielle to set him up. A stretch, he knew—especially considering that this apartment could belong to anyone—but he wanted so badly to understand Danielle's motive.

Only seven pictures were available for Cohen to look through, and their quality left something to be desired. Two old-fashioned bedrooms with dated furniture were featured, along with one tiled bathroom and a tiny backyard complete with two chairs surrounding a grill that Cohen assumed must serve as the garden view. Three other shots illustrated the kitchen, the staircase, and an outside angle of the apartment taken from the street.

Cohen couldn't see one person in any of the pictures, nor did he notice anything out of the ordinary. The apartment actually appeared quite tidy. All the while, something nagged at Cohen, and he flipped again and again through the pictures. The mouse finally received a rest as Cohen stared at the bathroom picture. Immediately looking toward the mirror, Cohen hoped to catch a reflection of the photographer. Unfortunately, the reflection in the mirror showed only the toilet and the left half of the shower, nothing of any value.

Dismayed, Cohen leaned his body back and let his head rest against the back of the chair. He had missed something; he could feel it. Cohen lingered on the picture again, taking in the light blue tiles lining the walls, their design imitating an ocean, and the medicine cabinet.

"No…"

Cohen almost fell off his chair as he zoomed further into the image. From his new vantage point, Cohen noticed a woman's jewelry hanging from the upper right hand corner of the medicine cabinet: a long golden chain, a ruby-red necklace, and a blue chunky bracelet. Zooming into the picture a little more, his pulse beat a thousand times per second and his heartbeat threatened to break through his eardrums. Danielle wore an identical blue bracelet the night of their hookup. Cohen closed his eyes and saw Danielle remove the same one from her wrist moments before intercourse.

It's about time, Cohen's gut responded. *You've found Danielle.* He found a piece of paper and a pen and scribbled down the address of the listing.

***

"Mier!"

Lieutenant Dolan didn't care that Mier was on a call and he sure didn't care that his tone of voice startled the Sergeant into almost dropping the phone. Dolan planned to give Mier a piece of his mind, and he strode into his office just the same.

Dolan stood by Mier's desk, waiting expectantly for the phone call to end. The last time Dolan had scolded Mier, well, he couldn't really remember the last time. The apprehensive look in Mier's eyes suggested that he knew exactly what was coming. Especially, Dolan assumed, given Dolan's notorious reputation as the hard-ass of the CPD. Dolan actually felt that "punisher" should be included in his job description, especially after handling situations like this one.

"Hey, listen, I've got to run." Mier hung up the phone not too hurriedly and stood from his sitting position. *Good*, Dolan thought to himself— arguments always proved more challenging if the two involved stood at eye level. Secretly, confrontations thrilled the Lieutenant.

"I'm assuming you can guess why I walked all of the way over to your office, Mier." Only one floor separated the two offices, and both parties acknowledged the ridiculousness in the Lieutenant's exaggerated tone. Mier did not take the opportunity to point it out, which convinced Lieutenant Dolan that he had already won this fight. Apparently, Mier decided to place his usually sarcastic personality on hold. In other words, Mier knew he was in deep water, and Dolan planned to make him swim.

"I know what you're going to say, Lieutenant, but I swear, I'm on top of it. I have everything under control."

Dolan laughed so sarcastically that Mier sat back down in his chair and folded his arms across his chest. Any attempt to appear in control of the situation had been silenced; Mier stood no chance against the Lieutenant.

"If you're so on top of your own game, Mier, then why the hell are three reporters sitting in my lobby waiting to interview me about Cohen Donahue?"

"Well…wait a minute…"

"If you thought I would be angry that you didn't tell me about Officer Donahue in the first place, imagine how much angrier I am that reporters are already on this case!"

"Listen, Lieutenant, I didn't tell you about Cohen because I assumed it would be cleared up quickly. I didn't think it necessary for you to stress over. And I'm sorry for that, I really am, it was a misjudgment on my part."

Lieutenant Dolan threw his hands in the air as if praising God that Mier admitted his fault.

"Cohen is under your watch, Mier, but don't forget for one second my role in that class's development."

"I know, Lieutenant."

"Good." Dolan made a move as if to leave Mier's office, turning at the last second.

"Snitches will absolutely not be tolerated under my leadership, Sergeant, and I assume you understand my meaning."

"Actually, Lieutenant, I don't think I do."

"Well then, let me spell it out for you. Someone snitched this story to the media. As far as I am aware, you're the only one in the department who knows of the accusation being made."

"If you think, for one second, that I have any connections in the media and tipped them off about Cohen's dilemma, Lieutenant—or are implying that in any way—then you are seriously mistaken."

"Hm." Dolan passively responded to the claim.

In reality, Mier had no idea why the media would want to speak with Lieutenant Dolan. If anything, Mier's standing as Cohen's immediate superior should have made his phone ring off the hook since the news was leaked. Eventually, Mier expected that he would have to deal with many pesky reporters. He had yet to receive one call.

"Well, Mier, then you'll be happy to hear that I called security and ushered the nosy sons of bitches all out of the building."

"Good call." Mier responded with an equally aggressive arm raise.

"They didn't go willingly, however, so I was forced to make a deal with them."

Negotiating with the media was always a risky idea. As Lieutenant, Dolan knew this first hand; he also knew that Mier would not support the risk. Dolan enjoyed watching Mier squirm and anxiously wait to hear the rest of Dolan's narrative.

"I promised the reporters that we would supply some answers tonight. I've set up a press conference to be held by Cohen's supervisor."

Mier sat in silence.

"Since you felt so confident taking on this case in the first place, Mier, I believe that would be you." The demeaning nature of the conversation had come full circle and Lieutenant Dolan knew that he pushed all of the right buttons. He could almost see Mier's heart threatening to jump out of his chest and through his shirt in anger. Both men struggled to maintain their composure.

"Are you sure about that, Dolan?" Mier's voice, although calm and confident, failed to fool Dolan, and Dolan watched as Mier continued to put on an act. "A press conference alone will bring in huge amounts of media and attention. Maybe we should just keep our mouths shut until—"

"You don't still get anxious at the thought of speaking in public, do you Mier? It has been a while since I've seen you take an opportunity to address such a large audience. I'm looking forward to seeing the results."

Dolan walked out of Mier's office door before Mier had time to respond. The look in Mier's eyes had been confirmation enough of the answer to Dolan's question—Mier despised public speaking, he always had, and it most definitely still gave him anxiety.

Dolan heard files fall to the ground as Mier swept them off of his desk in frustration. Dolan smiled, slightly amused at the situation. By choosing not to tell Dolan that trouble existed in his own department, Mier had crossed a line. Especially considering that the officer in question was one that Dolan trained so recently.

Dolan knew that he succeeded in getting under Mier's skin. First and foremost, accusing anyone in the department of maintaining media relations was serious. As a police officer, using media for monetary gain was one of the shadiest activities possible. Despite Mier's many years of loyalty to the CPD, the accusation had been made. Of course, Dolan did not really think that Mier had informed any news crew of Cohen's situation. In fact, just earlier that day, Dolan passed by Mier's office in time to hear Mier telling another CPD officer to "mind your own damn business." The phrase originally held no meaning to Dolan. He now assumed someone inquired about Cohen's recent absence in the department.

No, Dolan didn't think Mier capable of speaking to the media, but Mier didn't know that. If anything, Dolan knew that his little tantrum would motivate Mier to clear his name. Mier would search for the real snitch in order to prove his innocence, providing Dolan with an opportunity to then fire the real culprit. Dolan applauded his own creativity.

Chapter 19

Sitting in Leila's car, Cohen pulled out Danielle Smith's address: 175 South Fillmore Street. Fillmore would be north; Cohen's foot eased slowly onto the gas pedal. Ever since his conversation with Mier, Cohen hadn't been able to keep Danielle off his mind.

Although initially Cohen associated Danielle with rage, since looking at the pictures of her apartment, his sentiments had begun to transform. Seeing Danielle's living situation reminded Cohen of her humanity. She had a home and people who loved her. Danielle must have set him up for a reason, possibly in an effort to feel safe. Whether rational or not, Cohen had begun to worry about Danielle's safety as well as his own. He had always been a good judge of character, and when she first approached him at the bar, Cohen felt no suspicion toward Danielle. Naïve, maybe, but Cohen couldn't help but feel as if there had to be more to the story.

Still, the names Laura and Grace didn't ring a bell, and Cohen doubted that he had ever met the women. Mier failed to provide Cohen with any last names, most likely in an attempt to stall Cohen's efforts to reach out to the women. He pushed Laura and Grace out of his mind for now, knowing that he lacked sufficient information to track them down. Cohen barely had enough leads on Danielle, for that matter.

Noticing that it was 6 p.m., Cohen wondered if it was too late to visit Danielle's apartment. Sitting at a red light, he debated whether or not to hold off on the visit until tomorrow. Then, he

178

laughed bitterly at the reality of the situation. *I am a wanted man running from the police with a time limit on my freedom, and I want to wait until tomorrow?*

Acknowledging that tomorrow might not be an option was a heavy dose of reality for Cohen, but he continued laughing to distract himself from the truth. His usually casual and light laughter transformed into long and surprisingly sharp spurts. Cohen began to recognize his mind's coping mechanism in the presence of stress. He didn't necessarily like the results and he hoped that he would be able to hold it together long enough to at least find Danielle. Cohen felt emotionally and physically drained. The thought of sleep tempted him to call it a night, but he decided against it with finality. *Sleep later,* he told himself.

Curbing his laughter and rolling through the green light, Cohen turned right and attempted to take any back alley that he could. He did his best to avoid coming in contact with too many other drivers. Along the way, a mother and daughter carried trash bags out to the curb and Cohen wished he could switch places with them. While they ate dinner and cleaned dishes in their safe and secure environment, Cohen searched for the woman accusing him of rape. Worry and dread wormed their way into Cohen's subconscious and the spiral of self-doubt began.

This is a lost cause.

Cohen felt as if he were standing waist-deep in a churning ocean, watching as a wave formed and the current pulled him into the ocean's depths. He had two options: run toward shore, hoping that his speed and strength were sufficient enough to fight the wave's pull, or run straight for the wave and dive under the foam before it crashed.

As far as Cohen knew, the rape accusation could be only the beginning of a very messy web of lies. Cohen had no way of knowing what lay ahead—so he kept driving. His foot stepped on the gas before his mind had time to disagree. Cohen refused to sit back and wait any longer than he already had. He would tackle the wave head-on.

Parking two blocks away, Cohen's nervousness fully took hold. He parked his car outside of 167 North Fillmore and made eye contact with a woman walking her dog. Cohen refrained from waving, struggling between not wanting to appear too suspicious and not wanting to be noticed. As the woman made her way inside, Cohen moved toward the apartment listed on Craigslist. He did his best to walk behind any tree or large object that could serve as a shield for his body, hoping with all of his might that no police cars would drive by and recognize him.

After surveying the neighborhood, Cohen stood in the neighbor's yard across the street from Danielle's apartment. A U-Haul parked in the driveway provided a sufficient shield for Cohen's body. Just as his foot rose to move forward, Cohen's senses prickled as he noticed a police car take a right turn onto Fillmore. The vehicle drove slowly in front of the apartments and Cohen saw the driver speaking into the transmitter.

Police presence made Cohen feel more confident that the location had to be Danielle's living quarters. Not only that, but if the police found it necessary to patrol the area, Danielle might actually be inside. Otherwise, why would the department even bother?

It was dark enough now for the squad car to turn on its lights and Cohen prayed that his shadow wouldn't cast out from the side of the truck. He watched as the squad car approached from his right, vanished behind the U-Haul, and then reappeared to his left. The car turned a corner and disappeared. It must be patrolling the entire block.

Just as Cohen began a second attempt to approach the apartment, another squad car ambled around the corner. The cars worked in shifts, Cohen realized. He resumed his hidden position and counted the seconds between the moments that the first squad car turned the corner and the other car appeared. The lead-time was forty seconds. Cohen had forty seconds to run across the street and convince Danielle to let him into her home.

If Danielle did answer the door, Cohen hoped that she would let him into her apartment; although a large part of him doubted it would be that easy. Cohen acknowledged the very real possibility that Danielle would turn him away. His presence could bring more trouble into Danielle's life, and Cohen definitely didn't want to cause her any additional worry.

Despite the fact that Danielle was clearly set on pressing charges against Cohen, he couldn't shake the feeling that he and Danielle were in the situation together. His first judgment of Danielle, he remembered, had been that she wouldn't hurt a fly. Someone must have forced her involvement in this situation. Cohen felt sure of it. Something had to go right tonight. The universe owed it to Cohen. His gut told him this meeting would be a success.

The first police car, back again, made its way down Danielle's street, turned on its right blinker, and stopped at the stop sign at the end of the road. Just as the driver eased off the brakes and turned the wheel haphazardly to the right, Cohen pushed out from his hiding spot. Tired of feeling helpless, Cohen welcomed the risk as he rushed to the apartment's front door. He made it to the front step in less than ten seconds. The apartment was divided into two duplexes: left and right. Cohen rang the doorbell on the left-hand side. He heard the melodious chime through the wooden door.

"Come on Danielle, I don't have time for this." He muttered under his breath.

Cohen stressed at the silence answering the chime. He began knocking on the robin's egg blue door—knocking nine times with increasing intensity until he finally saw movement behind the glass. An elderly woman, not Danielle, cracked open the door. Feeling deflated, Cohen scanned her features: dark gray hair, wrinkles surrounding the edges of her mouth, and a very small stature. At first dismayed, he looked closer and saw the same squinty eyes that he had noticed on Danielle's face. This woman had to be Danielle's relative, maybe even her mother.

Realizing he now had around ten seconds before cop number two reappeared, Cohen flashed his badge and his firearm for effect.

"Hi ma'am. My name is Duncan Terry." He did not wait for an invitation into the house. Rather, Cohen gently pushed his way past the woman and shut the door behind him. He mentally counted to forty seconds as the lock clicked into its hinge.

The apartment looked exactly as it had in the photographs online. A neat chaos defined the decor, mirroring the tidy suburban façade of the apartment. Cohen momentarily realized how much he missed his own living space, knowing that it might be a little while until he could return home without risking arrest. Pushing the thought aside, Cohen began his attempt to uncover any information he could about Danielle.

"Mrs. Smith..." not noticing any confusion at the mention of her name, Cohen assumed he spoke to Danielle's mother and finished the sentence. "I have some questions for you in regards to Danielle."

For the first time since entering the apartment, Cohen fully recognized how wary Mrs. Smith appeared. He took in her tiny, hunched shoulders and grimaced at the worry that flowed freely from her pores. Having a daughter involved in this type of a situation could produce that effect, Cohen guessed. Cohen's heart clenched at the sight of the vulnerable woman, while he struggled to keep his focus on the task at hand.

Focus, Cohen, no time to let emotions get in the way.

"For the last time, Officer Terry, Danielle is not here. I don't know how many times I have to tell you police personnel that," Mrs. Smith answered in a shaky yet firm voice. "And please, I believe I also asked you all to leave us alone. Yet here you are in my apartment while two cop cars circle my block."

183

"I'm sorry for your situation, Mrs. Smith, but in order to help Danielle—"

"You don't want to help Danielle! None of you do! And even if you did, you couldn't!"

None of us? Cohen watched as Mrs. Smith's once lucid facial expression drifted into confusion. At first glance, Cohen associated Mrs. Smith with old age and weakness. Now, he saw that the woman teetered between passivity and destructiveness. Her eyes shot daggers in Cohen's direction before her gaze began darting to the four corners of the room. Cohen doubted Mrs. Smith even registered his presence anymore. Her mouth began moving up and down and her hands held each other in her lap as she took a seat at the kitchen table. Mrs. Smith appeared to be having a conversation with herself.

Cohen had an eerie feeling and felt all too ready to leave this apartment.

"Why couldn't we help her?"

"He said he would help her," Mrs. Smith continued, wrapping her arms around her upper body. "He said that if she worked one more appointment, had one more client, she would be free to leave the business. And look what this has done to her! Look what it has done to us!"

Body-shaking sobs emerged from Mrs. Smith and Cohen hoped they wouldn't lead to a heart attack. He could see the physical stress his presence had added to Mrs. Smith's night, and he didn't like the look of it. Clearly, this setup had left multiple victims in its path. Danielle's actions took a toll on her mother as well. Cohen questioned the woman's sanity and felt for her at the same time. Desperate for more information, Cohen tried again,

"I'm sorry, Mrs. Smith, I don't understand. You said 'he'—who is he?"

Right on cue, Cohen saw a police officer park and step out of his car before making his way to Mrs. Smith's door. Cohen wondered if he had been spotted, but assumed that the officer would be in more of a rush had that been the case.

Shit. Cohen looked around for a way out, dismayed to realize that the front door offered his only escape route. He could hide, but the chances of Mrs. Smith not mentioning her meeting with "Duncan Terry" to the approaching officer seemed slim to none. Mrs. Smith continued to sob into her hands and Cohen was reminded of a small child waking up to night terrors. He and Mrs. Smith had some things in common after all.

As four knocks sounded, Mrs. Smith raised her head and her eyes snapped back into lucidity.

"Well now, who could that be?"

Now fully aware of her surroundings, she began moving past Cohen toward the door to open it for the officer. Feeling stuck, Cohen pulled out his firearm, stepped in front of Mrs. Smith, and blocked her path to the doorframe. Cohen, now holding his firearm at an angle pointed toward the ceiling, stood in shock. He didn't remember deciding to move his legs, let alone deciding to pull out a weapon in an attempt to scare an old woman. He shook off his apprehension and pointed to the now vacant kitchen chair.

"I can't let you answer that, Mrs. Smith. I'm sorry to scare you but please…please, sit down at the table."

Cohen's heart all but broke in two as he watched her body tremble through her tears. Mrs. Smith turned and walked back toward her pink chair without any protest. This time, her shoulders didn't hunch, and Cohen noted her attempt to sit straight and erect. Mrs. Smith had completely transformed over the past few seconds. Cohen appreciated her attempt to appear strong. He had been there once, convincing the world he was okay after his dad died. The only one to see through his act had been Bre. After that experience, Cohen found that he could recognize almost anyone's attempt to postpone reality.

Wanting to reach out and comfort Mrs. Smith, Cohen took a step in her direction, not entirely sure how he would accomplish the task when he reached her side. Her flinch stopped him in his tracks. The next four knocks on the front door, much louder than the first set, reminded Cohen of his limited time. He glanced at the door and then back at Mrs. Smith, not sure how to continue the conversation. Mrs. Smith answered for him.

"Police officer my ass, you're working for him! Why are you not letting the other officer into the room?" Mrs. Smith spit the words with such vehemence that Cohen knew she must perceive him as a threat to Danielle. Yesterday, Cohen solved a crime and helped the city of Chicago by putting a criminal behind the bars. Today, he was associated with "him"—someone even Cohen had begun to fear. Deciding in his final seconds that Mrs. Smith would only reveal information to someone she trusted, Cohen decided to try an honest approach.

"My name isn't Duncan Terry, Mrs. Smith. It's Cohen Donahue, and I promise you, I did not hurt your daughter."

Her head snapped back against the chair and Mrs. Smith squared her shoulders at Cohen. Pure determination crossed her face as she clamped her mouth shut. Cohen couldn't tell whether his strategy worked. With nothing left to lose, he offered a little more.

"That police officer trying to speak with you?" Cohen continued, pointing his finger toward the knocking at the door, "He would arrest me the second he saw me. I did not hurt your daughter," although something told Cohen that Mrs. Smith already knew this, "and I really just need to understand what is going on here."

Mrs. Smith simply stared. Her stature turned cold as ice and her trembling slowed down. *So much for honesty*...Cohen regretted.

"Please, Mrs. Smith, if Danielle is involved in this mess, she could be in trouble. We are on the same team here—I think I can help her. I know I can."

Cohen almost stopped mid sentence, taken aback by the sincerity and honesty in his voice. He knew he had planned on helping Danielle. He hadn't been aware, however, of the extent he would go to do so. Deep down, Cohen planned to put Danielle at the top of his priorities. He hadn't realized his determination until now.

"You're wasting your time, Mr. Donahue. He took her. And he will take you too."

The force of the words caused Cohen to take a step back, positioning himself directly in front of the long windows lining the sides of the front door, right into the officer's line of vision. Cohen realized his mistake and turned his head to make eye contact with the officer. Full on thrusts of the officer's shoulder against the door replaced the knocking and Cohen realized he had about five seconds to move. He put his gun in his back pocket, picked up a heavy kitchen chair, and threw it as hard as his body allowed against the kitchen window. A crack appeared in the glass, providing Cohen with enough leeway to hurl his body through the glass and hope it shattered. Mrs. Smith did not move from her position at the table.

Just as his body successfully broke through the glass and Cohen braced himself for the two-story drop, the front door came crashing in. Two police officers ran into the apartment toward the kitchen.

Landing proved surprisingly less painful than Cohen suspected. The ground broke his fall nicely and he felt no extra pain from the pile of bricks positioned under his ribcage. Realizing that he must be in shock, Cohen took advantage of the numbness and propelled himself off of the grass and forward.

"What in the hell!" Cohen heard a man's voice yelling at him from inside the apartment and he hoped that Mrs. Smith had stalled the officers, although he doubted she would. Cohen did not take the time to glance back at the apartment as he ran, knowing by now the police officers must already be making their way toward the front door in pursuit of a supposed rapist.

Don't think, just run, Cohen told himself. His mind moved a mile a minute as he ran in the opposite direction from the front door. Cohen jumped the white fence lining the Smith's backyard and his legs took his body left down a long alley. Finally, the fall caught up to him and his body roared with pain. The deep ache began just slightly in his legs. By the time it reached Cohen's ribcage, Cohen worried that he would drop from the excruciating pain, making himself the easiest target the CPD might ever come across. Exiting the alley and hearing the police climb the fence, Cohen knew he only had one option. If he tried to hide, more police officers would have the opportunity to arrive on the scene. Chances of Cohen being caught would increase dramatically.

One more block, you can't stop now. Allowing his mind to picture his dad, Cohen found just enough strength to push himself toward Leila's car. He started the engine and pulled around the corner before any police had a chance to follow his tracks.

The car moved, yet the pain took away any sense of direction that Cohen had left. His ribs screamed for help at the point where the bricks had connected with bone. The pain he felt while breathing almost proved unbearable as the edges of his vision began to go black. Cohen made a sharp left onto a back street and kept his foot on the gas, still conscious enough to hear an increasing number of sirens sound throughout the neighborhood. At least now he knew his status from the department's perspective. Apparently, they were actively searching for Cohen. If Mier found out that Cohen fled from the police, coupled with the fact that he visited Danielle's residence, Cohen did not doubt that Mier would rip Cohen's head off.

Letting his subconscious take over the steering, Cohen reached his hand up to his forehead and felt a thick, sticky substance. Blood coated the left side of Cohen's face; in his rush, he hadn't noticed the injury until now. Looking at the new coloring of his hand while simultaneously steering the wheel, Cohen's world turned black.

Chapter 20

Mier finished up his work for the day and walked toward Dolan's office. He willed his nerves to dissolve, taking increasingly deep breaths and finding some comfort in the fact that today's press conference would have a podium for him to stand behind. For some reason, presenting to an audience while standing on an empty floor always made Mier's knees quake. By the time he reached the middle of his speech, the shaking had always spread from his knees to his legs.

Having something to stand behind helped Mier speak tremendously. *You're only talking about your job. You're the expert here,* Mier reminded himself. The media tended to be ruthless, however, and that fact alone caused the fear to rise again in Mier's stomach.

Lieutenant Dolan stood in his office and exited to meet Mier in the hallway. Mier knew his nerves were visible to anyone within a twenty-foot radius, and he hated that Dolan would see him this rattled. Dolan joined Mier's stride, apparently feeling no need to offer any words of comfort.

"You ready?"

"As ready as I'll ever be."

Mier opened the department doors and released a sigh of relief at the sight of the relatively small crowd waiting. With only about fifty media relations present, Mier felt his pulse begin to calm. His imagination had concocted an audience filling the entire CPD lawn. This crowd, he felt more confident that he could handle. Before they separated, Lieutenant Dolan placed a hand on

Mier's back. "Go get 'em, Sergeant," Dolan teased, with sarcasm enough for the crowd.

Cameramen and women fell silent and reporters drew notepads out of their bags. All stared at Mier as he approached the microphones. Dolan walked around the back of the crowd unnoticed, placing himself next to an anxious Officer Duncan.

"I saw all of the reporters gathered on the lawn. I wasn't aware we were having a press conference today, Lieutenant."

"Wanted to keep it quiet. No other officers know about the event, mainly in an attempt to limit any officer contact with the media."

"Probably a good idea." Duncan focused her attention back onto Mier.

Lieutenant Dolan was more than familiar with reporters' common tendency to twist an interviewee's words before airing segments. By limiting the CPD audience, he hoped to avoid that scenario from occurring altogether. If one of the new recruits really had tipped off the media in the first place, giving that officer a chance to attend the press conference would provide him or her with ample opportunities to get some face time.

"Thank you all for being here tonight. My name is Sergeant Mier. Cohen Donahue joined my unit a few days ago. The CPD holds that Donahue is innocent until proven guilty, and we plan to stand by our officer. Officer Donahue did not display any misconduct while under my watch, rather quite the opposite—"

"What about the incident on his first day of work when Cohen Donahue shadowed a fellow officer? Did Officer Donahue not demonstrate a complete disregard toward Officer Duncan's directions?" a slender male reporter wearing ridiculous, oversized glasses asked, looking at Mier with a certain air of mockery.

Mier froze, his gaze immediately finding Duncan standing behind the crowd. She wore an equally dazed expression. This reporter knew too much information. No one should have known about the incident besides Duncan, Mier, and Lieutenant Dolan. A sheer sense of panic spread between the officers. The tension could be felt in the crowd and cameras held their positions at the ready. There was a snitch in the department, and it was becoming more and more imperative to find out who it was.

"I will not be answering any questions at this time. The CPD will update you with any further information as we come across it. Thank for you for your understanding and support."

Mier stepped down from the podium hurriedly and walked back toward the front doors of the department. Reporters shouted questions at his back but none dared to follow him. After they saw the glare he shot at the reporter asking the question, Mier was allowed to pass without too much hassle.

Mier rubbed his head in an attempt to clear his sudden headache. After this conference aired, the whole world would know that Cohen messed up on his first day of training. It didn't matter that the mistake Cohen made was small; the media cared only about creating a story—about finding a bad guy. They had their story all right, and Cohen would soon be cast as the villain.

Mier turned to close the front door and looked out at the small sea of reporters. Most of them now moseyed back to their cars. Before the door swung completely shut, through the smallest crack, Mier made eye contact with another CPD officer standing on the outskirts of the lawn—an officer who should not have made an appearance at that night's event. The door shut.

"What the…"

Mier could think of no reason for Spencer to have been present at the event. In fact, Spencer shouldn't have even known that the press conference was taking place. Mier couldn't think of one person from the CPD who would have delivered the message to Spencer. Unless, Mier realized, Spencer heard about the press conference not from a coworker, but from someone working in the media business.

"Bingo." Suddenly, Spencer's possible relationship with the media looked all too convenient in light of the recent leak. Mier shook his head and made a mental note to discuss his suspicion with the Lieutenant.

***

Cohen woke in a deserted parking lot and looked around for any clues regarding his location. He saw the lake to his right and knew that he must be at least fifteen minutes away from the Smiths' apartment. Actually, the area looked pretty familiar, although Cohen couldn't comprehend its relevance. Confusion set in as he tried to remember maneuvering Leila's car to that location. He only remembered leaving Danielle's apartment, getting in the car, and then there was nothing but blackness, blackness and sirens.

A deep throbbing in his ribcage served as Cohen's first hint of reality. Although it was not as bad as when he first felt the pain, Cohen doubted his ability to walk comfortably, let alone run if needed. He closed his eyes for comfort and rested his head on the back of the headrest, surprised to feel his skin tighten on the left side of his face as he relaxed his facial features.

"Jesus."

His reflection in the mirror explained the sensation. Blood covered the entire left side of Cohen's face. He attempted to wipe it off, but the blood merely cracked at his touch. Apparently, Cohen had been out of it long enough for the liquid to dry. Deciding to leave it until later, Cohen replayed his conversation with Mrs. Smith in his head. The clock in the car displayed 9 p.m., and Cohen guessed he must have left Danielle's house around 6:30 p.m., meaning the police had been looking for him for the past two and a half hours. At this point, Cohen would bet money that their efforts had at least doubled. Officers tend to carry pride in their pockets; the fact that Cohen escaped from two officers would not be forgotten easily.

And then there was Mrs. Smith's warning: *"He took her. And he will take you too."*

What the hell did she mean by that? Two questions continually replayed in Cohen's mind: who was "he," and where did he take Danielle? Mrs. Smith had been vague in her answers, suggesting to Cohen that, more than anything, this woman feared revealing too much information, even if her daughter's safety was involved.

Cohen had no idea how to even begin solving the puzzle. He knew only that somewhere along the road, Danielle became involved with the wrong crowd. Now, a man held her captive, and that same man very possibly wanted Cohen dead.

When Cohen first pulled out his gun, Mrs. Smith had accused him of "working for him." Her response initially confused Cohen. Now, he tried to make sense of her reaction. Clearly, Mrs. Smith had a negative experience in her apartment with another man. It seemed possible, Cohen thought, that Danielle's kidnapper visited the Smiths' apartment before Cohen's visit. Mrs. Smith could very well have been witness to Danielle's kidnapping, causing her to associate Cohen's odd arrival with the traumatic event.

Cohen pulled out his disposable phone and dialed a number from memory.

"Duncan here."

"Officer Duncan," Cohen inhaled sharply, surprised at how his ribs ached when he spoke. "It's Cohen Donahue; I need your help."

Silence. The pain spread up the right side of his body.

"Duncan…" another sharp inhale, "you said when I screwed up on my first day that I reminded you of yourself—picture yourself in my situation. I'm being framed, and," Cohen doubled over and his voice lost its volume. The pain was terrible and he feared he would black out again if he continued to speak. Cohen didn't think that he had broken any bones, but his injuries were not minor.

196

"Christ," Duncan responded.

Taking that as an invitation to continue, Cohen muttered quickly in an attempt to beat the pain, "I stopped by Danielle Smith's apartment and her mother mentioned Danielle's 'clients.' I think she is a prostitute and I'm guessing Laura and Grace were involved in this business somehow as well. I need you to reach out to all of your connections on the street and find out the name of Danielle's pimp."

The determination in Duncan's response rang clear: "Keep your phone on." Cohen ended the call and swiveled his head to the left and the right. He looked at the road providing the only entrance and exit to the deserted piece of land where he was parked.

Okay, first things first, Cohen thought; he needed to collect himself. He needed medicine and a place to sleep. Though the police force was clearly on the hunt, Cohen knew he needed to recuperate at least a little bit. Hopefully, no one from Mrs. Smith's neighborhood had noticed Leila's car parked down the block. If the officers didn't have an ID on the car, their search for Cohen would prove much more difficult. Knowing he had enough strength for another twenty-minute car ride, Cohen began driving to one of the only places he felt safe.

This time, he didn't bother parking two blocks away. Rather, Cohen stepped out of the car onto the driveway and staggered up to the blue door. Cohen wondered if he should knock or use Leila's house key. He couldn't be seen standing outside, but something about barging into Leila's house seemed wrong. Especially considering the heart attack she'd probably have at seeing a man with blood all over his face in her home.

Cohen took his chances and knocked as if he were merely coming over for a dinner date, not because he was running from the police.

Moments before Leila came to the door, Cohen realized that by this time, Leila had no doubt heard about his situation. *She knows I had sex with Danielle*...he turned his body to leave just as the door pulled back to reveal the first comforting sight Cohen had seen all day. The second he made eye contact with Leila, Cohen's worry transformed into heart-wrenching guilt. Her entire face was etched with concern, and though she obviously tried to appear nonchalant, Cohen could tell that she was deeply hurt. Cohen noticed something else behind her feigned facial expression. Embarrassment? That made him want to turn back the clock more than anything in the world.

"My God. Are you okay?" Leila broke the ice, although Cohen's appearance clearly suggested otherwise.

Before Cohen could answer, a bounding bark sounded through the night and Pumpkin came running from the TV room up to Cohen's side. As if able to sense Cohen's pain, Pumpkin's tail wagged uncontrollably, yet he refrained from jumping on Cohen per their usual greeting. Cohen looked at Leila in shock and she blushed in response.

"I didn't think you had a chance to make arrangements for him before you heard about...well, everything..." Leila explained while offering Cohen her body for support. They made their way to the couch in silence, Pumpkin following at their heels.

When Cohen reached his seat, he wanted to say thank you to Leila, to apologize. As Pumpkin jumped in his lap, however, exuding an innocence that overwhelmed Cohen, all he could do was wrap his arms around his dog.

"Hey boy."

"Cohen, could you please tell me what's going on here?" Leila tried in a quiet yet firm voice.

"You're safer not knowing anything. I'm sorry, but, the more I find out the more I realize how large this thing could be." Cohen sucked in some air and continued despite Leila's concern at his response. "You know that by helping me, you're incriminating your—"

Leila cut him off, "I assumed you'd be back here, so I made up the couch for you to crash on." She shrugged, as if any other human being would act similarly. The cushions lay on the ground and a blanket covered the entirety of the couch. Cohen let the genuine kindness of the action soak into his heart.

"Thank you, Leila. Your help—it means more than you know." He tilted his head toward Pumpkin and patted the ground next to the couch. Pumpkin leapt at the invitation and lay next to his owner. Seeming to understand that Cohen would not give her any more information, Leila looked at Cohen and disappeared for a minute. She returned holding a glass of water, Advil, and a wet cloth.

Without a word, Leila's fingers gently pulled Cohen's face toward her and she dabbed the wet cloth over his wound. Cohen wondered how this woman could know exactly what he needed without him even asking. Her elbow brushed against his collarbone and he momentarily forgot about his pain. His physical pain, that is, as his emotional guilt caused a certain torment to spread throughout his body.

"Leila, I…with Danielle, I wasn't thinking. It didn't mean—"

"Cohen, please," Leila begged, leaving no room for negotiation.

"I need you to understand. I don't expect you to forgive me, but please, you have to hear me. I was stupid and lost and confused."

Leila stood from the couch, signaling an end to anything else that Cohen might attempt to say. She placed the medicine and water on the side table next to the couch.

"You don't owe me an explanation, Cohen. We are friends, okay? I'm here to help, that's all. Get some sleep."

Leila's cheeks matched Cohen's blush. She moved to turn off the light in an attempt to hide her awkwardness. Cohen finally took the hint, although he couldn't help but notice that Leila's body language contradicted her words. Deep down, Cohen knew Leila still felt something for him. He also knew that those feelings wouldn't matter if Leila couldn't look at Cohen without feeling the pain he caused.

Cohen's brain and heart joined forces, encouraging him to yell at Leila, to tell her that he wanted to be more than friends, that he found her attractive in every sense of the word: smart, witty, funny, and beautiful. The speech played out in his mind, but his mouth remained still—sleep paralyzing his ability to speak.

It will have to wait until tomorrow, he told himself, succumbing to the wave of nausea. *I can't be just friends with this woman,* Cohen realized before falling asleep for the night.

Allowing herself one glance back in his direction, Leila watched as Cohen swallowed more than the suggested dose of pills. His head lay on the pillow and she waited for his breathing to stabilize before she whispered, "Goodnight, Cohen."

Cohen slept soundly and woke the next morning feeling stiff, but able to maneuver much better than the day before. He slowly rose in hopes of talking to Leila. It was still early enough that Leila might not have left for work. He glanced into the kitchen and realized that he had missed the boat, based on the coffee and note placed on the kitchen counter. *Not another note,* Cohen immediately thought of Danielle as he grabbed the coffee and turned to read the piece of paper:

312-998-7865

Understanding Leila's gesture, Cohen's disappointment in himself and gratefulness toward Leila's persistence overlapped each other. Leila still wanted to help.

As a friend, Cohen reminded himself.

Chapter 21

Mier stayed up all night thinking about Spencer's presence at the press conference. He knew what he had to do, but he also worried that Lieutenant Dolan might not be so quick to jump on board. After all, if the press conference proved anything, it was that Dolan didn't exactly trust Mier at the moment. Mier imagined himself explaining his "gut feeling" to Dolan in the morning and grimaced at the thought. He could almost picture Dolan laughing right in his face at the lack of evidence. Mier knew it and Dolan knew it: a snitch had been sharing information with the media, and that snitch was a Chicago Police Department employee. Once the snitch had been let go, a huge burden would be removed from both Cohen and the department.

Walking to Dolan's office that morning, he gained enough courage to muster three hard knocks on the thick wooden door. Mier envied Dolan's office door, especially when comparing it to the thin glass separating his office from the outside world.

"Come in!" Dolan barked.

From the now open doorway, Mier saw Spencer sitting in the chair opposite Dolan's desk, looking ashen and scolded. Dolan paced behind his desk, his face red from exertion—most likely from an argument.

"I could come back later…"

"What is it, Mier?"

"Actually, I was hoping to speak with you in private, Lieutenant." Dolan looked at Mier exasperatedly, motioning toward the door.

"Spencer, step into the hallway and wait until we are finished please. It should only be a few minutes." Dolan's eyes dared Mier to question his time assumption.

"Okay, Lieutenant."

As soon as Spencer was fully out of earshot, Dolan started on a rant.

"That kid thought it was okay to skip an hour of his shift yesterday to watch a press conference! He left his partner completely hanging—faked some sort of illness or something."

Okay, Mier thought, *maybe this will be easier than I thought.*

"This new class couldn't be anymore trouble if they tried to be. Hell, at this rate, Leila will be a convicted felon by the end of the day!"

Dolan finally allowed his weight to fall dramatically into his chair. His head rested on both of his hands.

"I sensed from day one that Spencer and Cohen had animosity toward each other. But it just made no sense. Why would Spencer skip out on his training to hear details about Cohen's case?"

"Excuse me, Lieutenant, you sensed animosity between Cohen and Spencer?"

"Oh, sure. I never had enough time to figure out the source of the problem, and it appeared to fade slightly over time, but those two seemed to genuinely hate each other's guts. On a few occasions, I thought they might actually throw some punches." Dolan shook his head as the pieces of the puzzle began to fall into place in Mier's mind.

"That actually helps support my theory, then, Lieutenant. I saw Spencer at the conference last night and, for some unexplainable reason, I got the feeling he had been feeding the media information."

Dolan raised his gaze as if seeing Mier for the first time.

"Think about it: no one else knew about the press conference. We sure as hell didn't pass along the information, so he must have heard about it through his media relation. And now that I know Spencer and Cohen didn't get along...I know we don't have any solid proof here, and that we have bigger fish to fry, but I really think Spencer is our guy, Dolan."

As Dolan took in Mier's words, Mier noticed for the first time how old Dolan actually looked. He seemed tired, and Mier knew that the Lieutenant must be desperate to put Cohen's case behind him.

"I hate to say it, Mier, but I was thinking the same thing. One gut feeling and the outcome could be negative. Two gut feelings...chances are you've won the lottery."

The thought of cutting an officer loose based on nothing more than hearsay enveloped the room with thick guilt.

"Maybe it could just be a temporary suspension, Dolan." Mier offered. "No need to completely cut the guy out of the program, just long enough for Cohen to get back on his feet."

Dolan nodded his head in agreement. "I'll take it from here, Mier." Mier stepped out of the office and didn't stick around to hear the rest of Spencer and Dolan's conversation. Making eye contact with Spencer as he passed proved impossible. Mier couldn't imagine actually having to place the guy on suspension. A familiar anxiety threatened to ruin Mier and he attempted to steady his breathing.

For Peter, he reminded himself yet again. With Spencer gone and no more snitch to worry about, things would run a lot smoother. Mier returned to his office. Within the hour, rumors spread that Spencer had packed his bags.

***

Cohen knew that he shouldn't return to his apartment. Based on the two squad cars patrolling Danielle's house, he guessed his own apartment had even more surveillance. The stench of his clothing had become unbearable, however, and he needed to feel the safety that a person could only find in his home. Although Cohen had only inhabited his apartment for two weeks, it was the closest thing he had to the feeling. Not only that, but Cohen was optimistic that he would find some clues in his apartment. With no other avenues available, he didn't have any other options.

His watch glowed, showing 6:30 a.m. The morning felt young and suffocating. The birds began chirping hours ago and the sun now inched its way above the buildings. It was a perfect morning to sit by the lake while sipping a cup of coffee; and yet, Cohen would spend it hiding from the law in his very own apartment.

Assuming that his apartment had already been searched, Cohen thought it possible that the police might have moved on from patrolling his area to searching the streets. If he was lucky, Cohen might be able to get inside his apartment without any problems. After all, surely the CPD wouldn't expect him to return to his home while he was a wanted man: that would be careless. But Cohen was desperate.

Thankfully, Cohen's knowledge of his apartment building gave him an advantage over the police. On his first night back in the city, Cohen had locked himself out of the building. Instead of waiting for someone to come along and let him in through the front door, he found himself climbing through a broken window on the basement level of the building. He had dropped into the basement and found the staircase leading upstairs. Cohen would do the same this morning.

Thankfully, no officers appeared anywhere in sight as Cohen walked to the window. After falling through the opening, a little harder than he had the first time, and making his way up the stairs, Cohen stood at his door. He hadn't seen any neighbors during his ascent and he quickly reached out and jiggled the handle open.

The living room and kitchen appeared just as Cohen left them. His dishes from breakfast rested in the sink and the water in Pumpkin's water bowl sat still and undisturbed. Pumpkin was still at Leila's, and Cohen wished he could have some company. The past few days had been lonely. With just Cohen and his belongings in the apartment now, everything seemed so foreign. Cohen felt like a different person, like an intruder in his own house. He looked at his things and envied the happy-go-lucky man who had lived there merely a day ago.

One thing hadn't changed: Cohen pulled on a gray T-shirt and worn jeans. Before looking for any clues, Cohen recognized his need to eat and made himself a sandwich. Famished, he allowed himself fifteen minutes of solitude before trying to piece together the story slowly forming in his head. The bread tasted a little stale, but Cohen devoured the meal, adding potato chips to his large plate.

The fact that I have to hide, in my own apartment, Cohen started thinking before he could scold himself for holding a pity party. He looked around the room. Something still nagged at him from yesterday. Cohen swallowed the last crumbs of his food and retraced his footsteps from the beginning of the day to the end. His voice made the apartment appear less solitary.

"I went to interview Leo. Mier called, telling me to hide out. I returned the squad car, went to Leila's, and then back to the office where I talked to Mier. Mrs. Smith suggested Danielle was a prostitute, I had a little run-in with the police, and then I slept at Leila's."

Oh, and Leila wants to be just friends.

The memory flooded Cohen's mind, blocking the chance at the formation of any logical thoughts. Deciding to think about it later, Cohen walked into his room and looked for a sweatshirt to wear. He reached under his bed for the discarded clothing when his hand touched something rough: the cardboard holding Peter's belongings.

The box lay at Cohen's knees within seconds. The worst thing about this accusation was that Cohen did not have his dad for guidance. Bre popped into his head, but it had been so long since

207

they'd last talked. Cohen didn't want their next conversation to be a negative one.

It had been at least a year since Cohen maneuvered his way through the contents in the box. He picked up the newspaper sitting on top of the pile. The page facing up displayed Peter's obituary. Cohen looked back over the familiar words. His hands smoothed the creases where the newspaper had been folded over the past five years. The newspaper's worn state proved Cohen's love for his father, if nothing else.

As he placed the newspaper back into the box, he saw a slight crease not noticed before. It looked as if one of the corners had, at one point, been dog-eared inward. If so, that corner did not mark the obituary article, but rather the article placed on the opposite side of the piece of paper. Cohen turned the paper over to read the contents of the article someone had thought necessary to mark.

"One More Mobster Behind Bars, Thanks to the CPD"

The picture provided with the article appeared old and dated. Cohen looked closer at the text, fumbling through the words. Apparently, the case involved two criminals: a drug dealer and his brother. Only one of the brothers had been convicted of smuggling drugs. Due to a lack of evidence, the second brother walked away a free man. In the first sentence, Cohen saw a familiar name: Jeremiah Diaz.

Alarms went off in the back of Cohen's head and he felt his heart move in slow motion. Jeremiah

Diaz, the man who attempted to shoot Officer Turner, the man who shot Peter. In the same newspaper as his father's obituary existed the story of how Peter had been injured, and Cohen had never noticed.

Feeling that the article could prove useful, Cohen kept reading. Nothing more caught his attention and he lifted his head toward the ceiling in frustration. Before putting the article back in the box, Cohen took a second look at the picture on the left side of the article. Three men stood next to each other in front of a run-down house. They didn't wear smiles or touch each other, nothing to suggest kinship of any kind. They just stood there, as if the photo had caught them in the midst of an everyday activity.

Looking closely at the picture, Cohen took in the features of the two men and the smaller boy next to them. He guessed that the boy was around fifteen when the picture was taken, maybe a few years younger. Lingering on each man's face in the picture, Cohen felt rage building up inside him. Jeremiah shot his father over his drug money. The caption on the bottom of the page read: "From left to right: Jeremiah, Coda, and Michia Diaz (son of Jeremiah)."

A flash of a vivid memory hit Cohen so rapidly that his hand dropped the paper. The boy's face in the photograph exploded in his mind, developing into its current day state. The boy must be around twenty now, most likely still involved in the drug trade. It couldn't be.

Looking at the photograph a second time, and much closer than before, Cohen felt confident:

the boy in the photograph—although much younger than when Cohen had crossed his path—was the Latino man that Cohen delivered to prison on his first day working with Duncan. *I would recognize that smirk anywhere*, Cohen assured himself. Michia had one hell of a smirk on his face that day.

None of this made any sense. Peter was on the scene when Jeremiah Diaz was arrested, and Cohen arrested his son, Michia Diaz, five years later. Cohen willed his memory to take him back to that day. He pictured himself opening the door to take Michia into the jailhouse. He heard Duncan yell through the open window.

"Hurry up, Donahue!"

Michia could easily have recognized Cohen's last name and connected him to his father. Turner mentioned that Jeremiah was killed in prison. Could the recent attacks on Cohen be an attempt to get back at Peter for putting Jeremiah in prison in the first place?

"Don't I get to make a phone call?" Michia's question echoed in Cohen's memory.

Who had Michia called? It didn't add up. Cohen put Michia in prison, and the next day Danielle accused him of rape? Something about this story did not sit right, and Cohen couldn't seem to shake the feeling that his situation related somehow to the newspaper article.

Cohen sat and digested his finding. Confused, Cohen knew that he needed to make a phone call. He also realized just how desperate he had become for information. Cohen dialed the number for the Chicago Police Department. Only one person would be able to recall the details from that day five years ago.

"CPD, Officer Turner speaking, how may I assist you today?" Funny, Turner's voice sounded so normal when not scolding Cohen at work. Pulling every ounce of courage he had left, Cohen began.

"Officer Turner, it's Cohen Donahue, please don't hang up. I really need your help."

Silence.

"Cohen," she whispered, "did you not understand our conversation the other day? I have strict orders not to talk to you. I could lose my job by helping you."

"Listen, Officer Turner, your plan to get me to drop out of the Department is a cop-out, and you know it. If you really want to repay my dad for saving your life, why don't you see if you can help his son before his ass is hauled to jail for a crime he didn't commit?"

Cohen felt Officer Turner absorbing his words and he knew that he had reached her on some level.

"Keep talking." She responded.

"The case you and my dad worked on together, when he was shot, there was a little boy named Michia. He was Jeremiah's son…" Cohen left his sentence open, not sure what exactly he hoped to get out of this conversation. He hoped Turner could fill in the unknown.

"Yes, I remember the boy."

"What happened to him? I mean, after Jeremiah was arrested—after Jeremiah died—do you know anything about that?"

Two seconds elapsed before Turner responded. Cohen noticed that her voice had gotten progressively quieter. Had she wanted to rat Cohen out for calling her, Turner would have done so already.

"After Jeremiah's arrest, Michia lived with his uncle. I can't recall his name."

"Coda?"

"That's it."

"Do you remember anything else weird about the case? Any follow up contact from any of the family members?"

"Nope. Never heard of them again. Like I said, Jeremiah passed away in prison. That's the last I heard."

Cohen thanked Officer Turner and rattled off his disposable cell phone number for her to call in case she remembered any more information. He went to hang up before remembering something.

"Oh, and Officer Turner, one last question: who gave you orders not to speak to me?"

"Sergeant Mier."

The line cut and Cohen released a huge sigh that he hadn't been aware his lungs were holding. *Miracles really do happen,* Cohen thought, still in shock that he convinced Officer Turner to help. He shook his head at the length that Mier was going to make sure that Cohen didn't incriminate himself to anyone.

Although Cohen knew his situation had to relate to the arrest made five years ago, he hesitated to connect the events. His father died that day, how could that not be enough revenge for Jeremiah's incarceration? Cohen shuddered at the thought.

With Peter gone, Cohen would be the only Donahue left to settle old scores with. Still, Cohen felt there had to be more to the story.

Having nothing to do now but wait for Duncan's response about Danielle's pimp, Cohen drove Leila's car outside of the city, thankful that she lent him the car on a full tank of gas. He parked in a deserted lot, about half an hour away from the skyscrapers. The sounds of the city only made Cohen feel more isolated. He needed to separate himself from the commotion—get peace and quiet so that he could think. Since taking a run wasn't exactly realistic right now, the small road trip would have to do.

Cohen spent the next hour so lost inside of his head that he might as well have been asleep. He tried to put all of the pieces of the puzzle together, but some things just didn't seem to fit. Cohen was so distracted, in fact, that he didn't see the blue truck pull into the same isolated parking lot. The blue truck lined up directly behind Leila's parked car, accelerated to 25 miles per hour, and crashed directly into Cohen.

Chapter 22

What the fuck?

Cohen fought through his confusion and attempted to regain his bearings. The car, thankfully still right side up, must have shot forward at the impact. The back end of the vehicle was wrapped around a telephone pole situated on the outskirts of the parking lot. Cohen's shock wore off and his panic increased. One minute he had been sitting in the car and the next he found himself stuck behind his seatbelt, Leila's car wrapped around a pole.

Attempting to turn his head to find the source of the collision, Cohen realized the strain of the movement made it impossible. Cohen felt his body losing control of its motor functions. He wanted to scream for help. Instead, his head fell to his chest and he came dangerously close to passing out. He used everything he had to remain conscious, listening for any sounds around him. Whatever hit him could still be within close distance.

Cohen heard an engine stalling. At the sound of another car, Cohen was flooded with relief, comforted in the knowledge that help must be coming. As if in answer to his plea, he heard feet shuffling toward his car. Someone stood just outside the driver's side door and Cohen could hear a man grunting as he pried the door away from Cohen's body. Some of the pressure suddenly released as the door opened, allowing much of the pain to subside.

The seatbelt strained tighter around Cohen's shoulders as his upper body fell forward. He heard the fabric being cut and waited, his head still sagging, along with the rest of his limp body. A set of hands grabbed him under his arms and jerked Cohen's body from the car. The gruff nature with which Cohen was removed from the car finally allowed his vocal cords to yell, not so much from the pain, but from the sudden release of so much pressure.

Nothing but silence followed the noise and Cohen's body dropped against the solid concrete. Through mere slits in his vision, Cohen saw a large man looming over him, looking Cohen up and down. The man's hand moved directly for Cohen's gun and removed it from the holster. Cohen realized something wasn't right. *Why would anyone take an injured man's gun, unless they planned to use it?* His question was answered all too quickly as the butt of the gun came down on Cohen's head.

Waking to aching pain was becoming a very common occurrence for Cohen. He took his time registering that all of his limbs still had mobility, his searing headache the real problem. His body swayed with the movement of a car and the scene came rushing back. Another car hit Leila's car. Cohen remembered the man taking his gun. He was now unarmed.

A foot nudged Cohen's head impatiently and Cohen reeled in alarm. Opening his eyes to take in the car's floor, Cohen struggled to hold onto consciousness. His head throbbed; Cohen had never wanted Advil more. He felt blood on his leg and wondered where it had come from. The foot stubbornly continued to push his head from side to side. Cohen originally assumed he was in the car alone; apparently, he had company.

Taking a deep breath, Cohen rotated ninety degrees and put a hand over his mouth to stop a groan from escaping from his lips. The van looked huge; he guessed it must seat ten people, although all of the seats had been removed, leaving a large open space. Two women sat in the back corner of the van—the one closest to the back door sat erect with her foot ready to deliver another kick. The other woman appeared to be unconscious, her body situated neatly on the floor. Cohen turned enough to see the top of the driver's head over the partition separating the front seat from the back.

The woman nudged him again and Cohen looked in her direction. Both women's hands were secured to the side of the van with chains. Tape covered their mouths and bruises lined each of their faces. Cohen did not recognize them. The kicker sat erect and at the ready; despite the bruises coloring her skin, she looked determined and strong. Her small frame and skinny face did not fool Cohen. He wondered for the ten thousandth time how this all connected. Not wanting to alert the driver with his voice, Cohen nodded his head to signal that she had his attention. She began touching her chin to her chest in a repeated movement.

Okay, she is trying to tell me something here, Cohen thought. *That, or she is having a seizure.*

The woman glared so intensely at Cohen that he knew he should pay attention. She continued with the movement until Cohen finally rested his gaze on her necklace. Around her neck hung a gold chain, with an L pendant dangling on her chest. He made eye contact with the girl; her gaze pleaded with him to understand.

216

L. L. L.

Cohen's mouth fell open and his stare widened in awe. There, sitting in the back seat of the van with him, were Laura and Grace—the two other women that Mier mentioned were involved in the setup. Now fully realizing the gravity of the situation, Cohen tried a different route. He mouthed a question to Laura, "Where are we going?" as he inclined his head toward the blacked-out van windows. Tears began to flow heavily down her cheeks, serving as the only answer Cohen needed. It didn't matter where they were going: they had to get out of there. Cohen had to figure out an escape plan.

He nodded reassuringly toward Laura, wanting to convince her of his determination. Immediately after nodding, Cohen inched toward her. If only he could find something to break the chain binding her hands, maybe both of them could take on the monster of the man driving. Halfway to his destination he realized the chains would not break without a substantial amount of force, force that Cohen would not be able to muster alone. Not to mention that he couldn't make any noise if he didn't want to attract their kidnapper's attention. He sat back and tried to think of another plan.

His mind raced back in time to the classes he took only a week ago at the CPD. One of the instructors had spoken of his experience of being held in a hostage situation.

"I'll leave you with three useful points to remember if you're ever held hostage," the officer had said. *"One, avoid the situation at all costs."* Cohen almost laughed at the irony. Seeing as he sat

217

in the back of a van, he couldn't do much about that one. *"Two, find an escape route."* Cohen looked around the van. Besides the two front doors, the van had a back door. He glanced at the partition and didn't think his body would fit through the gap between the top of the wall and the top of the car. *Okay, one potential exit.*

"Hi boss." The man driving interrupted Cohen's strategizing. "En route with Donahue in the back seat."

Laura started crying harder, although no additional sound left her mouth. The tears flowed at a steady stream and Cohen pretended not to notice. For some reason, he guessed Laura wouldn't appreciate the extra attention.

"No sir, hit him at about 25 miles per hour, just hard enough to knock him unconscious. I'll finish up with the girls, then bring him to you. Bye." The flip phone snapped shut.

Cohen allowed himself one glance in Laura's direction. She had heard the conversation just as well as Cohen had, and understood the man's statement. Their kidnapper planned to get rid of Laura and Grace. Cohen would come along for the ride.

As the realization of her impending death sunk in, Laura's posture changed from a victim's to one of pure strength. Cohen admired the new fire that lit her face, and he agreed with her mindset. Maybe they could escape from their captor after all. As he returned to brainstorming, Cohen struggled to remember the last tip the police officer had given in the class. He wished he hadn't slept through those courses. If only he had realized their potential importance.

The man driving pulled the car over and Cohen faked unconsciousness. The driver told his boss that Cohen would be delivered after he finished with the girls. Cohen realized that no matter what, he would be safe for at least a little longer. His kidnapper planned to deliver him alive, giving Cohen more leeway to try and free Laura and Grace. Something told him that this monster of a man would get in big trouble if he presented a dead Cohen to his boss. For someone willing to go through this much trouble in tracking Cohen down, the man in charge would no doubt want to inflict a little torture on Cohen himself.

Think, Cohen. Think!

The kidnapper stepped out of the driver's seat and walked toward the back. Keys jingled and the lock slid out of its hinges.

"And third, when all else fails, use momentum."

The door opened and Cohen pushed his entire body at the giant standing directly outside the door.

***

The initial momentum of Cohen's body did throw the man off guard. He stumbled backwards and fell to the ground, giving Cohen enough time to make his escape—had he wanted to escape, that is. Laura and Grace still sat in the back of the van and Cohen would not be leaving without them. To Cohen's horror, he realized that, although the

219

officer providing the three steps had given good advice, he gave it thinking of a single-hostage situation. Cohen hoped his momentum stalled the kidnapper long enough for three hostages to get away.

Cohen jumped into the back of the van, looking for any object he could use to knock the man unconscious. Any kind of weapon would prove sufficient. Laura joined his search, her head scanning the van. She jerked to the left and Cohen saw a crowbar sitting under the driver's seat. He ripped the tape from Laura's mouth before lunging for the bar. Laura began screaming and Cohen's fingers connected with the metal.

Just as Cohen brought the bar out from under the chair, the man grabbed his right leg and wheeled Cohen onto the gravel outside the van. The air left Cohen's lungs and he felt the man grip his shoulders. Somewhere in the van Cohen had dropped the crowbar. He had heard the metal clank against the floor as it fell. The giant lifted Cohen with no apparent difficulty and flung him back into the van. Connecting with the wall of the van, Cohen scrambled before feeling the man jump on top of him and grab his right hand. Laura continued to scream and the man paid her no mind. Apparently, they were too far from civilization for anyone to hear.

Despite Cohen's writhing, the man taped his entire arm against the headrest behind the passenger seat. He wrapped the tape so many times that Cohen did not stand a chance of pulling free. When he finished and stepped back to view his handiwork, a chuckle left his lips that chilled Cohen to the bone.

The giant gave a quick pat to Cohen's left cheekbone.

"You trying to be the hero with these two whores we got back here, Donahue?" The man chuckled again and this time pivoted, delivering a punch to Laura's stomach.

She balked in surprise and hunched forward in pain.

"You bastard!" Cohen shouted before launching himself toward the man in rage. The tape securing his hand pulled his body abruptly backwards. His left hand moved to unsecure the tape but was unable to find the end. He tore at the tape in desperation—the trio's only chance at an escape had just vanished, and now Cohen would watch Laura and Grace suffer because of his failed attempt.

The man, apparently bored with the two victims, unlocked Grace's unconscious body from the chains and threw her like a rag doll over his shoulder. "I'll be back for you, beautiful," he said, nodding his head at Laura and blowing a kiss her way before striding off into the distance. As soon as he disappeared, Laura moved her feet to the edge of the van. Cohen realized for the first time that she wore no shoes. He followed her movements as her toes wrapped around a metal object and flung it in Cohen's direction.

"The keys!" he cried. "He left the keys, the idiot. Good eye!" Cohen picked up the key ring with his free hand and started to cut the tape with the object's sharp edges. He had to move fast. Their attacker would be back sooner rather than later, and

221

this was the last chance Laura and Cohen had of escaping. Cohen continued to think out loud.

"We don't have too much time here. Who the hell knows where we are, anyway? Once I'm done freeing myself, I'll unlock your chains and we can make a run for it." Cohen didn't expect to hear a reproach.

"Hey, listen, he's coming back soon. Throw me the keys and make your arm look like it's still fully taped. He is going to take me next—"

"No, Laura, we can fix this!" Shock filled Cohen's voice. Laura could survive this; Cohen knew she could. He braced himself for one final jerk of his hand that would surely free it from bondage.

"Cohen! No offense, but I have a little more experience in this kind of situation than you do. You need to trust me."

Cohen's eyes locked with Laura's and he relaxed his arm into the position it held moments ago.

"After he takes me, pull your hand loose. Then you need to look out the back door and wait for my signal, okay? I have an idea, Cohen, and once I give the signal, you need to act."

Cohen wanted to protest, to know how Laura would manage to escape when the guy with muscles bigger than her entire body had a hold on her. Instead, he decided to trust the woman partially responsible for his current situation. He threw her the key ring and her foot moved it back into place.

"What should I do after your signal?"

"If you can't figure out what to do after I nod, then you really are as stupid as these guys say.

We will both be saved, I promise. Oh, and Cohen, Danielle needs to be found. She needs help."

Before any further plans could be discussed, the man appeared between the two back doors. Cohen took in his features and realized how ugly he really looked. The giant's shaggy beard did nothing to hide his two disproportionately small ears. The guy seriously needed a shower. "You two get to know each other while I was gone?"

"Please…please don't do this." Cohen begged.

"Let me help you out a little bit, Donahue. Grace and Laura set you up. We told them to file a police report, and they did. They know too much, so they have to go. In other words, it was about time they disappeared."

"Who the hell are you?" Cohen tried desperately to stall.

"You know, now that I think about it, your time to disappear is approaching pretty quickly as well, Donahue. God knows I can't wait to see that."

The giant grabbed for the key ring and found it exactly where he left it. Yanking Laura roughly, just as he had with Grace, the man threw her over his shoulder before carelessly dropping the keys in the back of the trunk yet again. Cohen wanted nothing more than to pummel this man through the floor. As soon as he took a step away from the van, Cohen pulled his hand free from the headrest. He stepped back toward the door of the van and took in the scenery.

They seemed to be on some sort of a cliff. The grass spread wide and wild, suddenly disappearing to nothing but air merely 500 feet in the distance. Cohen could only guess how long the ensuing drop-off could be. Some trees shot up from the ground, but not many. Cohen saw water past the drop off; they must be overlooking Lake Michigan. The area looked oddly familiar. Cohen remembered his high school friends tempting him to travel to Starved Rock one weekend, and after seeing pictures of the water below the drop-off, Cohen had opted out. He didn't know of any other cliffs remotely close to Chicago, but Starved Rock was located two hours east. He couldn't have been unconscious for that long, could he?

Wait for her signal, Cohen reminded himself. His eyes glued to Laura, her body now lifted over the giant's shoulders. The two of them stood on the ledge and Cohen really hoped that Laura knew what she was doing. He still didn't see how any plan she concocted could possibly have gone this far, but right now he had no choice but to trust her. Just as the giant looked like he couldn't support Laura's frame anymore, his elbows bent and Laura found Cohen. Two quick, very sure nods were given seconds before her body was tossed over the ridge like a sack of garbage.

"NO!" Cohen screamed and dropped to his knees. The man turned his head at the noise and looked shocked to see Cohen kneeling in the back of the van. His hands grabbed for the keys in his pocket before realizing his mistake of leaving them in the van.

Cohen saw the man coming and forced his body to jump into action. He grabbed the keys from their position on the floor, ran to the front seat of the car, and jammed one key into the ignition. Just as he floored the gas, the man reached one giant hand toward the doors on the back of the van. The giant yanked open a door handle and attempted to throw his body into the vehicle. Looking in the rearview mirror, Cohen saw the large lump of a body lose its grip on the door as the car turned sharply left, sending gravel flying in all directions. The man tumbled to the ground and screamed profanities into the air. Fortunately, they were too far from civilization for anyone to hear.

As Cohen navigated back to the city, his body hummed with adrenaline. He had no idea which direction to head, but he followed the river to his left. The tears finally came as Laura's words echoed through his entire body. Their meaning was obvious and clear now. Cohen let the words reverberate through him: *"We will both be saved, I promise."* In those last fateful moments, Laura had given up her fight. After all of her suffering, she had been ready to experience some peace. At least now she had that.

Cohen's mind flashed back to Laura suddenly transforming from afraid to determined. Laura had chosen to sacrifice her life for Cohen's, the one person able to possibly save Danielle. *"Danielle needs to be found. She needs help."* Laura's gift would not be in vain. Cohen's determination matched hers; Danielle seemed to be the one missing piece to this entire game, and Cohen knew he needed to find her.

Cohen drove along the road—just him, the lake, and his newfound determination. The buzzing of his phone was the least of his worries.

Chapter 23

Foliage. Cohen had been driving for almost two hours and he had yet to see anything but green grass and trees. Deciding to assume that he had been at Starved Rock, Cohen navigated the car west and hoped beyond hope that he would eventually find his way back to the city. Cohen planned to arrive within the next hour, and he hadn't considered his plan of action if the skyline never appeared. Knowing that a gang of hit men most likely waited for the van to make it back into the city, Cohen felt adrenaline rushing through him the entire drive. The two hours flew by in a blur.

Given his clenched body, Cohen's muscles strained at any and all movements. Cohen took his foot off the gas and let the car cruise. His frame of mind had solidified over the past few hours. Before watching Laura and Grace die, Cohen thought this nightmare would all be over once he cleared his name. Once the police realized his innocence, Cohen would be able to return to his normal life. Now, he knew that nothing could be further from the truth. Cohen just witnessed the murder of two women. One of those women had sacrificed herself so that Cohen could escape—so that Cohen could find Danielle. He would be damned if he stood by while a similar fate befell Danielle.

Cohen felt responsible. Had he not moved back to Chicago, Grace, Laura, and Danielle might still be living normal lives. He let the guilt wash over him, expecting it to propel him the extra mile. Craning his neck and stretching his arms over his head, Cohen's cell phone fell out of his sweatshirt pocket. He picked it up to find one text message from Mier:

Stay out of sight. Working on it.

Thanks for all the detail, Cohen thought to himself. Cohen debated calling Mier to tell him about what had just happened with Grace and Laura. Not only that, but also about the run-in on the bridge the other day, about Officer Turner's warning regarding the black Jeep, about everything.

He wanted so badly to have someone to talk details over with, but deep down, Cohen knew that Mier wasn't that person. Mier had Cohen's best interests at heart, the past few days had proven that. That also seemed to be part of the problem. If Cohen told Mier about his plan to save Danielle, Mier would no doubt try to talk him out of it. In fact, Cohen felt that Mier would do whatever it took to keep Cohen safe. Instead of responding to the text or reaching out in any way, Cohen put the phone back into his pocket.

Despite good intentions, Cohen couldn't help but feel simultaneously frustrated with Mier. "Working on it," seemed a little vague. The car veered too far left and Cohen corrected the angle, thinking for the first time of the car he left back in the parking lot: Leila's car. Cohen had no doubt the vehicle had been totaled, but Leila expected the car to come back in one piece. Cohen realized he had another phone call to make. Sure, it could definitely wait, but Cohen convinced himself that the car was of the utmost importance. He wasn't ready to admit that, in reality, he simply needed to hear the woman's voice on the other end.

"Herzog here."

"Leila, it's me." Cohen's body throbbed from his stiff muscles, but it was no comparison to the deep ache growing in his heart and spreading throughout his body. Cohen hadn't known it was possible to have such strong feelings for a woman he hardly knew.

"Listen, a hit man found me earlier today, and I was in a parking lot with your car when—"

"Oh my God, Cohen. Are you alright?"

"I'm fine. I just wish I could say the same for your car. I'm so sorry, Leila. It's wrapped around a telephone pole. I know this wasn't part of the deal, none of this was, but I wanted you to know that I will replace the car, with interest."

"Cohen, where are you?" The concern in Leila's voice was impossible to hide. "Do you need me to pick you up?"

Leila did not even mention the car and Cohen wondered if she even heard him describe its state. Despite the wreckage of her vehicle, Leila cared only about Cohen's well being. Cohen realized yet again how much he regretted his actions with Danielle. Leila, without a doubt, was the most compassionate person he had ever met.

"It's okay, really. I stole the guy's car—the guy who kidnapped me. I just wanted to make sure I warned you far enough in advance for you to plan transportation for tomorrow."

Silence lasted for a few seconds and Cohen held his breath. He hoped Leila didn't read into the real reason for his call: that he desperately needed a little hope in the darkness of his situation.

"You're telling me, that you're riding in a stolen car right now?"

"Um, yes…"

"Did you stop to consider that your kidnapper could have stolen that car from someone else in the first place? Meaning that cops in the city most likely have an ID out for it?"

"Well, I was going to ditch the car eventually, but—"

"Not to mention, you stole it from someone whose boss more than likely had a tracking device on the vehicle."

"That's a good point, but—"

"Did you really not think about any of that?"

Cohen hadn't thought of that, and his inner police officer scolded himself. Leila was right. At this point, driving any vehicle was risky, not to mention one most likely stolen with a tracker in place to boot.

"Well, when you put it that way…"

"Cohen, where are you? Let me help." Leila's tone suggested that she would not take no for an answer. Even if Cohen did decline her offer to help, Leila would find a way to supply some guidance.

The temptation to see Leila again, to hear her voice, see her smile, proved too much for Cohen. He caved within seconds.

"Give me forty-five minutes to ditch the car. I'll meet you at Michigan Avenue Bridge."

***

Leila hung up the phone and stepped out from the ladies room where she sought refuge after seeing an unfamiliar number appear on her caller ID. Her heart raced and her hands felt clammy and damp. She scolded her heart for still jumping at the thought of Cohen. Clearly, after his night with Danielle, Cohen wouldn't be interested in getting anywhere near another woman, and Leila didn't blame him. To be honest, after the past few days, she wasn't sure she wanted to become involved with any men either.

She did know, however, that if something happened to Cohen while she sat on her ass at the CPD, Leila would never forgive herself. Her determination scared her, especially considering that Cohen would never be anything more than a friend.

When Leila heard Cohen's voice on the other end of the call, she hoped he had finally come to his senses and called to take Leila up on her offer to help. Even she couldn't hide her disappointment when she learned his actual motivation for the call: to apologize for the destruction of her car.

None of that mattered now. Clearly, if Cohen proved delusional enough to think it was safe to drive around in a stolen van, he needed all the help he could get. Leila knew of only two people in the entire office whom she could trust. One would meet her shortly by the Michigan Avenue Bridge. The other would be in his office, still working tirelessly to help Cohen in any way possible.

230

"Hey, Sergeant Mier, could I speak with you for a second?"

"Make it quick, Herzog. A single person can only hold the media and investigating officers off for so long."

"It's about Cohen, actually. He needs a car and mine isn't doing so well at the moment. I know it's a lot to ask and that it could be incriminating, but…"

Mier looked up from the endless documents spread out on his desk. His office phone rang; he made no move to answer it.

"Leila, I told Cohen to talk to no one but me throughout this process. He has now included you in the case and therefore put your reputation, not to mention your job, in danger. I'm sorry, you know I would help Cohen in any way that I can, but right now I am busy with the media and the other police officers searching for him. Cohen should be staying put in a safe spot and absolutely not driving around on the streets of Chicago."

Mier had a point, and Leila questioned her ability to convince him otherwise.

"Listen, Sergeant, I completely agree, but…right now, Cohen is sitting on the street waiting at the Michigan Avenue Bridge. All I plan to do is pick him up and bring him to a safe spot. Better I pick him up than some other police officer—one who's trying to put him in prison, don't you think?"

It wasn't until Leila brought up the other officers that Mier's facial expression began to soften.

"Damn it. I guess leaving an innocent man on the side of the street won't do anyone any good. I wish I had time to go pick Cohen up myself, Leila, but I'm honestly too swamped."

"Understandable." Leila breathed a sigh of relief.

"Let me go out and grab some files from my car. You know, in the off chance that my car ends up in the same state that I'm assuming yours is in right now."

"Probably a good idea."

"Leila, you have one hour before I want to see my car back in its spot, with no Cohen Donahue anywhere in sight. Am I clear?"

Leila nodded and smiled, "Thanks so much, Sergeant Mier."

Mier took his keys and placed a package under his arm before moving to leave his office. When he came back, holding a handful of his files in a cardboard box, Mier handed Leila the keys.

"Please be careful, Leila. I'm sure you realize how big a mess this is becoming."

Leila understood Mier's warning, knowing that she had to proceed with caution, both in terms of protecting Cohen, and protecting her heart.

Chapter 24

Cohen turned the wheel of the van toward the lake and shifted the gear back into neutral. He stepped out of the car and watched as the tires moved toward the water. If there had been a tracker on the vehicle, Cohen would rather it be underwater than on solid ground. He turned away before the van could get any closer to the edge of the cliff. Even though it was just a vehicle, Cohen couldn't handle seeing something else fall from the ledge. Leaving the demons behind him, he started his walk toward Michigan Avenue Bridge.

To decrease his chances of being seen, Cohen walked in the brush along the side of the road. Even if his kidnapper had called his entourage for backup, they would have no idea where to start looking for Cohen. The sunken van might give them some clue, but Cohen planned to be long gone by that time.

His disposable phone vibrated harshly and Cohen glanced at the caller ID, expecting the caller to be Leila. The number that appeared did not belong to Leila, however, and Cohen stalled. *No way*. He recognized the number, knowing it was too much of a coincidence. He answered the phone, welcoming yet another trip down memory lane.

Answering the phone a little too tentatively, Cohen greeted the caller.

"Bre...?" He knew he recognized the number, but something about the randomness of the call caused Cohen to doubt his memory.

"Well now, don't sounded too excited, Cohen!" At the sound of her voice, Cohen felt the majority of his worries disappear, if only momentarily. After remembering the positive effect that Bre had on his spirits, Cohen wished he had reached out to her earlier. Giving the first hearty laugh he had in days, Cohen responded.

"Oh come on, Bre. It's great to hear from you. It has been way too long, I haven't seen you since…"

Cohen stopped mid sentence, remembering when Bre handed him his father's box of possessions at the airport. Cohen took a seat on a stump and settled himself for the conversation. Sensing his discomfort, Bre picked up the conversation.

"Listen, Coh, I've really missed you. I'm sorry I haven't called; I know it's not an excuse, but…it's just hard sometimes, you know?"

Oh boy, did he know. Cohen wondered if Bre could feel him nod his head slowly in affirmation. Cohen realized that Bre must have called him for a reason. He highly doubted this was simply a social call, and he waited for her to continue.

"Listen, to be blunt here, I turned on my TV this morning to see your face plastered all over the news."

"Oh, great." The reports had finally become top news. The last Cohen had heard, Bre lived a little bit out of the city. The fact that she saw the reports suggested that the story had spread far.

"What the hell is going on?"

"More importantly, Bre, how did my hair look in the picture?" Bre responded to Cohen's joke with silence. Apparently, she hadn't called to hear

Cohen's smart-ass humor that she had become familiar with during his childhood.

"Sorry," Cohen offered, "I've been having some weird reactions to stress these days."

"Well I don't doubt that. This story has gotten big, Coh."

"Jesus."

"Why don't you explain to me exactly what the hell is going on here?"

"If I could tell you, Bre, I would."

Silence echoed through the phone.

"Well, I'll tell you this much, I sure didn't raise a man capable of committing any crime as serious as rape and abuse. So, Cohen, how do we fix this?"

Hearing Bre simply assume his innocence made tears swim beneath Cohen's eyelids. Cohen knew he did nothing wrong, but having someone else trust in his character without him even having to confirm—that had yet to happen. Bre knew Cohen better than anyone else. Cohen knew he would always have at least one ally familiar with the real him.

"I don't know, Bre. I don't have the slightest idea who is setting me up, or why. Small clues are falling into place, though. I had a little run-in with a black Jeep a few days ago and then today a huge man kidnapped me. Grace and Laura, the two other women involved, they're—they're both dead. I saw them…" Unable to describe what he saw, Bre took over the conversation after ten seconds of silence.

"Black Jeep, huh?" Bre stated this more than she asked it, her tone a combination of matter-of-fact and whispered suspicion. "I think I can clear at

235

least that part up for you. In fact, now that I think about it, I do remember Peter talking about a black Jeep. Would you be able to meet up with me a little later?"

Cohen agreed to connect with Bre. He didn't know if he would have a car that far into the night, but it shouldn't be too difficult to figure out.

"Let me move some plans for the night around. I'll call you back within the hour to set up a time to meet. Of course, it will have to be a secluded location…"

Something struck Cohen for the first time and he blurted out the question just as Bre got ready to end the call.

"Wait a minute, Bre. How did you get my disposable phone's number?"

"I called the CPD and Officer Turner gave it to me. It was always hard to work with that woman; apparently, you won her over. She seemed like your biggest fan."

Cohen chuckled. "She's paying back an old debt to my dad," he responded. Bre did not respond for what felt like an eternity. Cohen assumed that his knowledge of Tuner's working relationship with his father was a surprise to her.

"Turner filled me in on the day my dad died, that's all."

"Cohen, your father was more concerned about your safety than anything in the word, you know that, right?"

Cohen didn't respond. People had been bringing up Peter a lot over the past few days. It had become clear that Peter was involved in this mess somehow, though it was not yet clear enough for Cohen to determine how, exactly.

"Let me ask you something," Bre continued, "do you remember those nights your father wouldn't come home? When you would come stay with me at my place?"

Cohen's breath stopped short. His heart beat so loudly that he worried about his ability to hear Bre's next words. How did Peter's nights away from home have anything to do with this?

"After solving big profile cases, your dad would rent a motel room and stay away from your house for a few nights."

"Why?" Cohen wanted to ask so much more, but he could only afford the one syllable.

"In case anyone out for revenge trailed him. He wanted to make sure that no criminal ever found out his real residence because, well, because that would put you in danger. People wanted your dad dead, Cohen. He couldn't bring that home with him. It would have been too risky for you."

"I always thought he needed a break, from Mom, from me, I don't know."

"Staying away from you on those nights was the hardest thing your dad ever had to do."

"Bre, why are you telling me that now? You lied to me about it when I was younger…"

"Oh Cohen, I didn't lie to you. Not about that. I had no idea where your father would disappear to; he didn't tell me either. He said it would be easier if I didn't know. All that mattered to Peter was keeping you safe. Eventually, that became all that mattered to me as well."

"Why does my dad keep coming up, Bre?"

"Tell you what. Let me call you back in an hour and we can schedule a time and a place to meet. Okay?"

Cohen ended the call with an uncomfortable feeling in his stomach. What else had Bre lied about? He had lost touch with the woman, despite the relevant information that she clearly knew. As the days wore on, Cohen found himself constantly doubting his instincts about whom he should trust. Bre was one of the strongest people he knew; something felt wrong here. In the midst of his thinking, Cohen noticed the blinking voicemail icon. He heard Duncan's voice.

"Donahue, I have the information. You're looking for a woman named Desire Morrey. I have an address for an apartment building at 1565 Washington Park, the South Side. Apartment 3K. Be careful, Donahue."

Desire Morrey? The name didn't ring a bell and Cohen felt oddly relieved. With the way things had been going, he wouldn't have been surprised to hear that Danielle's pimp was Peter himself. The universe had intertwined so many parts of Cohen's life into this case that he had no idea where the line would be drawn.

His next step would be visiting the address provided by Duncan. Hope flickered in Cohen for a second as he realized that Danielle might be at the location Duncan had given him. A car idled just fifty feet in the distance under the bridge. Cohen recognized the black Camry as Mier's, smiled at Leila's success at replacing her car, and took off to jump into the passenger seat.

Chapter 25

The door shut and Leila stepped on the gas. She looked Cohen's way as if to confirm his presence in the car, not bothering to ask for details of his recent encounter. Neither spoke for the first few minutes as Leila drove west. Cohen turned his body and faced Leila head-on, finally racking up enough courage to tell her everything, to apologize, to beg for forgiveness. Leila saw it coming and cut him off.

"I ran into Charlie on my way out. I didn't mention the fact that I was going to meet up with you, but I told him about your car troubles. We only have Mier's for an hour, and then Charlie said you could use his after. You should be set for the night now. Where are we headed?"

"Oh, great, ah thanks. 1565 Washington Park, a set of apartment complexes."

Leila nodded her head and began to drive in that direction.

"Funny, growing up in the city, my parents always warned me to stay away from the South Side of Chicago. The crimes, the theft, the deaths—they were terrified of it. I actually never disobeyed them. Well, until now, I guess." Leila allowed a quick laugh before launching into more serious matters.

"So, can you fill me in on what's going on? I know it's complicated, but if you're up to talk about it, I'm ready to listen."

Cohen's slight smile suggested that he welcomed Leila's question.

"Well, I guess I'll start from the beginning…" Cohen described everything that had happened since he saw Leila last. He told her every detail, making sure to leave nothing out this time around. Leila's eyes grew slightly when he mentioned the full extent of the first mugging. Her eyes continued to grow all through his story and looked as though they would burst when Cohen mentioned meeting Laura and Grace in the back of the van. He ended the story with a short description of the women's tragic death, although he kept that part of the narrative short. For some reason, Cohen felt that speaking too in depth about Laura and Grace's murder might dirty their memory, at least for now.

"I am seriously impressed you're still alive right now," Leila responded when all had been said.

"Tell me about it."

"How are you holding up?"

"I'm actually trying not to feel too much right now. Seems to do the trick." Cohen hoped that Leila would take the hint that he didn't feel like bringing any emotion to the surface right now. Her lack of further questions suggested that she understood.

Leila's phone announced the destination on the right and she pulled her car into a dirty parking lot. Two brown, four-story apartment buildings rose from the ground, looking out of place and nearly destroyed. Their roofs appeared slightly crooked and boasted an odd layering effect. The buildings rested in the middle of nowhere. Leila parked the car and Cohen heard Laura's voice in the back of his mind. *"Danielle needs to be found."*

"I'll try and make this quick." Cohen reached for the door handle and pulled it as Leila's hand latched onto his arm.

"You're kidding me, right?"

"Leila, look. At just about every place I've gone to over the past few days, I've run into some macho guy looking to kick the shit out of me. You're safer in the car. I'll be gone for ten minutes, tops."

"Like hell." Leila stepped out of the car and continued walking toward the apartment door despite Cohen's reluctance to join in her pursuit. She looked over her shoulder into his annoyed glare and shrugged her shoulders in defiance. Had Cohen not been frustrated that Leila was willingly putting herself in danger, he would have thought her actions cute.

Cohen looked up and around in an attempt to check for any security cameras. He didn't see any, realizing after the search that the chances of this apartment having any sort of security cameras were low. Cohen didn't doubt this place had seen its fair share of crime. He hoped his and Leila's departure would come sooner rather than later.

An alarm vibrated in Cohen's pocket and he looked down at his phone to see that it had only 5% battery left. Annoyed that he hadn't thought to ask Mier for the phone's charger, Cohen sighed before turning it off to preserve the battery. If someone had to reach him, they would leave a message. Besides, Cohen didn't want to have any interruptions while speaking with Desire.

"Ready?" Cohen asked as he joined Leila at the elevator and pushed the button for the third floor.

Leila nodded. The hallways were exactly as Cohen would have suspected after seeing the building's lack of a lobby. The cramped walls immediately made him feel claustrophobic. The hallways were wide enough for one body to walk through at a time. Cohen stepped in front of Leila and made his way to 3K. If anything bad did happened here, which Cohen almost expected, he didn't want Leila to have to get around his body in order to escape. The lights flickered and Cohen knocked on the door and waited.

A scuffling sounded from behind the door and an old, ragged, chain-smoking female voice greeted the knock: "Nico, is that you?"

Opting to remain somewhat anonymous, Cohen responded. "No. It's Peter Donahue."

A deafening silence followed; Cohen watched as a shadow covered the peephole in the door and then disappeared. The woman had seen Cohen. She now had the advantage.

Let's see who Danielle's pimp really is, Cohen thought, relieved to have heard a woman's voice rather than a man's. A few seconds passed until the woman pulled back the door. Cohen nearly lost consciousness.

"Mom?"

"Long time no see, Cohen."

Cohen leaned back against the wall and willed his eyes to see someone else. He hadn't seen his mother in over fifteen years, yet there she stood, somehow involved in this entire mess. Her face appeared more sunken in, her skin had more wrinkles, and she looked even more evil than Cohen

242

had remembered. Leila confirmed Cohen's fear by placing a firm hand of support over his arm.

Theresa gawked at the sight, smiling broadly for effect. "Well, what a happy little reunion this is!" she said sarcastically. "Did you come all this way to tell me you're in love? Oh wait! Don't tell me! You knocked this whore up and now you want some motherly advice?" Her mock happiness ended just as suddenly as it began, replaced by a permanent grimace. "I guess the apple doesn't fall too far from the tree after all."

Her vulgar, crude voice brought back all too familiar memories for Cohen. Theresa glared directly through Leila and Cohen shakily pushed his body from the wall and cut off her line of vision. He could deal with that evil stare, but Leila shouldn't have to.

"Glad to see you haven't changed a bit, Mom. Actually, we are here trying to keep my ass from being sent to prison for a crime I didn't commit. You have any insight you'd like to share in regards to the situation?"

Theresa let out a combination of a grunt and a cough, suggesting that her smoking had finally caught up to her. Cohen knew this interaction would not be a good one.

"Could we talk inside, Mom? It is really important."

Theresa turned and walked back into her apartment, leaving the door open. Cohen wanted nothing more than to turn around and walk back to his car. Going to prison might actually be easier than this confrontation. Assuming the open door was the only invitation they would receive, Cohen turned toward Leila.

"Offer still stands to wait outside. This won't be pretty in here."

Leila reached out and gave Cohen's hand a quick squeeze. "Hey, I'm right here with you."

No judgment, just pure support. Cohen knew he definitely did not deserve the added comfort that Leila supplied, but he felt overwhelmed with gratitude at her steadfast presence. They turned and walked into the apartment together. A lingering smell made Cohen want to vomit. A mixture of sewage, trash, and sex accosted his nose. Leila sat on a ripped couch in the middle of the small, mustard-yellow living room and Cohen followed her lead. *Get this over with*, Cohen told himself.

"Mom, are you Desire Morrey?"

"You came here to ask what my street name is?" Theresa laughed so disgustingly that Cohen gripped the armrest on his chair to keep himself from leaving the room.

"Enough with the games, Mom. Are you or are you not?"

"So what if I am?" Theresa looked at Leila, apparently already bored with the confrontational tone that her son was using. "Are you comfortable, sweetie? We have plenty of clients waiting if you'd like to take a shot."

Had Leila not just witnessed Theresa's sarcasm minutes before, she would have thought the offer was genuine. Leila opened her mouth to respond, but Cohen beat her to the punch. He stood and closed the distance between him and his mother in one stride. He towered over her and she looked at him with defiance, reminding him of a child in timeout.

"If you keep talking like that, I'll call the CPD over here in seconds and invite them to see what kind of establishment you're running. Let's just stay focused here so we can both get on with our separate lives."

Cohen paced the room now, unable to sit back down. He stopped, placed his hands on his hips, and looked at Leila. He silently pleaded with her to leave, but recognized her determination to stay. She nodded for him to continue.

Theresa had never been smart. Even a person with a below-average IQ score would realize that if Cohen called the police, it would also result in his arrest. Cops were hunting for him this very minute, after all. Theresa had yet to put the pieces together, and Cohen doubted she ever would.

"Tell me what the hell is going on. Start from the beginning. How did you end up here?"

"Why don't you ask your father that question? You two seemed to get along so much better without me, anyways."

Cohen realized that his mom hadn't heard of his dad's passing. *Good,* he thought, *she doesn't deserve to know that information.* Cohen pulled his phone out of his pocket and pretended to start dialing 9-1-1. Despite the phone's sleeping status, Theresa took the hint.

"Oh, fine. We'll take the happy trip down memory lane. Get comfortable, because it's a good one." She continued before either Leila or Cohen could react.

"On the night that I met your father, I was taking care of some business."

"You were looking to seduce someone?" Cohen interrupted bitterly.

"Conveniently, Peter was also looking for a distraction," Theresa continued with an annoyed sigh. "Prostitutes can spot men like Peter from a mile away, you know. So we did the dirty."

She let loose a low chuckle. "I bet that son of a bitch never thought he would see my face again. Unfortunately for him, I got pregnant and we married. That's our love story in a nutshell."

"Did he know you were a prostitute?"

"Hell no, and I didn't plan on telling him, either. I couldn't risk having the wedding called off. Before your dad, I only had two main clients. They weren't too difficult to get rid of."

"Who were the clients?"

"Wouldn't you like to know?"

Theresa smiled so eerily that Leila squirmed where she sat. Cohen noticed and he reminded himself to keep this quick.

"So then what, Mom? You were unhappy with your life and became a drunk? Dad got sick of it and kicked you out one day, so your only option was to come back here? To run a prostitution ring?"

"I wasn't unhappy with my life, you little bastard. Maybe if I wasn't reminded day in and out of the biggest mistake I ever made, I would have been a little more chipper."

The meaning of her words sunk in, and Cohen hated that they stung.

"Right, so I was your big mistake?"

"Don't worry, honey, at least your daddy loved you. I could see the way he looked at you and that made me jealous. And then, your dad decided he wanted to throw a barbeque for his CPD buddies."

Cohen's heart rate increased at the mention of the barbeque, the day that everything fell apart. He had never considered his mother's side of the story, but suddenly felt curious.

"You and Dad got in a fight at the barbeque. You left the next day."

"Let's just say, your dad found out about my professional interests," she winked at Leila, "and decided to throw a fit. Then we fought, we screamed, and I made threats I was determined to keep."

"What kind of threats?"

"Nothing too crazy. I simply threatened to make your life a living hell. I knew exactly how to push your dad's buttons. And my God, did I push them."

Cohen flashed back to the arguments that took place at the barbeque and he lacked the strength to even swallow. His entire childhood threatened to come back and overwhelm him. This time, something told him the perspective wouldn't be pleasant.

"I knew that you were the one thing Peter loved most in life, so I went for it. I made one remark against you and your dad snapped. He told me that I had to get myself out of that house, by the next day, or he would throw me out on the street himself."

Cohen knew that his mom was withholding some of the storyline, but he didn't care. He wanted to hear the bare minimum, and nothing more. His agenda for coming here involved getting answers from Desire Morrey, not reliving his childhood.

"If you could have seen the look on your dad's face." Again with the chuckle, she continued, "I mean, really seen it. He was not fooling around. So, that night, I called one of my two clients from before. I said I needed an out and he told me to wait until tomorrow, said he would send a car to pick me up. That was that. I packed my things and I waited. A black Jeep sat outside for ten minutes. I walked out and got in. I never even looked back."

Someone began knocking at the door and "Desire Morrey" walked to answer it. She let a drunken, overweight, disgusting man into the apartment and led him to the second room on the right. The two exchanged no words and the man shut the door behind him. Cohen sat in humiliation and disgust, lacking the courage to look Leila in the eye.

"My client," Theresa continued, "offered to set me up with my own network of men. He would supply the customers, I would supply the prostitutes. All he asked for was a 5% share and the rest was for me. So I agreed to the business and began gathering women to keep his clients happy. Three days ago, this old client showed up and asked me for three of my girls. He said he had to carry out a plan he'd been working on for some time."

"So you just handed three girls over? Just like that?"

"Rumor had it that Danielle wanted out of the business, so I gave her an out. I thought that would teach her a lesson. Next thing I know, you

248

and Danielle are both on the news. Truly, Cohen, I haven't stopped smiling since."

Cohen had heard enough. He knew he needed more time to comprehend the information that his mother shared with him, and he wanted nothing more than to breathe some fresh air in place of the musky odor currently filling his lungs. Sensing his need to leave, Leila stood and walked toward the door.

"Where is Danielle?" Cohen turned to his mother. He had come for this information and he would not leave without it.

"She's gone." His mother's yellow teeth threatened to fall out of her mouth. "After I handed Danielle off to my boss, I knew I would never see her again."

Cohen willed his nausea to decrease. How could he be related to such a vicious monster? Despite his attempts at distancing himself from Theresa's characteristics, his similarities to the woman were depressingly apparent to Cohen. Aside from any physical characteristics inherited, Cohen realized that a part of his heart belonged to this woman as well. The part that refused to let anyone in, that refused to take a chance on love, and Cohen hated himself for it. No matter how hard he tried, Cohen could not forget that Theresa's blood ran through his veins.

For the hundredth time, Cohen wondered how Danielle could have gone through with this plan. Now, he had an idea. She had wanted out of the prostitution business. She didn't stand a chance.

"What about Grace and Laura?" Cohen asked, in an attempt to test his mother's story. He knew exactly what happened to Grace and Laura, and he would know immediately, based on Theresa's response, whether or not she told the truth.

"You better hope, for Grace and Laura's sake, that they're dead. What would happen to them alive would be much worse than dying. I haven't seen Grace or Laura since the reports went out. I heard they got picked up on the streets; no one has seen them since."

Okay, an accurate enough response. Cohen needed a few more pieces of information.

"Where would your client have taken Danielle? If I wanted to find her, how would I go about doing so?"

"Trying to play hero, huh? So much like your father. Well, except for those blue eyes of yours. Don't forget that I'm still in you too, sweetie pie." She mocked affection and blew a kiss in his direction. "I don't know where he lives. Find the black Jeep and follow it. Something tells me, in your case, it should be relatively easy to find."

"The black Jeep, huh?"

"It will lead you right to where you want to go."

Cohen's mind registered each and every experience with the car he had over the past few days: trying to run him into the lake, almost being hit by a black car on his walk to O'Reilly's. It was the same car that Peter warned Officer Turner about, the same Jeep whose scratched passenger door sent a reflection into Cohen's eyes as he watched his mother drive away all of those years ago. Cohen didn't need to meet up with Bre anymore; after speaking with Theresa, the story behind the black Jeep began clicking into place.

"One more question for you, Mom. What is his name? The client that picked you up on the day you left, the one that took Danielle. I need a name."

Theresa sat in silence, tilting her head while looking at Cohen. Anger flared in Cohen's stomach. He held his phone in the air, hoping his threat still held the same authority.

"If you lie to me, Mom, I swear to God I will call the police. Tell me his name."

"Coda," Theresa responded. "His name is Coda."

Cohen and Leila walked out of the apartment and shut the door. Theresa slowly rose from her chair and moved toward a landline hanging from the wall. The phone rang only twice before Theresa's call was rewarded with an answer.

"Did you take care of it?"

"I said I would, didn't I? Keep tracking the car; Cohen will be watching for the Jeep and he will follow it."

Theresa hung up the phone without waiting for a response. Her wicked, yellow smile inched its way across her face.

Chapter 26

Leila and Cohen did not speak for what felt like an eternity. Whereas before, Leila wanted nothing more than to avoid talking about feelings, she now waited anxiously for Cohen to open up. Seeing Cohen's mother had been a shock for Leila; she couldn't imagine how Cohen must be feeling.

Leila pulled the car to a stop at a stop sign. "Cohen?"

Cohen grabbed the door handle and opened the car door, only to slam it shut again with all of his might. He repeated the pattern four times until he finally loosened his grip. Leila could see early signs of his body beginning to tremble and tears jerked at her eyelids. Cohen's shoulders hunched and Leila watched as his hands took their familiar position on the top of his head.

"You didn't deserve that, you know. No one deserves to be treated like that," she offered, knowing that her words must contain very little comfort given the situation. Leila stared at Cohen with tenderness and compassion. Her hand reached out and grabbed Cohen's in a further attempt to offer support.

"I'm sorry, Leila. I'm sorry you had to see that…now you know the extent of my childhood. My mother not only left, she was also a prostitute and I was her biggest regret."

"Hey, no judgment from me, okay?" Leila couldn't handle the thought of Cohen feeling embarrassed at Leila knowing details of his past. She held his hand tighter and didn't move the car forward until Cohen nodded his head in acceptance.

As the car moved, Cohen leaned back against the seat as if letting all of his mother's hateful words wash over his body.

"I can't let her in, Leila. She's my mom and I just can't let her in."

"She doesn't deserve to be let in." The sureness in Leila's voice rang true to Cohen's ears. He couldn't allow his mother to make him feel worthless. Rather, he should feel grateful that the woman no longer had a large presence in his life. Cohen squeezed Leila's hand and she held back tears for the second time since returning to the car.

"Would you take a right turn up here? We need to make a stop at the department."

"The department? Cohen, for someone hiding from the police, that doesn't seem like the—" Cohen hastily pushed the door open for a second time and Leila swerved to the side of the road in alarm. He leaned his upper body out of the car before vomiting on the side of the road. Cohen pulled himself back into the car and looked carefully at Leila.

"Take a right turn, please, Leila." She drove toward the department with no further protests.

"I need to make a call; is it okay for me to use your phone?" Leila nodded and Cohen dialed.

"Charlie? Hey man, listen, could you come out into the parking lot, please?"

"Sure. Right now?" Charlie responded.

"Yes, and if you don't mind bringing your car keys out, that would be great. Oh, and please, don't mention to anyone that I called you. We are pulling in now."

Leila pulled the car into the closest parking spot and waited for Charlie to emerge from the back doors.

"So, what's the next move?"

Charlie stepped out of the doors as soon as the words left Leila's mouth. He walked briskly to the far corner of the parking lot. Cohen took his time before leaving Leila's comforting presence. He and Leila sat still, just staring. Cohen turned and his hand found its way to Leila's face. He ran his forefinger along her cheekbone before stepping abruptly from the car. Leila delayed movement momentarily, but eventually followed suit.

"Cohen, man, you shouldn't be here." Charlie glanced around the parking lot. "Are you okay? We've all been worried about you."

"I know Charlie, thanks for the car. Mier's going to need his back soon, and I can't exactly drive mine around right now. I wish I didn't have to ask, but I'm in a bind here."

"Hey, if worse comes to worse, I'll just say you stole the keys." Charlie handed Cohen his keys without a second thought. Cohen had never had friends like Leila and Charlie, willing to put their safety at risk to help him. He reminded himself to never take them for granted. Cohen began walking toward Charlie's car and Leila followed.

"So what? You're going solo now? Cohen, why don't you let us help you?"

"Leila, listen to me," he turned to face her; Charlie still stood within earshot. "I appreciate your help more than you know. You've done so much to help me. Both of you have. But I will not let you put your lives in danger on my account any longer—I just won't."

"But—"

"Please, Leila." Cohen pleaded quieter now, this time not wanting Charlie to hear his words. "I would not be able to live with myself if something happened to you."

Leila took a step back and froze. Cohen looked toward Charlie and carried out the next part of his plan. He had asked Charlie to come outside for two reasons, to bring his car keys, and to make sure that Leila went back inside.

"Charlie, would you take Leila inside and make sure she doesn't try anything that could get her killed?" Leila surrendered and handed Cohen her firearm, once again knowing without even asking how to help.

Charlie nodded, knowing very well how Cohen felt about Leila. Cohen knew that he could trust Charlie to keep Leila safe. Since watching the two of them interact on their first days in the department, Cohen got the feeling that Charlie harbored a crush on Leila as well. Cohen climbed into Charlie's car and pulled out of the parking lot.

Just as he hit the red light directly outside of the station, Cohen saw a black Jeep cross his path. Feeling that luck must finally be on his side, Cohen took a sharp right turn through the light and began his pursuit of the vehicle.

Keeping his car at least two cars behind the Jeep, Cohen waited for the Jeep to exit off of the main road. The car drove fast, dodging in and out of traffic and Cohen wondered if the driver suspected a tail. He took extra precautions when exiting and stayed far enough behind the Jeep that he could just barely make out the car in the distance. *Danielle could still be alive.* Cohen held onto this thought the entire time he trailed the Jeep. Something good needed to come from all of this; someone needed to be saved.

Although Cohen felt no physical attraction for Danielle, the thought of her in trouble made him sick to his stomach. Theresa had mentioned that Danielle wanted an out from prostitution. She had wanted a clean slate, and Cohen couldn't help but feel that it shouldn't be this hard for someone to get that in life.

As the Jeep took a left turn onto an extremely quiet dirt road, Cohen reminded himself that he would be dealing with criminals. His mother had shed a lot of light on the situation. This payback had been planned for a long time; someone had been watching Cohen for God knew how long. He hoped to see that someone at the approaching destination.

Ten more minutes passed before the Jeep took a slow left down what looked like a deserted driveway. Cohen took his time reaching the point and continued to drive straight past it. After two rundown houses passed by on his left, Cohen pulled his car to the side of the road and parked.

Thinking like a police officer, Cohen took note of his surroundings. If he ended up in need of a quick getaway, he would have to run a small distance to reach his car. Assuming these people had guns, Cohen doubted that he could avoid being shot. Knowing he couldn't afford anything but

256

confidence, Cohen pushed the thoughts out of his head and secured Leila's firearm under his belt.

He cut across neighboring yards and walked on foot through the woods until he saw a dirt driveway. It appeared long and winding, turning left and disappearing beyond a cove of evergreen trees. Assuming the driveway couldn't possibly extend too long, Cohen guessed he stood about halfway from the house—if a house even lay at the end of the dirt road. Cohen took a step out of the bush, planning to cross over to the other side of the driveway, when he thought he heard an engine coming from the direction of the house. He dove back into the woods just as the headlights shone his way, praying that the car did not see his shadow.

Though he couldn't say for sure if it was his imagination or not, Cohen swore he saw the black Jeep slow down as it passed directly across from him. Absolute silence followed and Cohen did not dare even risking a glance in the car's direction. After what felt like an eternity, Cohen heard the tires continue down the driveway toward the road. He released the huge mouthful of air he had been holding.

Cohen's heart beat so fast that he felt as though it would break through his shirt. *Stay calm*, he told himself as he forced his legs to continue walking up the road. Since the car had driven by, Cohen felt much more on edge, and much more aware. He rounded the final bend and saw a tiny house in the distance, its gray paint just as ominous as the dead lawn. Cohen wondered if grass had ever grown in this yard—it sure didn't look like it.

Checking his phone yet again to make sure that it remained off, Cohen made his way toward the house. He hoped that no security cameras pointed his way. A good fifty feet of yard stood between Cohen at the edge of the woods and the house. He moved swiftly, taking in the features of the house.

Two lopsided windows sat on the front of the home. The shades were drawn and Cohen could see through the plastic blinds that the inside lights were on. Crouching, Cohen maneuvered toward the back of the house. He saw no windows except for a small square of glass, its size totaling about half of his car's passenger side window. The tiny square was set low, apparently lending light into the basement. Cohen decided that the back door would serve as the best point of entry. Anything in the front of the house would be too risky, and no way could Cohen fit his body through the tiny back window.

Cohen reached the back door quickly. *This is insane*, he told himself, just as he felt the adrenaline hit his bloodstream. Cohen welcomed the feeling and stood straight against the siding of the house. His hand shot for the door handle to find it locked, the door secured in place. Cohen panicked and scolded himself for thinking it could be so easy.

Taking inventory, Cohen bent down and attempted to look into the small back window. He saw nothing but blackness. It was so black that Cohen guessed paper had been placed over the window; it was only 7 p.m., after all. Based on the extra effort taken to hide the contents of the room, he also assumed that, if Danielle were here, she would be in the basement.

For the hundredth time, Cohen considered calling the police. He thought of the pros and cons of the situation and decided to wait. If anything, he wanted to make sure that Danielle really was in the basement before he made the call. Not to mention that bringing the cops into this mess without any solid proof about Coda's involvement seemed preemptive. Cohen had to keep in mind how smart the mastermind of this crazy plot must be. He doubted that Coda would leave any evidence at the crime scene.

Cohen thought of the black Jeep that drove down the driveway not too long ago. Chances were, no one would be inside the house. Right on cue, the front door opened and Cohen heard footsteps walking across the porch and down the steps leading to the wooded area. Hearing the footsteps drift toward the left, Cohen inched along the right side of the house. He peered around the front corner and gained a visual of a man wearing a cap making his way toward the woods. Cohen's body froze. The man bent down and picked up a large branch. *Firewood.* Cohen noticed the front door hanging open and realized two things: he now had a way in, and this guy would be coming back, soon.

Move! He told himself.

Before Cohen had time to come up with a strategy, he found himself standing in the front entryway of the house. The disconcerting dead exterior had nothing on the eerie nature of the house's interior. Complete silence enveloped the structure. Absolutely nothing resided in any of the rooms as far as Cohen could see. No furniture, no pictures, and no rugs—the house had definitely not been lived in.

I probably wouldn't decorate a house I used for torture and killing either, Cohen thought to himself. He glanced out the window and saw the man coming back with enough firewood under his arm to keep a fire going for an hour.

Cohen had one second to pick a hiding place and he darted straight. The empty house lacked any objects to hide behind, but Cohen thought back to the black paper on the window and decided to take his chances. He made his way toward the door leading to the basement and pulled it open slowly. He prayed that the stairs didn't squeak under his weight as he stepped deeper into the basement. Surprisingly, his 175-pound frame did not result in too much noise during the descent.

Another noise, halfway to the bottom, however, broke Cohen's heart in half. A small, terrified whimpering sounded from the basement and Cohen knew exactly to whom it belonged. Moving quickly now, Cohen jumped down the last few stairs and turned the corner. There, in the middle of a tiny, square, cement room, lay a woman tied down to a steel table. Cohen recognized her immediately.

"Danielle."

Chapter 27

Danielle began visibly shaking the second that she made out Cohen's face. In her delusional state, she almost convinced herself that she was imagining his concerned features. Then Cohen placed a hand on her arm and she felt his touch. He was real. Tears sprung to her eyes and her gaze followed Cohen's finger as he signaled her to stay quiet. He placed his fingers around the edges of the tape covering her mouth and looked at Danielle to make sure she was ready. She nodded and he pulled off the tape as gently as possible. Danielle didn't make a sound. Cohen guessed it must have been a minimal amount of pain compared to what she had endured over the last few days. Danielle immediately opened her lips to mouth words to Cohen, but the footsteps upstairs silenced her as they creaked the floor directly overhead.

Cohen attempted to break the bindings tied around her waist, legs, and upper body. It was some sort of thick cloth. The binding didn't budge and he swept his gaze around the room, following Danielle's head when it twitched to the right. She jerked her head fiercely toward a wooden cabinet and, upon opening the doors, Cohen saw a thick butcher's knife inside. Not wanting to ponder the knife's purpose, he grabbed the handle and used the blade to cut through the fabric easily.

Even after the restraining ties had been broken, Danielle struggled to sit up as her body tried to remember how to move. Grabbing her shoulders, Cohen helped Danielle raise her back from the steel table. He grabbed her waist and lifted her shaking body to the floor, noticing for the first time the amount of weight Danielle had lost since he last saw her.

Cohen had to keep himself from recoiling at the sight of the bruises and cuts covering Danielle's entire body. The rags attempting to replace clothing hid nothing from his sight. Clearly, she had been through hell, and Cohen had no option but to get her out. One glance at the bloodstained table, now bodiless, filled Cohen with enough anger to kill the man upstairs.

Whispering, Cohen risked asking, "Is there any way out of here through the basement?"

Danielle gave a disheartened shake of her head. Cohen had been afraid of that.

"Listen," he joined Danielle on the ground, willing the volume of his voice to mirror his actions. "I have a car, parked two houses down from this driveway. Two houses north." Danielle tried her best to nod, wanting to believe that freedom existed two houses down while doubting Cohen's ability to take on the man upstairs at the same time.

Cohen noticed Danielle's panicked expression. She could hardly stand, and Cohen was asking her to run two blocks north?

"You're going to have to let your adrenaline kick in and use it to get you there, okay?" Cohen handed Danielle the knife. She would need some form of a weapon, and Cohen felt the gun Leila gave him in his belt holster. "My keys are in the front compartment—"

"Hey! What the hell is going on down there?" a voice shouted from upstairs. Danielle's shaking

262

turned into full-on spasms and Cohen grabbed her shoulders as the door to the basement opened.

"You have to keep running, Danielle. Don't stop." In one swift movement, Cohen swept Danielle off the floor and guided her to stand on the left side of the staircase. With no room to completely place her out of harm's way, Danielle would have to run around whatever commotion Cohen created in order to incapacitate her captor. The stairs creaked at the halfway point and Cohen braced himself for the next part of the plan; he would have to use his gun. He placed his hand over the holster, making sure it was still in his pants.

The chances of Danielle's captor also wielding a gun seemed very high. Cohen realized that if he opened fire right away and a shootout ensued, Danielle's chances of escaping would decrease dramatically. Cohen made a split-second decision to knock the man off his feet before pulling out his gun. That way, Danielle would have the best chance at escaping.

Cohen felt fully aware that using momentum hadn't been successful the last time, but he also acknowledged that this time would be different. Only one person needed to escape. It would work. He wondered if Laura had a similar feeling before she died.

A big, oversized shoe came into Cohen's view and the man set his foot on the concrete floor. Without even looking the giant in the face, Cohen threw his entire weight at the man, his determination adding a good extra ten pounds to the impact.

Connecting with the man's broad shoulders, Cohen felt the wind leave his lungs as the two men fell toward the ground.

"Ugh!" The sound escaped the man's mouth and Cohen knew his attack had been successful. Cohen heard Danielle's feet running up the steps and his heart surged with pride at her ability to run.

Cohen moved all of his body parts at once and stood to reach for the gun behind his back. He stepped up two steps to create more distance when a strong set of hands gripped his foot, pulling his body back down the steps. Before making contact with the concrete floor, a blunt object hit Cohen in the back of the head and his body fell slack.

Cohen felt the next kick delivered to his side as his captor attempted to gauge the extent of Cohen's consciousness. The pain spread, and yet Cohen's body lay unreceptive. The man, assuming Cohen to be knocked out, lifted the lifeless form all too easily. Cohen felt his body traveling over the stairs as the man brought him to the living room. With a loud thud, Cohen connected again with the floor. The giant had no qualms in stepping over the limp form; he even laughed as he did so.

Little did the man know that Cohen mustered all of his composure to remain limp. Catching the man off guard would be Cohen's best shot. Remaining still throughout the pain presented Cohen with a whole new definition of suffering.

Lying directly in front of the fireplace, Cohen's body grew hotter by the second. Relief surged when the man opened a window. More importantly, Cohen's confidence grew after feeling his gun still tucked behind his back. A cell phone vibrated in the next room and the large shoes shuffled to answer the call.

"Boss, you better come back here. You're never going to believe who showed up on our doorstep. The one and only Cohen Donahue."

Cohen allowed his left eye to open a crack—just enough to see the back of the man's head. His captor looked out the window and wore a backwards Twins baseball cap. No hair showed from under the hat and Cohen noticed the man's pale skin tone.

The speakerphone was activated as the man moved to crack another window in the room. His large, awkward figure struggled to get his fingers in between the frame and windowsill. Cohen held himself back from lunging, knowing that the phone call could reveal some helpful information.

Cohen heard the man on the other end of the phone. His voice sounded scratchy and quiet, yet simultaneously strong and authoritative. Goose bumps spread as Cohen continued to listen.

"How the hell did that happen?" The raspy voice asked. "Nico just left to do another drive by of the department, that's where the tracker says the sergeant's car is…"

"Listen man, I don't know what to tell you. Donahue must have switched cars. He's here on the floor, so who cares how the kid got here? Oh, and the bitch Danielle is gone, so we have to deal with that. I'll keep him alive for you, okay?"

Reassuring, the guy wearing a Twins hat wants to keep me alive. Cohen's insides boiled as his captor referred to Danielle as a bitch. It took all he had left to keep himself from jumping on this guy. Something told Cohen to wait a little longer.

Cohen kept a mental inventory of the helpful details already gleaned from the conversation. First, the man driving the black car wanted Cohen to follow him. Second, they had been tracking Mier's car. Cohen guessed the tracking device had been placed on the car while he conversed with his mom. Cohen wanted to laugh at his luck. By now, Nico would have done multiple drive-bys, wondering why Cohen had yet to follow.

He made a mental note to warn Mier to take the device off his car while he simultaneously cursed his mother.

"You better not fuck this up," the boss continued, "or I may just decide to teach you a lesson for missing your first opportunity to put him in the lake. I might have to replace Cohen's body with yours, and then all of your sister's work to protect you would be for nothing."

Cohen's mind flashed back to the moment when he jumped into the lake to avoid the black Jeep spiraling in his direction. The collision had been so close to happening, and Cohen now knew who had been driving.

"Whatever you say. Goodbye, boss."

A light exploded in Cohen's mind as a memory flashed across his eyes. He watched as Leila hugged her brother goodbye in the parking lot the day after National Night Out. He heard the familiar voice:

"Goodbye, Leila."

He saw himself lying on the grass as someone wearing a black sweatshirt beat him mercilessly:

"Goodnight, Donahue."

Both occasions had one thing in common: the same deep, distinctive voice. *It can't be,* Cohen's mind cried out. He remembered Leila explaining Emmett's presence at the CPD by claiming that Emmett wanted to build a relationship with her; could Emmett really have visited to check in on Cohen?

"Keep him there, Red. Do whatever you have to do."

Red: Emmett's street name. Cohen couldn't stop his body from recoiling slightly. From his position on the ground, his mind connected dots at lightening speed, not stopping to consider the likelihood of his assumptions. Leila's brother was involved. The man on the phone had warned Emmett that Leila's attempts to protect her brother would be in vain. Had Leila been working with these men in a last ditch effort to keep Emmett safe?

All this time, Cohen wondered how his attackers had known where to find him at precisely the right time. When the car tried to run him off of the sidewalk, when Danielle found him at the bar, when his cell phone was taken. Could all of those events have one thing in common?

Emmett first attacked Cohen after he said goodbye to Leila, Scottie, and Charlie at Gage. Someone broke into his apartment minutes after Leila left the barbeque. It all added up: Leila could have easily informed Emmett of Cohen's whereabouts.

Despite knowing that their connection had been real, doubt began creeping into Cohen's heart. No other explanation fit so perfectly in his mind. Cohen had fallen in love with the one woman who aided in the orchestration of this whole mess. He tried to stop himself from jumping straight to accusations, but the adrenaline of the moment made that completely impossible. It made sense: Leila had used him.

Emmett reached over and hung up the phone, keeping one arm under the windowsill, attempting to push it higher. Cohen saw an opportunity and he forced his mind to focus. He knew he had one chance to get out of this house, and this was it. He needed to get to safety, needed to reevaluate everything and everyone he trusted. Without a second thought, Cohen launched himself at Emmett.

Emmett turned at the commotion, only to see Cohen's right hand moving too quickly for him to deflect the punch to his nose. The crack echoed loud enough to guarantee a fracture and the window slammed shut. Emmett's right hand reached to cradle his nose while his left hand acted with a mind of its own, extending toward Cohen and clamping onto his neck just in time to prevent him from running. With one swift flex Emmett squeezed the air out of Cohen's throat and kept his grip tight as he pushed Cohen against a wall.

Cohen flailed, his world turning black yet again, and his body screaming for help. His body weighed nothing compared to his opponent. Kicking Emmett in the groin caused the steel grip to slip and Cohen reached for his gun. He dodged Emmett by staying low, but something held him back from shooting and he kicked himself, knowing he hesitated because Emmett was Leila's brother. Despite everything that Cohen believed Leila had done, his heart still couldn't comprehend the idea of her involvement. If he shot Emmett and the bullet hit any major organs, it would kill Leila as well as her brother.

Cohen stood and turned to run for the door, not making it before Emmett got a solid grip onto his legs, clamping down as if his life depended on it. Cohen maneuvered his gun while swiveling his frame to aim at Emmett, still not planning to use the weapon as more than a scare tactic.

Just as Cohen turned his leg in an attempt to pry it from Emmett's fingers, he felt a sinking stab as Emmett bit through Cohen's calf muscle. Cohen screamed a bloodcurdling cry, black circles closing around the edges of his vision. Desperate for help, Cohen fired the gun.

Emmett's hands went slack, allowing Cohen to run before his body fell to the temptation of turning to see where the bullet had landed. Deep down, he knew that he wouldn't be able to live with himself if he had killed Emmett. Cohen limped through the front door and made his way down the driveway, praying desperately that he had time to escape before the man on the other end of the phone call reached the house.

Chapter 28

Spencer drank his body weight in alcohol. He hadn't showered or eaten any substantial food since Dolan placed him on temporary leave. From his perspective, the CPD had been the only saving grace in his life. He needed an escape from his abusive father, from the drinking, from the lifestyle. The CPD had given him that, and now, after one mistake, that had all been taken away.

He should have continued his rounds yesterday instead of going to hear the press conference; Spencer knew that, but he also had to know what was going on with Cohen. No one told the rookie officers anything. Spencer didn't necessarily like Cohen, but he knew that Cohen would never do the things those women accused him of. He went to the press conference out of need. Spencer needed to hear details, and he needed to remind himself how easily everything could be ruined. The accusations would no doubt ruin Cohen's life, and Spencer needed a visual to carry with him always, a reason to stay out of trouble and protect his position as an officer. Spencer went to the press conference to protect his job in the long run. How ironic that it served as grounds for temporary leave.

Malice worked its way into Spencer's mind as the room began to spin. It had been spinning for the past twenty hours, and Spencer didn't see it stopping anytime soon.

After Dolan delivered his punishment, Spencer had wanted to inquire as to how long "temporary" would really be. How temporary was temporary? Knowing deep down that he couldn't bear to hear the answer, Spencer instead stood up from his chair, said nothing, and walked into the locker room to pack his belongings. Spencer's pride got in the way, once again, and now he'd been drinking for the past twenty-four hours, holed up in his apartment, not having seen a single soul. There didn't seem to be any foreseeable end to his habit.

"You did a very bad thing, Spencer, skipping your shift to come watch a press conference." Spencer mocked Dolan in every way possible, from his deeper voice to the pointer finger that he wagged at no one visible to the sober eye. All the while, Spencer cradled a glass of tequila in one hand.

"Now, I will have to decide on a punishment for you; do you have any suggestions as to how we should proceed?"

Oh sure, Spencer had some ideas. As far as he remembered, Dolan had some also. Right before Mier entered the office, Dolan had been adding extra shifts to Spencer's schedule to make up for the hours lost in his time of misjudgment.

"On top of that, I will be assigning you to car 35 for the next two weeks."

Spencer had mentally gagged at the thought of driving 35 around for two whole weeks. Just yesterday, a drunken teenager threw up in the back seat. The interior would most likely smell for some time. Spencer thought that punishment extreme. If only he had known what was coming.

"Fuck. Mier." Spencer blamed Mier for the entire mess. "You couldn't even look me in the eye like a man!" Spencer screamed, remembering how

271

Mier had exited Dolan's office with his eyes downcast, avoiding Spencer's gaze.

"You think your world is so perfect, Mier? You just live in a perfect little world, don't you? Well, maybe tonight we can change that."

Spencer stumbled over to the kitchen counter and grabbed his car keys.

"Maybe it's time someone paid Mier a little visit at the station." In his intoxicated state, Spencer never stopped to consider the ill effects too much alcohol can have on motor skills.

* * *

Brushing the last few branches out of his face, Cohen hurriedly made his way out of the trees and stood on the side of the street. Numbness spread throughout his body. Cohen crouched to the ground. In the rush of everything, Cohen forgot he had told Danielle to take his car. She would be long gone by now, and Cohen would have no mode of transportation to make a getaway. He surely couldn't call Leila, and in light of recent information, Cohen didn't feel comfortable placing his trust in anyone. No matter the details, Cohen couldn't stay put either; he made up his mind to continue heading south down the road. He would stay within the protection of the trees to decrease his chances of being spotted.

Just before he walked back under cover of the brush, Cohen looked up at the sound of an engine approaching. Sure enough, Charlie's car pulled up to the driveway and Danielle urgently waved him into the passenger seat. Cohen didn't

272

have time to feel shock. He quickly slammed the door shut and turned to Danielle for an explanation as she stepped on the gas.

"I was safer in that house than I am in this car, Cohen! It took me five minutes to get the engine started and then it screamed so loud I thought my ears would fall off!"

Amidst everything they had been through, Danielle and Cohen still had car troubles. He looked at Danielle incredulously and allowed himself a heartwarming laugh. Danielle followed suit and soon the entire car was filled with the happy sound.

"I didn't expect you to wait for me, you know. You really should have left, Danielle. Two other guys are on their way back to the house right now," Cohen explained.

"Well then, we better get on busier roads," Danielle joked. "You must be insane to have gone into that house, Cohen. You saved my life. Saying thank you just doesn't do it justice."

Cohen glanced at Danielle and noticed for the second time the bruises along her entire body. In the car's lighting, her cuts looked even worse than they had in the basement; some even seemed infected.

"You need medical attention. We'll drive to the hospital and you can call your mom when you get there. She is worried sick about you, by the way. Once you're cleared to leave, I wouldn't stick around here any longer than you have to. I'm guessing those guys will be looking for me before they look for you, so you should have a good chance at leaving Chicago. You could finally start over."

Danielle's right hand left the steering wheel and latched onto Cohen's forearm, giving it a tight squeeze that Cohen understood perfectly.

"And let me guess, you plan to distract them while I make my escape?"

"Whatever this is, it's between me and Coda. You, Grace, and Laura shouldn't ever have been dragged into this."

Danielle glanced over at Cohen at the mention of Grace and Laura and he sadly shook his head, transferring his gaze to the window.

"Grace and Laura, they were killed. I was with them when it happened," Cohen struggled to provide Danielle with closure. "They were very brave up until the end. The one thing Laura wanted was for you to be safe."

Danielle looked forward and squeezed her eyes shut. "That sounds like Laura."

She breathed. "You risked your life to come save me, almost got killed in the process, and you haven't asked any questions or blamed me at all for my involvement in all of this? I mean my God, Cohen, I set this whole thing up!"

"One of the first impressions I got after meeting you was that you wouldn't hurt a fly. You wouldn't hurt me, not unless you had to. Besides, I think I have most of it figured out. That guy in there, the one wearing a Twins hat—my coworker is his sister."

Referring to Leila as a coworker hurt Cohen more than Danielle knew. Cohen pushed the feelings aside.

"Leila?" Danielle questioned, obviously familiar with the name and therefore confirming Cohen's suspicion even further.

"Yeah, Leila. I can't believe I trusted her. I still do…I think…" Cohen struggled to word his emotions before giving up completely.

"I thought she…never mind, it doesn't matter anymore."

Cohen couldn't get himself to finish the sentence. He had been torturing himself for sleeping with Danielle, and now karma had played its role perfectly: Leila had been plotting against him the entire time. Again, he had a fleeting moment where he did not believe Leila could possibly be involved. He pictured the two of them on the night of his barbeque; they both had feelings for each other. Or at least, Cohen had thought they did. Now, he wasn't so sure.

Granted, after all was said and done, Cohen understood that his feelings for Leila could have in fact been deeper than whatever she felt for him. Even if she felt no romantic attachment, however, Leila would never hurt a friend. Someone so kind and loving could not go through with such betrayal. A small part of Cohen refused to believe it. Then, he remembered Emmett, and how much Leila's brother meant to her. Even the most selfless person, if forced to decide between protecting family or friends, would most likely choose kin. Cohen felt sure of it.

As Cohen brooded, Danielle's heart swelled with the reality of her freedom. She and Cohen rode in silence for the majority of the drive.

"You know, you're right about me." Danielle offered as she parked the car a few hundred feet away from the hospital. "I hurt you because I had to. Coda threatened to kill my mother if I didn't go along with the plan. I faked the texting conversations and seduced you in the bar because I had to. And I am sorry, I really am, but Coda follows up on his threats."

"Don't torture yourself over it, honestly. Had you not gone through with it, Coda would have just found someone else."

Danielle continued in spite of Cohen's forgiveness, "I left your apartment the morning after we slept with each other and couldn't go through with the rest. I made up my mind to run away instead of complying with Coda's demands."

"You what?" Cohen's shocked tone did not surprise Danielle.

"I ran home to my apartment and told my mom to start packing her bags." The tears came pouring back. "He came to my house and he tied down my mother and made her watch as he beat me. Then he drove me to the police station himself." Danielle let out one final sob before attempting to pull herself together.

"You don't know these guys, Cohen. They mean what they say."

"I'm beginning to know them," Cohen growled. His knuckles were ghost white and lined with red as he clenched his fists.

Cohen sensed that Danielle witnessed some horrific things in that basement cellar, so he didn't push for more details. Danielle placed a hand over Cohen's and he knew she would soon be gone from his life forever. Giving it one strong squeeze, she thanked him and opened the door.

Just before stepping out, Danielle turned to Cohen. "You know, I wouldn't be too quick to associate your friend at work, Leila, with any of this."

"It just makes too much sense, Danielle. Coda must have threatened to hurt Emmett had Leila not helped. "

She gave a knowing nod, "Red, I mean Emmett, I've known him since high school. Coda always kept him close, especially in the last few years."

"Why would he do that?"

"I've wondered the same thing myself. Everyone knew that Red had a sister training to work as a police officer. I don't know. Maybe Coda thought Red could get inside information from Leila one day, assuming you came back to Chicago. Which, unfortunately, you did."

"Or maybe," Cohen reasoned, "Coda kept Emmett close so he could threaten Leila into helping him someday." He pictured Leila back on the night of National Night Out as she poured her heart out to him about Emmett. She loved Emmett so much; that much Cohen knew. Had Coda wanted to manipulate Leila's love for her brother, he could have easily done so.

"Your guess is as good as mine. Even so, if you're willing to forgive me for setting you up, don't you think Leila might deserve the same? I mean, if Coda really did threaten to hurt her brother."

Danielle's words only served to confuse Cohen further.

"Hey, I guess it's none of my business. If I learned one thing from all of this, there are good people in this world and there are bad people. I wish I fought more to keep the good ones close." Deciding enough had been said on the matter, Danielle stepped onto the pavement and shut the door.

Even as she limped down the road, Cohen had no doubt that she would make it. Both to the hospital and out of whatever world she had tried so bravely to escape.

Chapter 29

Spencer waited for what felt like twenty minutes before Mier emerged from the building. In reality, it had been two hours since Spencer arrived at the department. He sat in his car with the windows rolled down. The alcohol still ran through his veins and Spencer had yet to make a plan of action. Obviously, some sort of confrontation would take place tonight. Spencer sure as hell wouldn't stand by as Mier bullied him out of a job.

The back door finally opened and Spencer craned his neck to get a good visual. Mier walked into the parking lot, looking exhausted and disheveled. His shirt appeared un-tucked and Spencer could almost see the dark circles under his eyes. Cohen's case had really taken a toll on Mier, but Spencer didn't care. It had really taken a toll on everyone. He reminded himself yet again of his current unemployed status.

Mier walked to his car and pulled out of the lot while Spencer followed suit, putting his keys into the ignition and easing his way back onto the roads. It had been a miracle that no cop pulled him over on his drive to the department, and Spencer hoped his luck remained constant. A moment of alcohol-induced distraction passed through Spencer's addled mind. When he came back to his senses, Mier's car was nowhere to be found.

After frantically searching for the lost trail, Spencer finally made up his mind to call it a night and drive home. Midway through his U-turn at a red light, Spencer spotted a black Camry in his peripheral vision. The car sat outside of a rundown bar called Jay's. Spencer doubted that Mier would go and get a drink at this hour, but he took his chances and decided to take a look. Making a right turn at the next light, Spencer pulled into the parking lot.

He parked at a ninety-degree angle to the window. Apparently, Mier had needed a drink; he sat at a table alone in the far left corner of the bar. Spencer watched as the bartender handed him a beer bottle. A few minutes later, another man entered the bar and walked over to Mier's booth. He wore khaki pants, artsy glasses, and a striped button-down shirt. The man and Mier embraced as if they were old friends. Bored with the interaction already and realizing he made a mistake in coming out this far, Spencer allowed himself to doze off in his car. His snoring sounded loud enough to wake a hibernating bear.

***

Now that Cohen knew Danielle would be safe, at least for the time being, he wanted nothing more than to end this vicious game. He didn't want to hide anymore, and he didn't want anyone else to get hurt in the process. This whole thing had gone far enough, and Cohen knew just how to end it. With everything that had happened, Cohen now had little regard for the outcome of his actions. He momentarily forgot his will to live, especially considering the betrayal he felt when thinking of Leila's involvement.

Cohen thought he loved Leila. No, he knew he had. Cohen finally found a woman he could picture himself making a life with and she had been using him the entire time. His heart wanted so badly to believe in true love; yet, right on cue, his tendency to shut down any potential opportunity to create an emotional attachment returned. It was almost easy, once he let his anger take hold; Cohen's vulnerable conscience was more than ready to blame Leila for the pain.

You let your guard down, and she fooled you.

Although he understood Leila's need to protect her family, it still hurt that she had used Cohen as a means to her end. How could he have been so oblivious to Leila's involvement? Cohen suddenly felt thankful that he refused any further help from Leila after the meeting with his mother. Ironically, Cohen had been trying to protect Leila. *As if she needs any protection*, he bitterly thought.

His anger toward Leila grew at an exponential rate, increasing with each second to the point where he needed an outlet. He needed to snap, to yell at someone and watch as his words took effect. Cohen acted on the rage that he directed toward himself for getting involved with a woman. That, and the embarrassment he felt at having believed he could find love.

Turning on his phone, Cohen was greeted with the 2% battery life that it had left. He dialed Leila's number. As always, she answered quickly. Cohen heard her voice in a new light, now knowing that her tone did not demonstrate concern for his well being, but demonstrated eagerness for information. She felt concerned all right, but not for Cohen.

"Cohen! I have been so worried. Did you find Danielle?"

Pause. Cohen debated how he wanted the conversation to play out. He decided to let raw emotion do the talking.

"As if you didn't already know that."

More silence, this time from the other end.

"Um, okay...where are you right now?"

Cohen laughed, a mean and hurt sound. "Why don't you do me a favor, Leila, and call Emmett. Tell him I'll meet Coda on the Belmont Harbor boating docks in twenty minutes. Or rather, why don't you call up your old pal Michia and see how he's doing. How is prison life treating him anyway?"

"You want me to call Emmett? Cohen, what in the world are you talking about?"

"Stop playing games, Leila. God damn it. How soon after you left my barbeque did you inform Emmett that I would be alone that night? Did you show him to my door yourself?"

"Cohen, what the hell!"

"I mean, my God, how could I have been so stupid? You told me your life story about your brother and I believed that after ten years he just randomly decided to stop by the CPD to chat?

"Correct me if I'm wrong here. When you told Emmett that you would meet him for drinks after my barbeque, you really just went home, right? You just needed an excuse to get out of my apartment before old Red arrived?"

"Coh—"

"Jesus, Leila, I know you needed to get close to me to protect Emmett, but did you really have to get that close?"

Cohen ended the connection and turned Charlie's car in the direction of the docks. Leila would deliver the message, he felt confident. More than anything, Cohen's heart was empty and lonely.

***

Leila hung up her phone after hearing Cohen's line go dead. Her breath had yet to reappear and she willed her hands to stop shaking. Cohen's entire rant hit her hard, but one comment in particular made her hair stand on edge.

The night Leila left Cohen's apartment to have drinks with Emmett, she sat at the restaurant for more than an hour before leaving. Emmett never showed up. He later claimed, "Something important came up." At the time, Leila assumed it had been gang related, and now she felt sure. If Emmett really did go into Cohen's apartment, he must have invited her to drinks to guarantee that she wouldn't be at Cohen's when he broke in. Still extremely confused as to how this all fit together, Leila leaned forward and placed her head on her desk. She waited for the nausea to leave, but the room kept spinning.

"You look like you're about to get sick, Herzog. Come out with it, what's up?" Leila looked up, startled by Mier's presence. He'd left the office an hour ago and she hadn't expected him to come back that night. The clock glowed with the late hour—11:00 p.m.—and Leila knew her night hours must seem a little strange.

She hesitated briefly before deciding that Mier was possibly the only person currently able to help Cohen. Leila began by explaining what Cohen had just said on the phone call. She told Mier everything, from the accusation to the message she was to deliver to Emmett. At the end, Mier's face looked just as bewildered as Leila felt.

"Emmett... Who the hell is Emmett?"

"My brother. Cohen said Emmett would deliver the message to Coda. But how does Emmett know Coda?"

"That little shit!" Mier thundered. "Under no circumstances are you to share that information with your brother, you understand?"

Leila shook her head as Mier took out his phone and dialed Cohen's disposable number. Leila had never even considered delivering the message to Emmett. Mier pushed the end button with force at hearing Cohen's answering machine after the first ring.

"I swear to God, if Donahue doesn't give me a heart attack he'll find another way to kill me. Stay here and try to figure out what in the hell Cohen was talking about. I'm going to go get him from the docks, the fucking idiot. Meet me at your house in an hour and we'll talk some sense into him."

Leila watched as Mier grabbed his coat and walked out the door. She knew she should follow his order and do some digging, but another comment Cohen made on the phone still nagged at Leila.

Why would Cohen have mentioned Michia? Leila recognized the name. She had been at the crime scene when Cohen put Michia into the back seat of his cop car. The only way that Michia and Leila could have connected would have been through the jailhouse, and that made no sense.

How could Coda, Michia, and Emmett all connect?

Leila saw one small glimmer of light in the situation and she looked up the MCC phone number in the directory. The booking officer took Leila's request and placed her on hold.

As Leila waited, Mier all but ran out of the department's back door, cursing Cohen and Peter as he did.

"Goddamn Peter and Cohen Donahue." He stepped into the parking lot and ran briskly toward his car, regretting his decision to park twenty rows from the entrance. Just as he pulled open the driver's side door, two hands gruffly grabbed Mier from behind. Mier found himself inside of the car quicker than he could yell for help. The door of the black Jeep closed, its white gash visible despite the darkness of the night.

Chapter 30

Twenty minutes passed and Cohen still sat in his car at the docks. There were a total of twenty-five separate docking areas. He could see all of them from his position. He and his dad used to come fish at this very spot all throughout his childhood. Cohen knew that it would provide complete privacy, especially under the cover of night. He thought back on everything that had happened over the past few days and realized that it really was something of a miracle he was still alive. So far, Cohen had beaten all odds by surviving multiple attacks.

He thought of Grace, Laura, and Danielle, each woman fighting so hard for what she believed in: a fair chance, life, and freedom. Laura had sacrificed herself so that Cohen could live, so that Danielle could live. The realization halted Cohen in his mental tracks as he finally realized his fault.

Laura died, so you could, what, offer yourself up to Coda? Cohen allowed his mind to dwell on Coda's power—specifically, his manpower. After everything Cohen had endured up to this point, his new plan involved waiting for death at the fishing docks? Coda had an army of hit men under his command and Cohen would surely die tonight if he didn't act soon.

Cohen accepted, for the first time, that Coda would not stop until Cohen Donahue had been killed. *Unless,* Cohen thought, *I kill Coda first.* The moral dilemma unsettled Cohen: either he or Coda would be killed. Cohen hoped there was another way.

Coda could be arrested, Cohen realized, although the reality of the situation settled in just as fast. The police had plenty of information to incriminate Cohen, but nothing against Coda. Thus far, Cohen only had stories. He could ask Danielle to come back and testify, but that would put her in additional danger, and Cohen wouldn't do that. *Besides*, Cohen thought, *even if I do kill Coda, someone else will take over his quest for revenge.* The circle would continue no matter what the outcome.

All of this time, Coda wanted Cohen to be delivered to him alive, and not so that he and Cohen could have tea together and swap stories. Coda wanted to hurt Cohen. He wanted to kill Cohen himself. As this realization kicked in, Cohen debated his next move. Leila's house was no longer an option. Before he could make a decision, his phone rang and Cohen saw Mier's name appear on the caller ID. One percent of the battery remained, and Cohen tried to make the call quick.

"Mier, could you meet me somewhere? I'm going crazy here and need to talk through some things I've found."

The voice that responded did not resemble Mier's in the slightest. Cohen's pulse increased as he listened to the man on the other end. The same raspy voice that he had heard speak from Emmett's phone not too long ago spoke to him now.

"I think we could make that work, Donahue. I've got Mier with me right now. He doesn't look so good, sitting in my backseat with my guys. A little birdie told us you're heading to the docks. You better not back out, or Mier dies. And besides, that would be the least of your worries."

He's bluffing. Cohen's mind attempted to find a loophole in the story. Just because Coda had Mier's phone didn't mean Mier was really with him.

"Let me talk to him."

"Hmm, pity you should ask. Let's get one thing straight, Donahue: we don't negotiate with you. This will go one way only, and that's my way. Now listen closely."

Cohen heard silence on the other end and then a blood-curdling scream in the background. Unfortunately, Cohen recognized the sound; Coda really did have Mier. Just as he opened his mouth to respond, the cell phone ran out of juice. The line cut and Cohen sat in complete darkness. So Leila had delivered the message to Coda—Cohen had been right.

Cohen knew one thing for certain: he would let no one else die for him. A second ago, Cohen convinced himself that other options existed. He tried to believe that he didn't have to wait for Coda to arrive with his army of men. Now, Cohen sat in his car and strained his vision to pick up any movement in the night.

Mier had been one of the first people to believe Cohen throughout this whole mess. Mier had been Peter's friend. Those two facts provided Cohen with all the determination he needed to finally face Coda. Mier would not die tonight, and Cohen would make sure of it. He utilized the remaining moments to mentally prepare for the impending meeting.

Three minutes passed before Cohen saw a black Jeep, visible through a small patch of light given by a light pole, pull up to dock ten. The car no doubt chose the middle dock in an attempt to avoid the city life on either side. No one stepped out of the car. The vehicle loitered, apparently waiting for Cohen to emerge from his hiding spot. Cohen grabbed his necklace, remembering its presence a little too late, and stepped out of his car. As he approached the dock, three men stepped out from the black car. Cohen recognized two of them: Emmett and the giant who killed Laura and Grace. Cohen assumed the third man must be Coda. Cohen was surprised at his slight figure and silver hair, all of which contradicted the force behind the voice heard over the phone.

"Where is Mier?" Cohen called, despite their distance of about twenty feet. Coda smiled and chuckled, clearly feeling confident that the situation was to his advantage. He signaled Emmett to the back seat of the car. Cohen pulled out his firearm and kept it trained on Coda the whole time, waiting for Emmett to pull Mier out from the doors. Emmett and the giant from Starved Rock also held guns. The giant swung an additional crowbar in his left hand.

Emmett pulled Mier out by his collar and forced him forward. The four men approached Cohen as a unit, walking slowly so that Mier could keep up. Cohen guessed that Mier's scream resulted from the crowbar connecting with Mier's knee. Emmett kept his gun trained on Mier's head while the giant aimed his weapon at Cohen. The four men stopped at a distance of ten feet.

289

"Let Mier go. We can deal with this ourselves." Surprisingly, Coda nodded his head at Cohen's demand. *So much for not negotiating,* Cohen thought to himself. Emmett released his grip on Mier's shirt and all but threw him in Cohen's direction. Mier faltered in his next few steps as he neared Cohen in response to the impact. Although Cohen wished Mier would take Charlie's car and drive to safety, he doubted that Mier would be ready to leave his side given the situation. Before he could make the suggestion, he saw a scowl of pain spread across Mier's face. Cohen subconsciously lowered his gun. That grimace…

In his last two strides, Mier faltered and Cohen reached to supply his struggling figure with support. Mier reached Cohen's side quickly. So quickly that Cohen couldn't have prepared for the punch that Mier delivered to Cohen's face. Cohen dropped to the ground in shock.

***

Leila clutched her cell phone to her ear, waiting for the booking officer on the other end to return to the phone.

Focus, Leila, she told herself. She listened as the officer's voice came back, babbling on about how tired she felt and how much she "would really like to just call it quits tonight." The woman assumed that Leila felt the same and sounded wounded when Leila didn't contribute to the chitchat.

"Listen, I'm in a bit of a hurry here…"

Deciding that she no longer wanted to speak with Leila, the officer complied with Leila's request.

"Michia's first call after being placed behind bars...ah, yes, here it is: 312-777-8675."

Leila jotted down the number but did not recognize the sequence. Her gut told Leila that the number belonged to Coda and she made a mental note to check the source after this call ended.

The officer babbled on about something or other while Leila's mind moved a mile a minute. Michia had called this number, most likely Coda's, and then Coda must have passed on the information about Cohen's return to Emmett.

If so, then Emmett came to the CPD to confirm that Peter Donahue's son had returned to Chicago. It added up, and it definitely made sense. Leila began to interrupt whatever the officer on the other line had delved into.

"Hey—"

"After that, we have a visiting record from Griffin Mier at 8:30 p.m. that next night."

So wrapped up in her own thoughts, Leila almost didn't hear the woman's last words. Her legs felt like jelly and she let the phone slip out of her hands. *Griffin Mier? Why would he have visited Michia?* The phone stayed on the ground; Leila's hands shook too much to grab it. Something felt wrong here, very wrong, yet Leila couldn't let herself believe anything just yet. Walking toward Mier's office, Leila's mind went blank and she reminded herself to breathe.

Griffin Mier. She attempted to put the pieces together but the story still seemed off. Michia called Coda from prison, and then Coda called Mier? That made no sense. Not to mention, then how would Emmett fit into all of this?

Leila opened the door to Mier's office and let herself in, having no idea where to start. She scanned the mess of papers on the floor and moved toward his desk. She jiggled the mouse, assuming any proof of his involvement would be present in Mier's email or some sort of word document. A password entry screen displayed.

"Damn it."

Leila worked her way to the filing cabinets when something on Mier's floor caught her eye: a note with handwriting that Leila recognized all too well. Willing her heartbeat to stop thumping so loudly, Leila moved closer and pulled the note free from under a pile of folders. Her body fell to the ground as her muscles numbed to nothingness. The note read:

10/11/14: Donahue is back—working in the CPD. Visit Michia Diaz. MCC. –Red.

The images poured into Leila's mind. She pictured Emmett on the day that she found him wandering the CPD halls. Leila had recognized the back of his head, meaning he had been walking toward the door. Emmett was leaving when Leila found him, clearly not concerned with finding his sister at all. Instead of stopping by in an attempt to make up for missing National Night Out, Emmett had come to deliver a message to Mier.

"Michia called Coda from prison. Coda then commissioned Emmett."

She considered the possibility that Mier was the villain, and everything fell into place—so easily that Leila kicked herself for not realizing it earlier. Mier pulled Cohen into the Intelligence Unit the day after Emmett appeared, not because of Cohen's ability, but because Mier wanted to keep him close. What was worse, Leila encouraged Mier's involvement. When she asked to borrow his car, Mier left with a package under his arm and came back with only files. Where had the package gone? Leila held her stomach, realizing that the package might have contained a tracking device.

You told Mier that Cohen would be driving to the docks. Suddenly, Mier's mock concern overwhelmed her vision. Leila realized the severity of the situation and knew she had no more choices left. She had no idea how much time, if any, Cohen had left. Leila ran down to the front lobby and grabbed a spare set of keys for car 65, but not before returning to the locker room.

Leila walked directly to Charlie's locker, bent down, and pulled the mat away from the floor.

"Charlie, for once, your idiocy might actually save the day." Grabbing the key and unlocking Charlie's locker, Leila took the gun sitting on the top shelf. At the very least, Leila hoped that Cohen still had her gun in his possession.

Chapter 31

Cohen struggled to gain his bearings. His head throbbed and he pushed himself to his feet. Mier took advantage of the element of surprise and Cohen fell for it. Just as he raised his body, Mier kicked Cohen's feet from under him and delivered two quick and forceful jabs to Cohen's ribs with his right foot. Cohen felt a crack forming in his rib and he clenched his jaw together to stop from screaming.

Although no sound erupted from his vocal cords, Cohen's mind screamed at him to take action. This couldn't be real life; Mier had helped Cohen with everything. *First Leila, now Mier.*

Mier delivered one last blow, this time to Cohen's left knee. Feeling his knee completely give out, Cohen screamed, it was a scream Cohen had never heard before. Cohen curled his body as a defense mechanism. Feeling pain but needing to stall, he realized the need for conversation. *Distract him Cohen,* he told himself.

"Mier! What the hell is going on?"

"Let me ask you something, you idiot. How many new recruits have you heard of getting promoted to the Intelligence Unit during their first week on the job?"

Cohen racked his brain; he couldn't think of anyone. "What are you trying to say, Mier? You pulled me up for ulterior motives? You said I would be a perfect fit for the job."

A deep, haunting laugh came out of Mier's mouth at Cohen's response.

"And of course you believed me, son, because you must take after your daddy, right?"

At the mention of Peter, Cohen noticed a darkness enter into Mier's features, one he had concealed so well over the past few days. Cohen suddenly remembered why he had stalled at Mier's scowl of pain only moments ago. His mind went to the picture currently in Cohen's wallet: everyone smiling, holding up his or her drinks. Everyone, that is, except for one man off to the side of the picture. That man, Cohen now realized, was a younger Mier.

All of those years ago, Mier wore the same grimace that he did today. Mier had chuckled at Peter's explanation about Theresa's absence from the promotional dinner celebration. For someone claiming to be friends with Peter, Mier didn't seem to exhibit very friendly behavior. Cohen wondered how much Mier really knew about his childhood. Tonight, he intended to get answers.

"You said you respected my dad, Mier. Let me guess—he got promoted to Sergeant over you, am I right? You couldn't handle being second place? You were never friends with my dad; you hated him."

The next kick connected with Cohen's head and stars appeared in the darkness. Cohen knew he had a concussion, but he didn't care. Mier kicked him out of anger, meaning that Cohen must have struck a nerve. Cohen's assumption about the promotion had been right, and he decided to continue on that path.

"My dad deserved that promotion, Mier," Cohen tried. The struggle to speak only increased, but the words contained more and more determination. Cohen hoped to push Mier's buttons, anything that would make Mier talk.

"Your dad was nothing but a lazy piece of shit! I saw the way he was in the office, pretending that everything at home was great, that he had a wife who loved and cared for him. The dirty son of a bitch!"

Mier paced now, his body pivoting from side to side. Cohen concentrated so hard that he could almost feel the wheels turning in his brain. Why would Mier bring up his mother? Either Peter had vented to Mier about the lack of love in his marriage, or Mier had spoken to Theresa. Through a process of elimination, Cohen assumed his dad wanted nothing to do with Mier. Cohen attempted to move his body and almost blacked out in the process.

Wait it out, he told himself, clearly in no state to make a run for it, especially considering the presence of the three hit men.

"Mier, did you know my mother?"

Cohen did not expect such a simple question to be accompanied with such a loaded answer. Again, Mier let loose a laugh that could have landed him in a mental hospital. He grabbed the front of Cohen's shirt, lifting his upper body off the ground as Cohen struggled to keep his head upright. Cohen ground his teeth together, not wanting to provide Mier with the satisfaction of hearing his pain.

"Oh, Cohen, have you really forgotten?"

"Forgotten what?" Cohen asked through clenched teeth.

"I was surprised at first that you didn't recognize me, but now, after all of this?"

Cohen knew that he had missed some vital piece of information, but he couldn't get his brain to focus long enough to figure out the details. When Cohen had first met Mier, he recognized him from somewhere. Cohen doubted the recognition came completely from comparing him to the scowling man in the photograph.

Sensing his confusion, Mier continued, "Tell me this Donahue, because it's something I always wondered: did you ever eat the food your old man prepared for you at the barbeque?"

Without any warning, the images Cohen's mind had fought to keep below the surface over the years came flooding back:

Cohen hides under the kitchen table, crying. His dad chases a man from the house. Cohen's mother sits on the living room floor bawling. The man turns to the seven-year-old Cohen before leaving and says his goodbyes. "Have a great day, son."

Mier wore a smile matching the one he wore at Peter's barbeque party all of those years ago.

"You bastard!" Cohen yelled. The memories overtook his emotions, but Cohen wasn't yet able to fully comprehend the details. Mier had done something to upset his parents that day, but what had it been?

"We loved each other! She told me things she didn't tell anyone else, she told me everything. And then your father ruined it all!"

Cohen realized that Mier was talking about his mother. Mier must have been a client of Theresa's.

"She was a prostitute, Mier. You meant nothing to her. Look how easily she left you for my dad!"

Mier threw Cohen's upper body back down against the dock and the pain shot all the way to his toes. Mier and Coda were Theresa's two clients.

"Are you telling me you went through all of this just so that you could get back at my dad for stealing your promotion and your lover?"

"That's half of it." Mier looked at Cohen with malice.

All right, this guy is off of his rocker, Cohen thought, annoyed by his vague answer and desperate for more details.

"You're crazy, Mier."

"I mean really, Cohen, do I have to spell everything out for you? Why do you think two people who despise each other get married?"

Cohen had thought about this before, so many times. His dad did not seem the kind of man to marry a woman on a whim. Something must have happened, and deep down, Cohen knew he had been the reason. His parents had a one-night stand resulting in a pregnancy. Peter took the honorable action by marrying Theresa when he found out about the baby.

"Because she was pregnant, Mier. Is that what you want me to say? My parents got married because of me."

"Peter always was such a martyr, wasn't he?" Mier began walking in circles. "Especially, if I remember correctly, after finding out that his one son wasn't, in fact, his son."

The entire world rotated around him and Cohen worried about his ability to continue the conversation.

"What the fuck are you saying, Mier?"

"Your mom and I were in love, Cohen. She came to me saying that she was pregnant, with *my* baby. I. Didn't. Want. You. So she seduced your father and told him the kid was his."

"No…"

"When I received the invitation to your dad's barbeque party, I couldn't resist creating a little tension, stirring the pot. Your mom slept next to another man for too long, and someone had to pay. So I told Peter the true story behind our little fairytale."

"You're lying!" Cohen's pulse raced dangerously fast. *He's lying; he has to be lying.*

"Of course, with your blue eyes, no one ever doubted that you were your mother's kid." Deep down, Cohen knew Mier spoke the truth. He thought back to the days of his childhood, the days when he would ask God for his father's eyes. Apparently, Cohen had them all along. Mier's deep blue eyes pierced through Cohen now.

Mier smiled, relishing the successful delivery of such torturous information. Meanwhile, the three other men stood on the sidelines and watched, seeming bored and annoyed at the length of the confrontation before them.

"I'm going to kill you tonight, kid. For everything that your father did to me, and for everything that you did to me. You ruined my entire life, *my entire life*, and I'm going to kill you."

Mier closed the distance between himself and Cohen and put his whole body behind a punch to Cohen's diaphragm. The wind left Cohen's lungs and darkness replaced the light.

A few minutes passed before Cohen regained consciousness. He struggled to lean his chest forward, but felt a rope tied around his midsection restraining his movement. Sometime after passing out, he had been tied to a post on the dock. Cohen did nothing to protest. The strength he felt earlier had now completely vanished. He lifted his head from his chest and watched as four figures spoke merely feet in front of him, but Cohen didn't hear the words.

Mier is my dad...

Chapter 32

Spencer's entire body lurched awake alarmingly fast. He had been dreaming that he fell from a building. Just as his body was inches from the concrete, he awoke to find himself sitting in his car outside of a bar. Spencer's abrupt awakening shocked the booze into leaving his body. The time was 12:30 a.m., and Spencer wondered how he had been able to sleep for so long. One glance at the empty bar, Jay's, confirmed Spencer's assumption that Mier left hours ago.

Spencer's mind struggled to remember the details of his night; he remembered following Mier to the bar and falling asleep due to a lack of interest. Mier had met a man here…an old friend it appeared. Spencer put the keys in his ignition and started his car, moving his way slowly back toward his apartment. His body screamed for a sober sleep.

As he passed the department, his mind automatically transitioned to the event that ended his career: the press conference. He pictured Mier speaking to the reporters and couldn't help but feel a smile spread across his face. That one reporter— Doug, had been his name—really gave it to Mier. Spencer would never forget the look of terror on Mier's face when Doug asked his question. Suddenly, Spencer's car almost swerved into the center median as he realized, to his horror, that he recognized the man Mier had met at the bar.

I would know those fucking glasses anywhere. Spencer ripped his phone out of his pocket and started dialing the phone numbers of his fellow new recruit officers, not surprised that no one answered due to the late hour.

On his last attempt, he ecstatically responded to the only other officer awake.

"Spencer."

"Leila! Thank God. I know who the snitch is—I just saw Mier talking at a bar with the same reporter from the press conference."

***

Cohen strained against the ropes as Coda approached with a look of hatred and amusement across his face.

"Isn't this a sight for sore eyes? Cohen, buddy, it's about damn time you came back into the city. We've been waiting for your return."

Turning to his hit men, Coda theatrically asked, "How long has it been boys? Five years, right? Enough time for old Cohen over here to finish up college and training?" Looking at Cohen, Coda continued in a patronizing tone. "You have a fun time in college? Get with some girls over there?"

Stall, Cohen, do something. Cohen said the first thing that came into his mind.

"How do you think you're going to cover up my death, Mier?" He tilted his head around Coda's body. "An officer in your department turns up dead after being accused of rape? You suddenly can't walk without a limp? Doesn't sound too legit to me."

"Oh, I wouldn't worry about that too much," Coda saved Mier the effort of responding. He walked in Mier's direction and Cohen could see Mier's shoulders slump slightly at Coda's approach.

Mier feared Coda, yet he had worked with the man for this long just to secure a shot at Cohen.

"You raped Danielle, Cohen." Mier found his voice. "Leila will confirm that you told her you'd be at the docks tonight. She will tell everyone how I left to try and *help* you. Then, you attacked me."

Mier turned to Emmett and gave him a nod. Emmett responded with a punch to Mier's face, hard enough for Mier to take a few steps back, but not hard enough to knock him unconscious. Mier's eye would be black in the morning, and it would look as if Cohen had committed assault. Cohen thought back to Danielle's story, how she detailed Coda beating her to create a similar effect.

"I had to kill you in self defense." Mier continued, as if the extra explanation were necessary. For the first time, Cohen noticed that Coda, Emmett, and the giant all wore gloves; their fingerprints would be nowhere near the scene of his death.

With one twitch of his head, Coda signaled Emmett into action. Cohen saw a bandage around Emmett's upper left arm and assumed that was where his bullet hit not too long ago. Emmett took his time, walking two circles around Cohen before coming at him from behind. Cohen felt a stabbing pain in his side, not sure what object had been used to impale him. He screamed into the night.

"Isn't it a shame that no one will hear you out here, Cohen? I was a little surprised at your stupidity in picking this place to meet, but, then again, I couldn't be too surprised."

Emmett took one more stab, this time at Cohen's left side. Some of his ribs were definitely cracked now. Cohen hated that he had no way of fighting back. His gun now sat at the bottom of the lake and the ropes still restrained his movement. Cohen's mind fought to maintain consciousness. There were still so many things he needed to know.

"How do you and Mier know each other?" Any kind of movement resulted in a severe pain shooting through his body; yet Cohen retained eye contact with Coda.

"It was too bad really, that Peter died before we could kill him ourselves—eye for an eye, you know how it goes. His death really just wasn't enough for me. Especially not after I heard that Jeremiah died in prison. You can imagine my delight after getting a call from Mier over here, five years ago, asking if I would like to join forces to inflict a little payback on Peter Donahue."

Another swift punch was delivered, this time to Cohen's face. He felt his right eye swell in seconds. He guessed two more punches would knock him unconscious, five more and he would be dead. At least his questions were being answered. Cohen willed himself to keep his consciousness long enough to hear some more.

"Five years, Donahue," Mier jumped in. "We've waited five years for this."

Cohen looked at the black water standing still under the docks. Fitting, he thought, that his death would occur in such close quarters to his biggest fear. In the face of dying, the unknown element of dark water appeared much less daunting.

The giant wanted in on the action, and he took over Emmett's role. He swung his body over to Cohen's left side and delivered a kick to Cohen's hipbone so severe that Cohen's vision returned to darkness. After Cohen regained sight minutes later, his head still resting on his chest, he noticed that Coda now held a gun. Apparently, Coda decided that enough punches had been thrown; Coda would be the one to shoot Cohen. Cohen knew his world was about to go black, permanently. Despite the odds, he still hoped for a miracle.

Refusing to give Coda the satisfaction of eye contact during his final moments, Cohen kept his gaze focused on the black night behind the giant's body. He felt his Saint Christopher necklace around his neck and Cohen almost felt Peter's presence.

Keep staring into the darkness, Cohen, it will all be over soon, he told himself. He hated giving up, but his mind told his body to rest; this nightmare would finally come to a close.

Cohen heard stories of people claiming to see their loved ones before they died; yet he still felt surprised to see his dad and Bre appear in the distance, their figures slowly growing larger. The only two people that Cohen trusted in this world— at least now he didn't have to die alone.

Cohen drowsily muttered his last word before his world turned upside down, "Dad?"

"You've finally figured it out." Mier chuckled as Coda cocked the gun.

"Rest in peace knowing that you are a little bastard with a mother and father who hate your guts."

"Like hell he is."

Coda wheeled around so fast that he almost lost his balance. Behind him, Cohen saw a beautifully bronzed woman with chestnut eyes standing next to the very Peter Donahue himself. One of the newcomers had a gun aimed at Coda's head. Cohen knew his mind wanted to rest, but his heart held onto the dream. He watched as his dad and Bre crept closer to his body, keeping their sights aimed at Coda and Mier the whole time. Oddly enough, Peter's voice sounded extremely similar to Spencer's annoyingly high-pitched whine.

Cohen failed to hear Mier's next question, but he heard the response. "Come on Mier, why don't you take the gun away from Cohen's head? The last thing you need is for me to keep this little camera recording long enough to catch you murdering a fellow police officer."

"Spencer, you little shit."

"I'm sure your media friend would be more than happy to leak that footage to the world."

Cohen processed Spencer's face just moments before his consciousness drifted. He heard two gunshots and felt one rip through his arm. Before his body surrendered and he lost his grip on reality, Cohen registered Bre's brown hair flashing a tint of red.

Chapter 33

Cohen woke in a hospital bed with a splitting headache and sharp pains running through his side and legs. He tried to sit up, but felt a woman's firm hand gently push him back to the covers. The details of the night came rushing back to him: the guns, Coda, Theresa and Mier's relationship, his dad, and the flash of red hair.

"Cohen?" a feminine voice roused Cohen from his numbness. He emerged from his sedated state to find Leila standing next to his bed. Her red hair hung flawlessly around her shoulders, framing her face. She appeared determined as ever.

"Leil—"

Leila's mouth interrupted Cohen's sentence as her lips found his. Fully awake now, Cohen strained to lift his hand to Leila's face. She pulled away and stroked Cohen's chin with her hand.

"I would never have set you up, Cohen."

Feeling a need to explain, Cohen stammered, "Emmett…"

Cohen's memory still proved too foggy to remember how exactly Emmett fit into all of this, but he knew that Leila needed to be warned about something.

"I know, Cohen. I know all about it." Leila paused before continuing, "I found out that my biggest fear really wasn't a fear at all. Maybe serving some time behind bars will provide Emmett with a proper perspective." Cohen attempted to lift his upper body, wanting so badly to pull Leila into his arms. She hadn't betrayed him, and Cohen believed that with all of his heart.

"Get some rest," Leila gently pushed him back. "We can talk about everything later."

"But…my dad, and Bre, I saw them. They were there."

The look of confusion that appeared on Leila's face caused a sinking sensation to spread through Cohen's body. His dad and Bre had not saved his life. Based on the wary look spreading across Leila's features, Cohen knew that he had imagined the whole thing.

A nurse entered the room at that moment and stuck a needle into the IV, sending fluid into Cohen's arm. He wasn't ready to return to a coma-like state. Panic set in as Cohen reached for Leila's hand, falling just short of contact before darkness blocked his vision.

***

"Coh? You with me, son?"

Hearing his father's voice, Cohen fought even harder against the pull to return back to consciousness. The thought of waking up to a world without his dad again seemed terrifying, especially since his mind had conjured up Peter's return so recently. Struggling through the urge, Cohen's lids stayed clamped shut. For the second time in the past five hours, Cohen saw the most beautiful sight he would see in all his life. He and his dad sat at O'Reilly's Pub. Peter looked at his son with the same loving eyes that Cohen had missed so much over the years.

"You have some explaining to do," Cohen croaked through his woozy, dream-like voice. His lopsided smile was plastered to the side of his face and he struggled to convince his loopy brain to stay focused on the details of the dream.

"Hey, Coh, I love you man, and I only wanted to protect you."

"But why did I see you back there? Right before two shots were fired, how did you just appear?"

"I told you, Cohen. Your safety is my number one concern. I will never leave you, especially not when you are in danger."

A warm sensation spread across Cohen's neck and he realized that even now, he still wore the Saint Christopher necklace Peter gave him five years ago.

Cohen sat in silence, letting the strength of his father's presence flow over him.

"What happened with Coda? I heard two shots, but…" Cohen clutched his right shoulder where a bandage should have been located. Instead, he felt no pain, as if a bullet had never entered his arm. Cohen remembered hearing Spencer's voice and knew that he didn't need his father's clarification after all. Spencer's shot had saved the day.

"Let me ask you something, son, because who knows how long this dream will last: when are you planning on asking that little redhead to marry you?"

Cohen balked at the question, wondering how his dad always seemed to know Cohen's mind.

"No rush, just don't mess it up, son. Something tells me she's a keeper." Peter winked and Cohen slowly shook his head, unable to suppress a smile from spreading at the same time—a smile that hadn't been used to its full potential in too long.

"So with that, my boy, I think a toast is in order."

Cohen could only laugh at his dad's request, not surprised in the least when a flask emerged from his father's boot and two shot glasses appeared out of thin air. With a twinkle in his eye, Peter delivered the toast before they both gulped down the burning liquid: "To dodging the bullet."

At the reference, Cohen started laughing. He slowly began regaining consciousness, and yet his laugh did not show any signs of stopping. His eyes opened to see Charlie, Scottie, Bre, and Leila's worried faces staring back at him. Knowing that his abrupt transition from sleeping to fully awake and joyously laughing—especially given the circumstances—must have seemed alarming made Cohen laugh even more.

Not entirely sure if the giddiness stemmed from the thrill of being alive, toasting to the future instead of the past, or the love he felt for Leila, Cohen decided he didn't care. His entire body hurt from the unfamiliar flexes of muscle, and he wanted nothing more than to keep laughing. Cohen laughed as he looked at the four standing before him. Despite a lack of shared blood, they were his family and everything would be okay.

"Cohen...?" Bre slowly questioned.

"It's okay, Bre. Everything is okay." His laughter began to subside.

"You were just talking to someone in your sleep..."

"Let's just say, my dad hasn't left my side through it all."

Cohen didn't need a paternity test to prove it.

Made in the USA
San Bernardino, CA
08 April 2015